Praise for

DENISE SWANSON

Chef-to-Go Mysteries

"Once again, Denise Swanson demonstrates why her books are bestsellers. In *Tart of Darkness*, the first of her new Chef-to-Go mystery series, Swanson delightfully delivers murder, intrigue, and romance as she introduces us to Dani Sloan and a lively cast of supporting characters. Fast-paced and fun—as is Swanson's style—*Tart of Darkness* is utterly unputdownable. I cannot wait to revisit Dani's B&B in the next installment of what's sure to be a long-lived, well-loved series."

—Julie Hyzy, *New York Times* bestselling author

"Denise Swanson's new Chef-to-Go mystery series is off to a delicious start with *Tart of Darkness*. Readers will enjoy rooting for Dani and her young tenants as they work to solve the perplexing murder in this tasty tale, full of warmth and charm."

—Cleo Coyle, *New York Times* bestselling author of the Coffeehouse Mysteries

Welcome Back to Scumble River Series

Also by Denise Swanson

Welcome Back to Scumble River

Dead in the Water
Die Me a River
Come Homicide or High Water

Chef-to-Go Mysteries

Tart of Darkness
Leave No Scone Unturned

Winner Cake All

CHEF-TO-GO MYSTERY

DENISE SWANSON

Poisoned Pen
PRESS

Published by Poisoned Pen Press, an imprint of Sourcebooks
P.O. Box 4410, Naperville, Illinois 60567-4410
(630) 961-3900
sourcebooks.com

Library of Congress Cataloging-in-Publication Data
Names: Swanson, Denise, author.
  Title: Winner cake all / Denise Swanson.
  Description: Naperville, IL : Poisoned Pen Press, [2020]|
  Summary: "Dani Sloan is back in another delicious
  Chef-to-Go mystery!"—Provided by publisher.
Identifiers: LCCN 2019059978 | (paperback)
Classification: LCC PS3619.W36 W56 2020 | DDC 813/.6—dc23
LC record available at https://lccn.loc.gov/2019059978

Printed and bound in Canada.
MBP 10 9 8 7 6 5 4 3 2 1

Chapter 1

DANI SLOAN'S CRITICAL GAZE SWEPT THE FRONT parlor of the mansion she'd inherited from her grandmother's sorority sister Geraldine Cook. The Victorian settee's gold-and-red-brocade upholstery had been spot cleaned that morning, and the Eastlake side chairs' intricate, carved backs were free of dust.

She inspected the brightly colored Persian rug covering the hardwood floor and was pleased to note that, per her instructions, it was freshly vacuumed. Next, she checked the fan-shaped transom above the front casements. The glass sparkled in the mid-October sunlight.

Nodding to herself, she blew out a relieved breath. As far as she could see, everything was in place and there wasn't a speck of dirt anywhere.

Wait! Dani frowned and used the bottom of her shirt to rub a fingerprint off the silver coffee service sitting atop the ornate gilt-and-marble coffee table. Now, the setting was immaculate and ready for visitors.

Yvette Joubert, the most important client Dani's fledgling Chef-to-Go company had ever attracted, was due to arrive at three o'clock to discuss the catering she needed for her upcoming engagement party. If that went well, Ms. Joubert had promised to hire Dani for the reception, the bachelor and bachelorette parties, and the rehearsal dinner too.

Franklin Whittaker, Ms. Joubert's intended, was rumored to be the wealthiest resident of Normalton, Illinois. If his fiancée selected Chef-to-Go to handle their wedding events, the business would be in the black for the next year. Or possibly forever.

Pleasing Yvette and Franklin meant Dani was almost guaranteed additional bookings from their many friends and business associates. Their social circle would follow the couple's lead and hire Dani when they needed an event catered or wanted a personal chef for their dinner parties.

Blinking away the dollar signs dancing in her head, Dani looked at her watch. It was time to fill the coffeepot and bring out the platter of mocha truffle brownies, orange brown-sugar raisin swirl coffee cake, and her secret weapon: chai latte snickerdoodles. One bite of that cookie and Yvette would be eating out of her hands. Pun intended.

Dani just hoped the woman wasn't on a diet. So many brides starved themselves before their weddings.

Dani had been at one ceremony where the bride actually passed out as she walked down the aisle with her groom after the ceremony. When the paramedics arrived, the new bride admitted that she had been fasting and had had nothing in her stomach except broth for the previous week.

Dani ran her hands down her own generous curves. She'd long ago quit trying to conform to the reigning beauty standards. There was no way a chef could stay a size two, not that she'd ever been even close to any single-digit dress size since puberty.

Shaking her head at how far afield her thoughts had wandered, Dani refocused on the upcoming meeting and headed into the kitchen.

She was placing the heavy tray of desserts on the coffee table when the doorbell rang. After one last glance around the room to assure herself that everything was ready, Dani hurried into the foyer.

Swinging open the massive oak door, Dani gulped. The woman standing on her front porch was utterly dazzling. If you saw her in a magazine, you'd swear the image had been photoshopped. She was that gorgeous.

It was impossible to judge her age. She could have been as young as twenty-five, or as much as ten years older than that. The porcelain skin on her perfect face was flawless, completely unmarked by any hint of a wrinkle or a blemish. And her navy-blue eyes were framed in long, lush lashes that looked completely natural but had to be very expensive extensions.

As Dani stood transfixed, the stunning beauty raised a raven eyebrow, and in a lilting soprano asked, "Danielle Sloan?"

Mentally slapping herself, Dani nodded and said, "But please call me Dani."

"I am Yvette Joubert, but no one calls me Yvi." The stunning woman winked, then tucked a lock of gleaming, jet-black hair behind her ear and added under her breath, "At least not anymore."

Dani was trying to figure out if she should respond to that or not when Yvette tilted her head and asked, "You were expecting me, no?"

"Yes, I was. Sorry." Dani stepped out of the way. "Please come in." She gestured toward the parlor. "Right this way."

Once Yvette was seated, she glanced around the room and grimaced. "I'm not fond of antiques. I prefer glass and leather. This"—she waved her hand—"looks as if someone's granny died here."

Dani noted that Yvette's slight French accent seem to come and go. Was she faking it? And if she was, who cared? Dani silently scolded herself.

Needing to assure her prospective client, Dani hastily said, "These furnishings came with the house. I promise you that my food is not reflective of the surroundings. Would you like to see my modernized kitchen?"

"Thank you, but no." Yvette gave a theatrical shudder and giggled. "I make it policy to avoid that room whenever possible."

"I'm very grateful that a lot of people feel that way." Dani chuckled. "It's why the personal chef branch of my business is so popular. Busy men and women, who don't want to eat out or order in all the time, hire me to do the cooking for them once or twice a week."

"I've been hearing about that service from several friends." Yvette gracefully crossed her tanned, toned legs. "Chelsea Barnes raves about your food." Straightening the hem of her periwinkle sheath, Yvette added, "In fact, she and her husband are the ones who recommended your company to me. Trent mentioned that you had catered a faculty tea that was utterly exquisite."

Dani was pleased that the Barneses, who were regular personal chef clients, had recommended her. She also briefly wondered if Yvette's relationship with Chelsea was personal or professional. While Professor Barnes taught at the local university, Dr. Barnes was a famous plastic surgeon.

"That's very nice of them." Dani made sure her voice reflected her gratitude. "Word of mouth is so important in my line of work."

Yvette indicated her agreement with a regal nod. "I always take what people have to say about a product more seriously than any advertising."

"I do too," Dani said, then asked, "Shall we get started?"

"I hope you don't mind, but I asked my wedding planner to meet me here." Yvette glanced at the slim diamond watch on her wrist. "Unfortunately, she's driving down from Chicago and texted me that she won't arrive for another fifteen or twenty minutes."

"No problem." Dani gestured to the refreshments on the table and asked, "Would you like a cup of coffee and a snack while we wait?"

"That would be lovely," Yvette answered. "Do you have any stevia?"

"I do. It's in the kitchen." Dani rose. "I'll be right back."

After quickly transferring the light green packages of stevia to a crystal sugar bowl, Dani returned and offered it to Yvette. The woman had already poured herself a cup of coffee and, from Dani's glance at the tray, had to be eating her third snickerdoodle. Dani's secret weapon seemed to be working.

Once she had her own cup fixed the way she liked it, Dani grabbed her notebook from the table, settled back in her chair, and said, "If you'd like, we can use the time until the wedding planner gets here for you to tell me a little about yourself and the groom. That way I can be thinking about possible menu ideas."

"Excellent idea. Let's see." Yvette took a bite of cookie and chewed thoughtfully. "I was born in France, but my parents moved to the States when I was five and I've lived here ever since. I work for one of the top architectural and design companies. We were involved in several Chicago municipal buildings."

"I can see why my decor was so important to you," Dani murmured.

"Yes." With a look of repulsion, Yvette glanced around the parlor.

Dani was immediately sorry she'd reminded the woman of her surroundings and encouraged, "You were saying?"

"Although I am currently taking time off from the company to concentrate on my wedding, once an interior designer, always an interior designer."

"Of course." Dani agreed. "It's the same when I'm served a meal." When Yvette didn't respond, Dani continued, "From what you said earlier, do your tastes lean more to ultra-modern styles?"

Dani noticed that Yvette had finished her snicker-doodle and was now sampling the brownies. That had to be a good sign.

"Absolutely. I like sleek, clean lines, and I love white-and-black color schemes."

Dani made a note, then asked, "Do you or your fiancé have any food allergies?" She looked up in time to see a puzzled expression on her prospective client's face, and added, "Or anything you dislike?"

"The only thing I can think of for me would be lima beans." Yvette made a face. "Those are just nasty." She tapped her chin. "Franklin may have an issue with mushrooms, but I can't remember. It could be my first husband or my previous fiancé who hated those."

Wow! Dani blinked. She hadn't realized this was Yvette's third engagement.

She hid her surprise and said, "Okay. But let me know as soon as possible." She chuckled. "We don't want to poison the groom-to-be, right?"

"Right." Yvette giggled. "At least not before we're married."

Dani didn't have any idea how to respond to that. She was pretty sure the woman was kidding, but it was hard to be sure. Especially without knowing what happened to husband number one and fiancé number two.

Time to change the subject.

"What can you tell me about Mr. Whittaker?" Dani asked.

"Franklin owns over sixty businesses. Although most are regional, he's been expanding his interests across the country. But his passion is the Korn Kings, which is a member of the Middle America Baseball League." Yvette took a sip of coffee. "Since Normalton doesn't have a pro team and the town is located several hours away from both Chicago and St. Louis, that franchise is very popular and very profitable."

While Dani wasn't a fan herself, she was well aware of the Korn Kings. "I've seen their logo all over the campus." Although the university had its own college-level team, NU students were huge supporters of the Kings. "Maybe we could do ballpark-themed food for your engagement party."

"Certainly not." Yvette shot Dani a sharp look. "I want it to be elegant."

"Of course. I love doing that type of event," Dani hastily assured her, then in an attempt to distract Yvette asked, "How did you and your fiancé meet?"

"At a charity ball for the Chicago Fire Department. My previous fiancé was a CFD captain." Yvette finished her brownie and wiped her fingers on a napkin. "Franklin and I hit it off right away."

Dani was curious about what had happened to fiancé number two but refrained from asking. If he had died in the line of duty, she didn't want to remind Yvette of her loss. And if the woman had dumped him for the wealthier guy, Dani didn't want to have negative feelings toward her client.

Luckily, the doorbell chimed before she had to come up with another topic.

Jumping to her feet, Dani said, "That must be your wedding planner. I'll go let her in."

Yvette gave a queenly wave of permission and Dani hurried into the foyer and opened the door.

"Danielle Sloan?" the woman asked.

"Yes, but call me Dani."

As they shook hands and the woman introduced herself. "I'm Vicki Troemel, Ms. Joubert and Mr. Whittaker's event planner. Sorry I'm a little late. The drive from Chicago was a nightmare. You wouldn't believe the construction on I-55. As the wedding gets closer, I may have to move down here to avoid the traffic jams. I don't suppose you rent out rooms?"

"Actually, I do." Dani immediately liked the bubbly woman. Vicki seemed about Dani's age, and she had a similarly curvy figure. "Unfortunately, the rooms that are finished are already occupied. I lease them to three college student who help in my Chef-to-Go business."

"Well, the wedding isn't for another eight months so maybe we can work something out." Vicki spotted Yvette and headed into the parlor.

As Dani followed, she admired Vicki's suit—the saffron color flattered her nut-brown hair and fair skin. Suddenly self-conscious, Dani tugged at her own plain dark slacks and black-and-raspberry striped tunic. Maybe she should have dressed up a little bit more or worn her chef's jacket. That always gave her a nice aura of authority.

By the time Dani sat down, Vicki had already made herself comfortable on the other Eastlake chair. She slipped a tablet from its case and glanced between Dani and her employer, clearly ready to begin.

"I've told Dani a little about myself and Franklin so we can get started discussing the event." Yvette waited for Vicki to nod her understanding, then continued, "My fiancé and I will be hosting an engagement party the first Saturday of November."

"Wow!" Dani inhaled sharply. "That's only two weeks from tomorrow."

"Yes, it is." Yvette's expression was bland, but her tone was sharp. "I take it you can make yourself available for that date."

"Let me check." Dani took her cell phone from her pocket.

But before she could swipe it, to consult her schedule, Yvette lifted her chin and said, "I certainly hope we haven't wasted our time coming here. Chelsea assured me that you would accommodate me."

Dani started to tell Yvette that Chelsea had no right to say that but stopped herself. It wouldn't do any good to point out to Yvette, or, for that matter, to Dr. Barnes, that they weren't the most important people in the universe or that their needs didn't have priority over anyone else's because neither woman would believe her.

Dani may have only met Yvette an hour ago, but having previously worked in human resources, she was pretty sure she was reading her prospective client correctly. As with Dr. Barnes, this woman was the kind of person who wouldn't get it. Everything in her world would always revolve around her desires, and she'd expect that desire to be fulfilled at the instant she had it.

Instead of verbalizing any of those thoughts, Dani glanced at her calendar and said, "I am free, but in order to guarantee delivery, I'll need to put in the orders for my raw ingredients by Monday at the latest." She made a quick entry on her phone to save that weekend, then placed the cell on the coffee table.

"Our guest list is currently just a tiny bit shy of three hundred fifty, but there will doubtlessly be a few additions and probably top out at four hundred. I'll have a firm count soon." Yvette raised her eyebrows. "Can your company handle such a large number of guests?"

"Certainly." Dani crossed her fingers and hoped she wasn't lying.

She'd have to hire five or six more servers, as well as a couple of kitchen assistants. Maybe her friend Gray Christensen would be available to act as her sous-chef. His day job as the chief detective of the Normalton Police Department kept him busy, but he loved to cook and had offered to help out whenever she needed him if he wasn't involved in a case.

Dani inwardly winced. Spencer wouldn't be happy about that arrangement, but he'd just have to suck it up and understand what this kind of booking could do for her business. In fact, it would be an excellent test to see if Spencer was a good fit as a boyfriend or not.

While they had shared a hot kiss a couple of months ago, since that time they'd only been out on a few dates. Between Spencer's schedule as Normalton University's chief of security and Dani's overwhelming workload, neither had had much leisure time.

This was the stage in their relationship for her to be cautious. Before their feelings deepened. Not after she was irrevocably in love and would be crushed if things didn't work out.

"Dani?" Vicki's gentle voice brought Dani back to the present.

"Sorry." Dani inwardly shook her head. She needed to stop thinking about her romance and concentrate on her business. "I missed that last bit."

"I was saying that due to the number of guests and Franklin's ownership of a sports team, we're holding the party in a tent erected on the grounds of the ballpark. What type of menu would you recommend?"

Before Dani could answer, Yvette said, "By tent, she means a fully enclosed space with heating and a hardwood floor, not something you use to go camping." She pointed a finger at Dani and said, "Keep that in mind when you make your suggestions."

"Of course, and I assume you'll also have a mobile kitchen nearby?" Dani flipped her legal pad to a fresh page and glanced between the two women. "If not, then that will have to be arranged."

"We'll definitely take care of that, as well as anything else you need." Vicki typed on her tablet. "Do you have an idea how large a kitchen you'll require?"

"Not offhand, but I can get the information to you by Monday." Dani made a note, then said, "Just off the top of my head, how does this sound? Three or four appetizers with the cocktails, then once everyone is seated, we'll put out a large salad on each table with a basket of rolls. We can have two or three entrées along with sides and the guest can indicate their choice when they RSVP."

"Can you be more specific?" Yvette asked. "And we'll need a vegan/vegetarian option."

"Sure." Dani's mind raced. "How about one vegan, one meat, and one seafood main course?" When Yvette nodded, Dani suggested, "Pappardelle with pistachios and lime for the vegans, rack of lamb with a cauliflower-and-lavender sauce for the carnivores, and for the guests who prefer not to eat meat, a red snapper Livornese." When both women shot her a blank look, Dani explained, "Livornese is a tomato, onion, caper, and black olive sauce."

"That sounds wonderful," Vicki gushed and Yvette inclined her head in agreement.

For the next half hour, they discussed side dishes and appetizers, then Yvette said, "I want you to come up with a trio of really special desserts. Something no one else around here has had. Not some silly cake with those awful icing flowers."

"Well, I don't know what's been served at every event, but I can do something unusual." Dani mentally flipped through her recipes, then added. "Give me today and tomorrow to think about it."

"Fine." Yvette leaned forward. "Once that's settled, we can move forward."

Before Dani could respond, her cell phone started playing "I Fought the Law" and Spencer's picture flashed on the screen. She hastily swiped ignore, thrust the phone under her leg, and apologized, "Sorry. I thought I had it on mute. I must have accidentally turned the sound back on when I checked the calendar."

"No problem." Yvette's eyes glittered with curiosity, or maybe something else. "Was that your boyfriend?"

"Uh…" Dani stuttered, then settled on saying, "It's the man that I'm dating."

"He's an extremely handsome guy." Yvette's lips quirked up at the corners. "But that just makes a relationship with him more dangerous."

"I suppose." Dani didn't like the fascinated expression on the beautiful woman's face and resolved that Yvette and Spencer would never meet.

Dani escorted Yvette and Vicki to the door, and while Vicki waved and hurried away with a promise to meet up with Yvette later, the bride-to-be lingered. She stood in the foyer and made small talk until Dani was ready to scream and push her outside.

Finally, Yvette stepped onto the porch and said, "I'll call you Sunday to hear your wonderful dessert ideas, and if I approve, Vicki can stop by that afternoon to sign the contract and give you a check." She carefully picked her way down the steps, then turned and said, "Don't disappoint me."

A chill ran down Dani's spine. Something about the woman was definitely setting off her Spidey senses.

Chapter 2

SPENCER DRAKE QUIETLY OPENED THE DOOR AND walked inside the red metal building. He sniffed, surprised that the odor wasn't as bad as he'd expected. He'd been assured that his newly assigned charges' accommodations were the top-of-the-line, but he'd still anticipated an overpowering stench.

He might have been born a city boy, but his previous profession had exposed him to a variety of environments. In fact, just before his retirement from an elite law enforcement agency, his last assignment had been based in the rural community of Scumble River, Illinois.

Spencer had been undercover as the Tin Man, a member of the infamous Satan's Posse, a motorcycle gang suspected of supplying homegrown terrorists with weapons. They'd squatted in an old farmhouse that had reeked of the raccoons using the attic for their own private toilets. Not to mention the bikers' own nasty body odor.

When Spencer had been exfiltrated from the gang, a story was circulated that the Tin Man had been shanked doing time in Stateville Correctional Center and died in prison. There was even a small marker on an empty grave in the penitentiary cemetery to prove he was six feet under.

It was best for everyone concerned that the Tin Man was never resurrected, so when Spencer had accepted the position of chief of security for Normalton University, one of his demands had been that only his boss, the university vice president, know about his previous work. And even she knew only a part of the truth.

He had helped put away too many outlaw bikers ever to be entirely safe. If it ever became common knowledge that Spencer had been the Tin Man, Satan's Posse would descend on NU like an invading army. And they wouldn't leave until he and a lot of innocent bystanders were dead.

Sighing, Spencer opened his camp stool and settled behind a set of plastic curtains. Dr. Stuart, the head of the agriculture department, had told him that the curtains, along with several large fans, provided the necessary air flow for the building.

That had been an eye-opening meeting. Dr. Stuart had gone on and on about barns and agribusiness. He had emphasized to Spencer why he, and not one of his staff, had to oversee this vital surveillance.

Spencer shook his head. If there was any kind

of justice in the world, he would never have to hear another lecture about animal waste.

If only to get away from Dr. Stuart, Spencer had agreed to take the first shift. And now as he sat there, he rubbed his face and thought about how badly he needed some sleep. The nightmares had been bothering him again, and last night he'd been awakened by them every couple of hours until he gave up and got out of bed around 5:00 a.m.

How in the holy heck was it that he ended up doing more stakeouts in his role as chief of university security than in all of his years in law enforcement? Spencer had certainly never expected that when he took the job.

Evidently, there was more crime on campus than he'd been led to believe during the interview process. When Spencer had applied for the position, he'd been told that the administration wanted him to concentrate on protecting the students from sexual assault and encouraging those who were attacked to report the incident, which was a project he could fully endorse. After all, he had a niece attending the school.

But lately, the university's head honchos had their panties in a bunch about all the pranks being pulled by the newly minted sorority and fraternity pledges. They were especially panicked over a rumor floating around about the Greeks' next target, which was the raison d'être for Spencer's current location in NU's mascot barn.

This outbuilding was on the College Farm, which was situated on the northern edge of the university's property. Its position was quite a hike from the main campus, but distance didn't seem to matter to the inebriated students.

And while the agriculture department was responsible for the well-being of the livestock owned by the college, a couple of the animals were considered too important to be lumped in with all the rest.

The administration was petrified that the university mascots, Hamlet and Oinkphelia, were going to be hognapped. Or worse, dressed in silly costumes and photographed.

PETA had already expressed their displeasure that the Chester White pigs were paraded around during sports events. If the animal rights organization got wind that the pledges had tormented the swine by playing dress up, they'd try to rally the alumni against keeping the hogs as mascots. And that would hit the university right where it hurt—in the pocketbook.

Why Normalton University had chosen pigs for their symbol was beyond Spencer. None of the college's sports teams' names had anything to do with swine. The only reason he could come up with was that whoever had originally chosen the hogs was a displaced Manhattanite who thought that a school located in Central Illinois surrounded by farms had to have a pig as its representative.

Shaking his head, Spencer squirmed on his seat.

The tripod stool wasn't designed to be used for such a long stretch of time. Keeping his gaze glued to the mascots' pen, he reached into his duffel and retrieved a bottle of water. Realizing it was tepid, he wished he'd thought to include a cold pack in his preparations.

It might be mid-October, but it was still darn hot. Spencer couldn't recall the politically correct name for Indian summer, but whatever it was now called, they were experiencing that period of unseasonably warm, dry weather that often occurs in the Midwestern autumn.

As he took a lengthy gulp of the lukewarm liquid, sweat trickled down from Spencer's armpits. Sighing, he screwed the cap back on and tried to get comfortable. Next time, he would delegate this assignment to one of his officers, whether the powers wanted him to handle it himself or not. He snorted at the absurdity of his situation.

In his previous occupation, he'd put his life on the line every day in order to protect the public from the scum of the earth. Now he was waiting for some dumbass kid to try to take a hog hostage.

And even though he knew it was a huge waste of his time, he also knew that he'd sit there until his butt cheeks were numb and his eyes dried out because it was his responsibility to stop the swine from being harassed. When he'd applied for and accepted the job of chief of NU security, he'd sworn to himself he would perform his duties with the same dedication as he'd given his prior work. And if that meant spending the night with a pair of pampered pigs, so be it. Still, he had to wonder how his life had come to this.

As the barn's interior darkened and the shadows lengthened, the sound of a car door slamming startled Spencer from his near doze. Footsteps thudded against the packed dirt and he stiffened.

Spencer checked that he was fully concealed, gripped the high-powered flashlight that he could flick on to temporarily blind the intruders, then waited.

The overhead florescent bulbs cast a greenish glow in the center of the barn but didn't reach the corners. Anything or anyone could lurk in the shadows.

Metal rattled and the door squeaked. A few seconds later a young woman and man approached the pigpen. It was located in the center of the building's interior and the brightest spot in the barn. Each of the intruders held a large white plastic bucket.

The guy poked the girl with his elbow and made a face. "We're in trouble if Professor Stuart finds out that we were so late feeding them."

"Yeah." The young woman nodded, then in a fake baritone pontificated, "Hamlet and Oinkphelia shall be fed at 8:00 a.m. and 6:00 p.m. on the dot."

Shit! Spencer wrinkled his brow. All he needed was for these kids to run into a drunken frat boy and attempt to protect their charges against the raider. He'd be forced to intervene if they got into a physical altercation, but he didn't want to have to tip his hand until he caught the pledges in the act of swine swiping. That way he could have the police charge them with grand larceny instead of just trespassing.

When the pair quickly poured the contents of their buckets into the trough and hurried away, Spencer blew out a relieved breath. He returned his attention to the pigs and watched Hamlet and Oinkphelia jockey for the best cabbages, sweet potatoes, bananas, and apples.

As the hogs inhaled their dinner, Spencer let his mind wander through the last six weeks.

For a long time, the worry that the motorcycle gang would find him and go after someone he cared about had kept Spencer from dating, or even making friends. Bad enough his niece was on campus, but there was nothing he could do about that. However, choosing to make someone a target because of their relationship with him was another story.

At least until recently, when his attraction to Dani Sloan, his niece's friend, landlord, and employer, had caught him by surprise. It had made him realize that he was using his fear of gang retaliation as an excuse not to risk his heart again.

It really wasn't the criminals he was afraid of; it was the lack of good sense that he'd shown in falling for his ex-wife. Maybe if it hadn't taken so long to get free of her, he'd be able to forgive his lapse of judgment, but although the divorce had been swift, her attempts to gain control of every last asset he owned had gone on forever.

It made him wonder why he'd married his ex in the first place. Possibly it was because he'd started realizing that he had nothing in his life that was his. Being undercover so much, he couldn't even have a pet.

But his ex hadn't wanted him to quit and become just another cop. She liked the idea of his dangerous job. That was probably what attracted her to his best friend, who was a firefighter. His profession had the mystique she craved without the inconvenience of an absent husband.

Because of his disastrous marriage and worse breakup, he'd thought that he was far from being ready for a romantic involvement. And although he'd vowed never again to rush into a relationship with a woman, he couldn't seem to fight the appeal of Miss Cupcake. He'd known resistance was futile the minute he'd given the curvy chef that affectionate nickname.

He'd managed to control his feelings until she started spending a lot of time investigating a murder with a local hotshot police detective, but then jealousy had reared its ugly head and he'd realized that he'd have to make his move before he lost her to the other man.

He hadn't exactly planned the moment of his surrender. But when it happened and he'd impulsively kissed her, he hadn't been the least bit sorry.

That kiss had been earth-shattering. Now if they only could carve out some time to spend together, maybe they could move to the next step. Whatever that might be. Certainly, more than their current quick peck good-night.

The past six weeks they'd had to be satisfied with a few dates, some long phone conversations, and lots of silly texts.

That reminded him. Dani had never returned his call. He'd tried to contact her earlier that afternoon and had to leave a message.

Why hadn't she responded?

While Spencer only worked the weekends during big college events, Dani nearly always had either a catering job or a personal chef gig. But for once she was free.

As soon as Spencer found out Dani was available, he had cashed in a favor to get a reservation at the Reapers Supper Club. The restaurant was normally booked months in advance and it had been a miracle that the parents of a girl Spencer had rescued from a party that had gotten out of hand were investors in the place.

Ordinarily, Spencer would never have accepted such a gift, but the girl's parents had insisted, and since it didn't have any monetary value, he felt okay having them arrange a table for him.

At such short notice, he had no choice if he wanted to take Dani to the hottest spot in town. And he really wanted to impress her.

Fishing his cell phone out of his shirt pocket,

Spencer checked to see if he'd missed Dani's return call, but there was nothing. That was odd. Unless she was working, she always got back to him within a few minutes.

He frowned. As far as he knew, Dani didn't have a personal chef or catering job tonight. And the appointment with the prospective client she'd been so excited about should have been over long ago. According to Dani, initial consultations rarely lasted more than forty-five minutes. An hour was pushing it.

Spencer was pretty sure that Dani had said her meeting was scheduled for three o'clock, which was why he waited until nearly five to call her. And now it was going on seven and still no response.

Spencer started to dial her number but stopped. If his investigative targets arrived for the hog hijacking, he didn't want them to hear him talking on the phone. Instead he'd send her a text.

He quickly typed out: Everything okay?

Hmm. He didn't want to seem needy or controlling.

Erasing that message, he tried again. I nabbed a reservation at Reapers for Saturday night at 6:30. Hope you're still free.

Okay. That was better.

His finger hovered over the Send button. Did that message sound a little cold?

They weren't at the stage where he'd include the *L* word. But maybe a romantic emoji would be good. Spencer swiped through the options.

No. Not the one with hearts in the smiley's eyes. That seemed too silly.

How about the smiley holding the red rose?

No way. Spencer was pretty sure he remembered Dani saying that her ex-boyfriend always gave her red roses after they'd had a fight.

Spencer kept swiping until he saw the two smileys sharing a plate of spaghetti a la *Lady and the Tramp*. It was perfect. He tapped the image and sent the text.

Before slipping his cell back into his pocket, Spencer checked the time. It had taken longer than he'd thought to compose his message and it was almost eight o'clock.

He glanced at Hamlet and Oinkphelia. The porcine couple had finished eating and were now snuggled side by side, sleeping peacefully.

Spencer drummed his fingers on his thighs. He'd give the animal abductors until midnight to show up. After that, he'd set up the surveillance equipment he brought with him, put the hardened-steel, high-security padlock on the door, and call it a night.

Standing, Spencer stretched the kinks out of his back. If he gave in and did this again tomorrow night, he was bringing a more comfortable seat.

And speaking of comfort, he needed a bathroom break. If he were on a life-and-death stakeout, he'd use a can or a bottle, but a possible pignapping did not qualify for such extreme measures.

A quick walk around the barn and a scan out

the windows of the surrounding area convinced him that there wasn't anyone nearby. Easing open the door, he stepped outside, then engaged the lock behind him.

Once the barn was secure, he jogged toward the office building a hundred or so yards away, sure there would be a restroom inside. Good thing he had a master key.

He was just completing the pause that refreshes when the radio clipped to his utility belt squawked. That wasn't good. His people had been instructed not to contact him unless it was an emergency.

Frowning, he zipped up, washed his hands, then keyed the mic and said, "Drake here. What's up?"

"Chief." Lavonia Jools, Spencer's only female security officer, cleared her throat.

"That's me."

"We have a situation in Area 51." Lavonia's voice was strained.

The university's department of paranormal and psychic phenomena was housed in Fox Hall. It had quickly been nicknamed Area 51 and become the butt of student pranks.

When Lavonia didn't continue, he asked, "What kind of situation?"

Lavonia was a good officer and not one to panic needlessly. She'd been an army MP, but while used to dealing with drunks, sometimes the silliness of the college students threw her off her game.

"Uh." She cleared her throat again. "It's a little hard to describe."

"Ohhhkay." Spencer stretched out the word. "Start at the beginning."

"The alarm went off in Fox Hall's storage room," Lavonia said.

"I assume you called Robert for backup, then went to check it out."

Spencer would be shocked if she hadn't. Lavonia followed all of his rules, even ones she might not agree with, such as the need for two officers to respond to any alarm. What could have knocked her for a loop?

"Yes," Lavonia answered. "I mean no." She sucked in a breath. "I did call Robert into work, but I had to send him to the Towers. As you know, it's an all-female dorm and the eighth-floor RA found a drunken guy singing in the shower. When she asked him to leave, he walked down the hallway naked and into one of the suites."

"Was it occupied?" Spencer sprinted back to the mascot barn, grabbed the surveillance camera from his duffel, and quickly set it up.

"Yeah, the girl was able to exit without any problem but unfortunately didn't take her key, and the door locked itself automatically when she let it close," Lavonia answered. "While the RA has a key, she didn't feel safe trying to get the guy out of the room by herself. So Robert's dealing with that."

Spencer attached the high-security padlock and took off toward the lot where he'd parked his truck.

"The room's original occupant is fine," Lavonia added. "But she and the RA are shaken up."

"So I'm assuming you went to check on the alarm at Fox on your own." Spencer arrived at his pickup, beeped open the doors, and threw his duffel onto the passenger seat. "What did you find?"

"The thing is, sir." Lavonia paused. "I'm not sure what I found."

"Just give me a sitrep." Spencer slid behind the wheel and drove toward the main campus as he waited for Lavonia to respond.

Lavonia began her situation report. "When I arrived at Area 51, the entrance and exits were secure and there was no evidence of forced entry."

"So if someone was inside, you figured they had a key," Spencer prodded.

"Yes." Lavonia's voice was low, then there was a long stretch of silence and Spencer wondered if something had happened to the woman. Was she still at Fox Hall? Had she been attacked?

Just as Spencer was about to check, Lavonia continued, "I cleared the first floor and went on to the second, where the storage area is located."

"And?" Spencer was pulling in front of Fox Hall as he spoke.

"When I got to the storage room, I proceeded with extreme caution." Lavonia's voice cracked.

"Good." Spencer threw his truck into park, jumped out, and ran up the steps of the building. He fumbled with the huge campus key ring until he found the correct one and opened the front door. "I'm on the premises. Are you still in the storage room?"

"I am, but the thing is…" Lavonia paused then admitted, "The door closed behind me. It won't budge and I can't get out."

"Is that the emergency?" Spencer asked. He'd have bet money Lavonia wouldn't have called him because she got locked in somewhere. She'd have waited until Robert was free and had him grab the key from the security office and get her out.

"Not exactly." Lavonia's voice cracked again. "There's a young man dressed in some kind of Native American costume. He's pinned to the wall with a couple of tomahawks."

"Is he dead?" Spencer bent to grab his Glock from its ankle holster.

While the rest of campus security weren't allowed guns and were only equipped with Tasers and pepper spray, Spencer was licensed for concealed carry.

"No," Lavonia answered. "The hatchets are holding him in place through what looks like an animal skin shirt. He says he's unhurt, but the tomahawks are so deeply embedded in the wall, I can't pull them out and the shirt is impossible to tear. If someone can hold him up, I could probably get him out of the shirt. Or maybe we can cut him free of it with scissors."

"Did the vic say how he got mounted like a bug?" Spencer asked standing in front of the storage room's door. He inserted his master key.

"He claims that an Indian chief attacked him, then disappeared into thin air. The next thing he remembered was me asking if he was okay."

Chapter 3

ONCE YVETTE AND VICKI LEFT, DANI ATTEMPTED to relax. She'd tried reading the novel that she'd been struggling to finish in time for her monthly book club, and when that failed to keep her interest, she turned on the TV. After channel surfing through her entire Media Com package, she admitted that what she really wanted to do was start concocting distinctive desserts for her prospective client.

A few hours later, the tantalizing aroma of stout-infused chocolate cake topped with pecan-and-caraway streusel scented the air of her kitchen. As the cake baked, Dani assembled the dough for bomboloni. The hole-less Italian doughnut would be stuffed with matcha, pumpkin, and Baileys liqueur–flavored crème pâtissière.

While the bombolone dough rested in the fridge, Dani start her third and final offering, hand pies with apple-and-green-chili filling. This was the riskiest of the trio but also the most unique.

Dani assembled the pastry crust using her usual recipe, but instead of the customary water, she substituted apple cider vinegar. Just as she was cutting the dough into rectangles, the kitchen door swung open and Ivy Drake, one of her three boarders, trudged inside.

Ivy's heart-shaped face and pink cheeks made her look even younger than her nineteen years, but her usual dimpled smile was missing.

Ivy flung herself on the center counter stool and her voice was grumpy when she asked, "Why are you baking so late? We don't have any events for tomorrow."

While Dani explained about her prospective new client's demand for special desserts, Ivy reached for the plastic containers that held the leftover desserts from that day's lunch-to-go bags. One held the frosted peanut-butter cookies and the other had the healthier coconut, fruit, and nut bars.

Dani offered two choices for her takeout meals. Both had an entrée, side, and dessert each day and were packaged in her signature red-and-white-striped paper bags, but one option had less sugar, carbs, and fats, while the other was more indulgent.

The lunches-to-go were usually the most reliable part of Dani's income, and she was a bit worried that the number of customers had been down this morning, which was why so many sacks had remained unsold.

She could only hope it was because the college

kids were taking Friday off and heading out early for the weekend. Dani hadn't quite gotten the rhythm of when students would and wouldn't be on campus during the semester. And she'd forgotten that Normalton University celebrated Founder's Day on the third Monday of October. It appeared that a lot of the students took advantage of the holiday to leave the area.

Dusting the flour off her fingers, Dani paused before starting the hand pie filling and said, "What's up with you? You're home pretty early for a Friday night. Is Laz out of town?"

Dani was nearly a dozen years older than Ivy, who, having skipped a couple of grades, was already a senior at the college. But over the past year and a half or so, the two of them had drifted into a close friendship, especially after Ivy and her best buddies, Tippi Epstein and Starr Fleming, had moved in with Dani and begun to work part-time for her Chef-to-Go company.

Until a few months ago when Ivy had started seeing Lazarus Hunter, she'd seemed to prefer hanging out at the mansion to going out with her pals. Even now, a lot of evenings when Dani wasn't working at a personal chef gig, Ivy would lounge around in the family room with her, watching reruns of some cooking show.

At first, due to their age difference, Dani had been a little uneasy about the friendship, but once she acknowledged that they had a sort of big sister/ little sister relationship, she accepted it. She'd always wanted a sibling, but her parents had said that one child was enough of a drain on their time and money.

"Laz didn't show up at the library." Ivy finally answered Dani's question as she pried off both of the cookie containers' lids and peered inside to make her selection.

"And you were expecting him?" Dani clarified, wanting to make sure she understood before weighing in with an opinion or commiserating.

She'd been apprehensive when Ivy had started seeing Laz. He just didn't seem like the kind of guy someone as studious as Ivy would attract. And that had Dani worried that he would break the girl's heart.

While neither Ivy nor Laz admitted that they were anything other than friends, Dani was pretty darn sure there was more to it than that.

Still, Laz's fiancée had only been dead for a few months, so it was probably best he and Ivy kept whatever romantic feelings they had for one another on the down low. It was no one's business, and this way they kept the rumor mill from grinding out nasty gossip.

And, despite Dani's initial doubts, Laz and Ivy had been nearly inseparable and they seemed to get along really well. Enough so that Laz had introduced Ivy to his family during the university's orientation week. Laz's mother had been a bit cool toward Ivy, but his father had seemed welcoming. Ivy had even been invited to a second family function.

"Sort of," Ivy muttered.

Dani shook off her recollections and repeated, "Sort of…"

Ivy licked icing off of her fingers, selected another cookie, this time one of the nut bars, and continued, "He's been meeting me there every night after supper since classes started. We both work on our homework for three or four hours, then we go get a slice of pizza or some ice cream and he drives me home."

"Did you text him?" Dani asked. "The library is huge and if he couldn't get his regular spot maybe he had to go over to the law library."

"Twice." Ivy played with the gold skulls hanging from her hoop earring. "He never answered." She wrinkled her brow. "And he always texts me right back."

Dani hadn't been able to decide if it was a good thing or a bad thing that Laz had gotten into NU's law school. On one hand, she was happy for him that the rehab treatment that he'd gone through the summer between high school and college had been successful and he'd done well enough in college to gain admittance to the prestigious program.

On the other, it might have been good for Ivy to have a little space from him. With Laz farther away, she would have had a chance to gain some perspective on their relationship.

Now that Dani thought about his alcohol problem,

she wondered if the young man had had a relapse. That would explain why he'd stood up Ivy. Although Laz had been clean and sober for three years, he had slipped off the wagon the day his fiancée had been murdered. Maybe the pressure of school had made it happen again.

"Has Laz been stressed lately?" Between her prior occupation in human resources and living with three college kids, Dani had gotten good at easing into unpleasant conversations.

"You mean you're concerned that he might be drinking again." Ivy flicked a disappointed glance at Dani. "Don't you think that I'd notice that?"

"Addicts can be tricky." Dani sighed. Evidently, she wasn't as good as she thought at easing into sensitive topics.

Ivy's shoulders drooped. "I suppose. But even if he was hitting the booze, Laz would have let me know that he wasn't going to see me tonight."

"Maybe he was fighting the urge and decided he had to go to an AA meeting right away," Dani suggested. "I doubt they allow cell phone usage."

"That's probably it." Ivy beamed. "He'll call as soon as he's free."

"Definitely." Dani tried to sound convinced, but Ivy shot her a hard look.

The two of them were silent, neither exactly sure what else to say.

Finally, Dani straightened and said, "I'd better

get the filling going for these hand pies or I'll still be making them at midnight."

"Can I help?" Ivy asked, hopping off her stool and heading around the counter.

"Sure." Dani began gathering the ingredients, then handed Ivy a bag of Granny Smith apples. "How about peeling and slicing those while I get the seeds out of the green chilies and chop them up?"

"Absolutely." Ivy washed her hands. "I love seeing if I can get the skin off in one long spiral. My dad says that if you do that and drop it on the floor, it will form the initial of your soul mate."

While they worked, Dani sneaked a peek at Ivy. She was disturbed that her young friend looked so downhearted. Ivy's personality was generally so upbeat and bubbly, it was sad to see her like that.

"You know, you shouldn't listen to me about Laz. With my history with men, I'm not a very good judge." Finishing up with the chilies, Dani juiced a lime, then measured out the sugar, cornstarch, salt, nutmeg, allspice, and cinnamon. "Look at what happened with my ex."

About a year and a half ago, Dani had found out that her then-boyfriend, Dr. Kipp Newson, was actually engaged to someone else. She'd had no idea that she was his side chick until Ivy had done a bit of sleuthing on social media.

Finding it hard to accept that she'd been so stupid, Dani could only hope that she'd learned her lesson.

She massaged the back of her neck. Thinking about Kipp always made her tense. Especially remembering that his cheating hadn't been the half of it. He'd been much worse than she'd ever imagined.

Ivy's expression was full of guilt. "I'm sorry I had to be the one to tell you."

"No," Dani assured her. "I appreciate you looking out for me."

Although she hated to admit it and would never say it out loud, Dani had known something was off with her and Kipp. However, for once her father had liked someone she was seeing, so she'd ignored her own gut feeling until Ivy shoved the evidence of his infidelity in front of her face.

Before that undeniable proof, Dani had been unwilling to give up her father's hard-won and rare approval. He'd been more impressed when she'd introduced him to Kipp than when she'd graduated from college summa cum laude, and she'd wanted to bask in his admiration for as long as she could. Even if in her heart of hearts, she knew Kipp had been only using her for her cooking and her satellite television package.

Breaking into Dani's depressing thoughts, Ivy said, "Anyway, all that's behind you. My uncle would never deceive you like that."

Ivy was Spencer's niece, which was how he and Dani had met. But going out with her friend/boarder/employee's uncle was a tad awkward at times. Ivy was one of the reasons that, so far, Dani and Spencer's dates had ended with a chaste kiss at the front door.

Granted, thanks to the previous owner's desire for privacy and comfort, Dani had a secluded suite on the third floor. The cozy sitting room filled with relaxing furniture, the spacious bedroom with the amazing walk-in closet, and the huge spa-like bathroom straight out of HGTV were wonderful, but it didn't have its own entrance and the only way in or out was via the main staircase.

And although Dani was really nothing more than the college girls' landlord and employer, their parents had entrusted her with their daughters and she felt a certain moral obligation to provide a good example. Her boarders weren't allowed to have guys in their bedrooms, so Dani was unwilling to have a man in hers. Unless, of course, she could figure out a way to sneak him up there.

Dani snickered softly at her thoughts. Girls or no girls, she and Spencer were far, far from that type of relationship anyway. She'd never been one to jump into bed with the men she dated and she certainly wasn't about to start with Spencer. Even if the chemistry between them was hotter than a Fourth of July sparkler.

"I'm sure you're right." Dani finally answered Ivy's remark about her uncle.

"Speaking of which…" Ivy had finished with the apples, poured herself a glass of milk, and returned to her stool. "What's going on with you two?" She reopened the plastic containers of cookies. "I see Laz more than you see Uncle Spence and we're only friends."

Dani watched Ivy shove another peanut butter cookie into her mouth and shook her head. It amazed Dani that someone with Ivy's willowy figure could eat almost nonstop and not put on any weight.

"We're both busy adults." Dani paused, distracted by Ivy as she snatched another cookie from the bowl, dunked it in her glass of milk, and moaned her appreciation. "While you and Laz can study together, your uncle and I have to do our work separately. It's not as if I can ride around with him while he patrols or have him with me when I cook for my private clients."

"I suppose." Ivy tilted her head. "But you have tomorrow night off, right?"

"I do." Dani pursed her lips. She'd been wondering if Spencer would make arrangements to see her. "Oh, crap!" Dani patted her pockets for her cell phone and frowned when she didn't find it there.

"What's wrong?" Ivy used her tongue to rescue a crumb from the corner of her lips.

Instead of answering, Dani grabbed her purse from the table and emptied it onto the counter, then hunted around the kitchen.

"What are you looking for?" Ivy asked.

"My cell phone." Dani blew out a breath. "Your uncle called while I was with a client and I wasn't able to answer, then I forgot all about it." She checked her watch. "Shoot! That was nearly nine hours ago."

"Yikes!" Ivy twisted one of the bright-pink wisps of hair scattered among her long, blond strands. "I'm surprised Uncle Spence isn't here beating down the door to make sure you're okay."

"Most likely because he's working," Dani explained. "I think he said something about having to guard some pigs tonight. Can that be right?"

"Yep." Ivy giggled. "He probably meant Hamlet and Oinkphelia."

"You mean the college mascots?" Dani continued to search for her phone.

"Yeah." Ivy rolled her eyes. "Rumor has it there's a contest among the Greeks to see which of their pledges can capture the mascots and display them at their house. The winning sorority or fraternity members get to be the guests of honor at a big luau."

"They aren't going to roast the pigs, are they?" Although Dani wasn't a vegetarian, the idea of using the pets as the main course horrified her.

"Nah." Ivy shook her head. "But I do believe Hamlet will be dressed for the occasion in a Hawaiian shirt while Oinkphelia will be wearing a grass skirt and coconut bra. And both will be featured in a video."

Both women laughed until they were gasping for air. They were still breathless when the kitchen door opened and Tippi Epstein swept in.

Unlike Ivy, who wore plain Levis and a T-shirt

with DON'T DRINK AND DERIVE printed across her chest, Tippi was smartly dressed in an off-shoulder plaid jacket with a black, twisted top and skinny jeans.

The tiny brunette zeroed in on the cookie container and marched toward it as she said, "Caleb Boyd is a big creep McCreepster! I hate him and I never want to see him again!" She shot a finger at Dani. "If he comes to the door, do not let him into this house."

Tippi and Caleb were members of a pre-law fraternity and members of the same study group, but this sounded more like a boyfriend-girlfriend issue.

"What happened?" Ivy demanded.

"He asked Bryn to the Halloween dance." Although Tippi was petite, her personality was anything but small, and she was used to getting her own way. "Just because guys have one, doesn't mean they have to be one."

As Dani puzzled over whether the word Tippi was referring to was dick or asshole, Ivy snorted and Tippi's lips briefly curled upward.

"I didn't know you two were anything more than friends," Dani said cautiously.

"I...I..."

Tippi's triangular face usually reminded Dani of a cute little kitten, but not tonight. Now she looked more like a ticked-off elf.

"Thought it was more than that?" Ivy supplied, patting her friend's arm.

"Yeah." Tippi crunched down on a cookie, chewed,

and swallowed. Then her shoulders drooped and she said, "Between classes, studying, and the fraternity activities, we spend so much time together and he's so nice to me, I just thought…" She trailed off.

"I understand." Ivy's bright-blue eyes dimmed. "It's hard to tell if they like you, like you, or just think of you as a pal."

Both girls looked at Dani, who threw up her hands and admitted, "I have no idea how to tell either."

They were all silent for a few seconds, then Ivy said, "Well, Caleb's not the only fish in the sea."

"True." Tippi's olive complexion reddened and she added, "And it appears that I'm also not the only fisherman."

Before Dani could comment, the kitchen door opened again. This time it was Starr Fleming. The silver beads on the ends of her braids clanked as she stomped across the floor and joined her friends at the counter. Evidently her evening hadn't gone any better than Ivy's and Tippi's.

Dani thought about the study she'd just heard about on the news that said one out of every four Americans suffered from some sort of mental illness. Looking at her three boarders, she wondered if she was that one person. Voluntarily living with three drama-filled college girls had to be an indication of something about her personality. She'd been there, done that when she was in school. Did she really need a rerun of that soap opera?

Chapter 4

IT TOOK A COUPLE OF HOURS, AS WELL AS DANI'S entire stash of homemade pecan-caramel crunch ice cream and her last jar of gourmet dark chocolate hot fudge topping, but Ivy, Starr, and Tippi finally stopped moping about their love lives...at least temporarily.

They'd put their bowls in the sink, said good night, and trooped up the stairs to their rooms. Once they were alone, the brooding probably started up again, but Dani was too tired to worry about it and resolved to deal with the problem in the morning.

A few minutes later, as Dani cleaned up the kitchen, she could hear the water pipes knocking, indicating that the three girls had all turned on their showers at the same time. She cringed with each clang and reverberation.

Most of the mansion had been renovated before she'd inherited it, but the plumber she'd hired to fix the leaky faucet in Ivy's bathroom had told her that the whole place needed to be re-piped. He'd claimed that houses this old had galvanized pipes that were prone to burst and corrode as they aged. He'd warned her that it was a disaster waiting to happen and encouraged her to replace them. The sooner the better.

Sadly, Dani just didn't have the money right now to start such an expensive project. Not only would it cost her thousands of dollars, but her business would have to be severely limited for the entire length of time.

Such an extensive refit would involve shutting down the lunch-to-go and catering arms of her company for the duration, leaving her personal chef jobs as her only income, which was not an option right now. Even a week or two could be the difference between balanced books and ones in the red.

Maybe next June, during the summer lull, she'd have saved enough to afford new plumbing. Either that, or she might have to work up the nerve to take out a home improvement loan.

It wasn't that she didn't think she'd qualify. The mansion had been free of any kind of mortgage when she'd inherited it from her grandmother's sorority sister, Mrs. Cook, and her credit score was excellent.

It should be relatively easy to get financing, but the real issue was that Dani had never owed a dime in her life and hated the thought of going into debt now. Especially without a guaranteed salary to ensure she could make the monthly payments.

Dani had used her savings and investments for her company's startup expenses. She'd shelled out cash when she'd originally purchased her car—which she'd then traded in for the Chef-to-Go van. She wrote a check for the entire amount due on her Visa every month. And, with the girls' rent, she was able to cover the taxes, insurance, and buy groceries for the household.

True, it was a balancing act, but so far, she'd been able to keep all the plates spinning on their sticks. She shivered at the thought of having the financial obligation of a loan. The image of those dishes smashing to the ground terrified her.

Still, she had to get the pipes fixed. Luckily, when Geraldine Cook had decided to open a bed-and-breakfast, she'd had the house rewired to bring it up to code. Too bad she'd passed away before she got to the plumbing.

Dani grimaced at that. She should be grateful to the wonderful woman for naming her as her sole heir, not griping because the inheritance wasn't perfect. Clearly, she was too tired to think straight.

Yawning, Dani finished up in the kitchen and headed for the stairs. Thank goodness tomorrow was Saturday and she didn't have to get up by 6:00 a.m. to start the lunch-to-go prep or cook the girls' breakfast before they left for their eight o'clock classes.

She was halfway up the steps when she jerked to a stop and ran back down to the main floor. When the girls had all begun crying on her shoulder, she'd forgotten all about her missing cell phone and Spencer's call.

He would be wondering what happened to her. She definitely needed to find her phone before she went to bed and let Spencer know she was okay. Otherwise, he'd be at her door as soon as he was off duty.

Dani was kind of surprised that he hadn't stopped by to check on her already. Unless she was working, he was used to her returning his messages immediately. His lack of reaction must mean he was still pigsitting the NU mascots.

Now where had she last seen her phone?

She paused at the foot of the staircase and tapped her chin. It had chimed during her meeting with Yvette and her wedding planner, which had been embarrassingly unprofessional, and Dani had shoved it out of sight beneath her leg. Had she seen it since then?

Nope!

Dani hurried down the hallway and into the parlor. Flipping on the switch for the chandelier, she blinked when the bright light blinded her. As soon as her eyes adjusted, she scanned the room.

She blew out a relieved breath when she spotted her cell phone lying beneath the chair she'd been occupying. It must have slipped off the seat and fallen on the floor when she got up to escort her prospective clients into the foyer. She probably hadn't heard it thud because of the thick Persian carpet.

Thank goodness!

She did not want to have to hunt it down. Swooping up the black rectangular device, Dani immediately swiped the screen, then punched in her code to listen to Spencer's voicemail.

"Hi! I thought you'd be done with your meeting by now, but it must be running long. I'll have my phone with me at the surveillance so give me a call when you're free. I have some great news."

Dani glanced at the time. It was past midnight.

Thinking that Spencer might be home asleep and not wanting to wake him, she thumbed the text icon to answer him, but saw that he'd beat her to it.

I nabbed a reservation at Reapers for Saturday night at 6:30. Hope you're still free.

Dani's pulse sped up. The smiley faces sharing a single strand of spaghetti were adorable, and the Reapers Supper Club was known for its romantic atmosphere. Spencer was sending a definite message arranging for them to eat there. The vintage furnishings and 1940s music in its lounge were reputed to put couples in the mood for love.

Her hand shook as she composed her reply.

I'm still free and I wouldn't miss dinner with you at Reapers for anything!

Her finger hovered over the Send button. Was her response too much? Maybe she needed to include an emoji to lighten it up a little.

She scrolled through her choices but didn't see

anything that said *I'm eager for our date but not pathetically eager*. Finally, she settled on a cat winking and after adding it to her message, she sent the text to Spencer.

Instantly, she wished she could delete it and try again. Did he even like cats? He'd mentioned having a dog when he was a boy, but nothing about a cat.

Crap! She was overthinking it. This is why she didn't like dating. It screwed up her self-confidence and made her second-guess herself.

As she climbed the stairs to her suite, she assured herself that her text had been fine. And by the time she had finished brushing her teeth, washing and moisturizing her face, and slipping into her nightshirt, she'd calmed down and was getting excited about spending time with Spencer without the threat of someone walking in on them and interrupting their conversation, which happened at the mansion on a regular basis.

Then, just as she was climbing into bed, her gaze landed on the closet door.

Shoot! It had been so long since she'd been out on a really important date. She didn't have a thing to wear.

~

The next day, Dani awakened to the sound of her cell blaring the Jackson 5's "I'll Be There." It was the ring tone she assigned to all her customers' phone numbers and she groaned.

Blinking awake, she checked the time and saw that it wasn't even 8:00 a.m. yet. So much for her plan to sleep in and have a restful morning.

Which of her clients was calling at such an early hour on a Saturday? Had Dani forgotten some breakfast event that she'd promised to work?

She mentally ran through her schedule, but there was nothing on her agenda. No lunches-to-goes to prepare, no personal chef gigs, and no catering jobs she had to work. This was one of the rare days that she was entirely free from professional commitments.

The third time the music played, she reached for the phone and saw the name of Yvette's wedding planner. Hastily she sat up and, not wanting to sound half-asleep, cleared her throat before she answered.

Then she swiped the icon and said in her best professional voice, "Chef-to-Go, Dani Sloan speaking."

"Vicki Troemel here." A pleasant alto floated out of the cell phone's speakers. "I hope this isn't too early to phone you."

"Of course not. I'm an early riser." Dani swung her legs over the side of the mattress and got to her feet. "But I am a little surprised to hear from you. Weren't you traveling back to Chicago yesterday evening, or are you calling from there?"

"No. I'm in Normalton. My original intent was to go home, but the meeting with Franklin and Yvette ran so long that I was afraid I'd fall asleep if I tried to drive up I-55 that time of night," Vicki answered. "Good thing my mantra is to always be prepared and I keep a packed overnight bag in my trunk."

"That's my motto too." Dani was pretty darn sure the woman hadn't called just to chat about their mutual preparedness so she asked, "What can I do for you?"

"What I'm hoping you can do is tell me you're free next Saturday."

"Why?" Dani asked gingerly.

She somehow doubted that the wedding planner was asking about her schedule in order to hire her for her own use as a private chef. Although maybe she had another client in town that needed some catering.

"Yvette and Franklin would like to move up their engagement celebration." Vicki's grim tone conveyed her feelings about the matter and they matched Dani's.

"How in the world do they expect that to happen?" Dani sank back down on the bed. "Forget all the components for the event, but the guests may not be willing to drop everything to attend the party."

"Most of the invitees are directly employed by Franklin, somehow owe their livelihood to him, or hope to get something from him in the future. And Yvette's portion of the list is mostly those men's wives and girlfriends." Vicki chuckled. "They aren't friends like you and I would have at our party."

"And when you have the amount of money that he controls, those kinds of people would miss their mother's funeral to be at his event." Dani filled in the blanks the wedding planner had left open. "Okay, forget the guests. How about the tent, lighting, furniture, music, and all the other accessories, along with the personnel needed to install them, available on such short notice?"

"Yvette's orders are that anything we can't rent, I should just buy." Vicki paused and added, "Plus the company we're using has the contract to provide all of that kind of stuff to the Korn Kings' training camp. Believe me, they will pull their equipment from another event before they'll disappoint Franklin or his bride-to-be."

"Wow." Dani whistled. "Well then, let me check my calendar. One sec."

She put the wedding planner on hold and pulled up her schedule. The upcoming week was relatively light. Just a birthday party on Sunday, Monday through Friday's lunch-to-go bags, and one personal chef engagement. If she didn't accept any other bookings for the next seven days and was able to get the food ordered within a couple of hours, she might be able to do it. But she'd need help.

Returning to the call, she said, "I am free that day." The other woman cheered, but Dani cut her off and continued, "However, in order to do this, I'll have to charge double the price that I originally quoted to you guys because I am going to have to hire additional staff, including a sous-chef, and none of that is going to be cheap."

"Not a problem," Vicki said quickly. "Let's say triple your initial estimate since we don't want you to feel you have to skimp on anything. I've been told by the happy couple that the sky is the limit budget-wise."

"I'm not expected to provide the china, crystal, silver, or linens, right?"

"Correct. We've got that covered with the same company responsible for the tent and other equipment," Vicki assured her. "Just text me a list of the type and number of plates, as well as the type and number of flatware that you'll need for your menu."

The wedding planner's voice was almost giddy and Dani wondered why the woman was so relieved. There were other caterers in Normalton. Although, perhaps not on such short notice.

"Speaking of the menu, I'll need it approved by Yvette before nine so I can place the food orders by ten. Oh, and a firm guest count," Dani cautioned. "Will that be a problem?"

"Absolutely not." Again Vicki sounded a little too cheery, but Dani shrugged it off. "We'll go with four hundred as we'd rather have leftovers than not enough. And Yvette agrees to the entrées, sides, and appetizers that we discussed yesterday. Did you come up with the desserts?"

"Yes." Dani crossed her fingers for luck. "How does hand pies with apple-and-green-chili filling, stout-infused chocolate cake with pecan-and-caraway-streusel topping, and an assortment of bomboloni filled with pastry cream flavored with matcha, pumpkin, and Baileys liqueur sound?"

"Amazingly delicious!" Vicki gushed, then said, "Let me run those by Yvette, then I'll come over to sign the contract and give you a check for two-thirds of your fee before nine. I believe that is the standard deposit for an event that is within a week away?"

"Sorry, but no. I'll need the full amount due because of the short notice."

"No problem," Vicki said almost before Dani stopped speaking.

Dani was about to disconnect when a question popped into her head. Was it unprofessional to ask?

Shrugging, with so little time left, she doubted they'd fire her for a minor infraction so she decided to go for it and said, "One more thing. Why the change of date?"

Vicki blew out a long, noisy breath, then her tone dry, answered, "Yvette just found out that the original Saturday she chose was All Saints' Day."

"So?" Dani scratched her head. "Does her religion forbid parties on that day?"

"Not at all." Vicki chuckled. "But with Halloween the day before, she was afraid that it might somehow, don't ask me how, taint her party."

"Maybe she was afraid people would come in costume." Dani rolled her eyes. "Anyway, I'll expect you before nine."

Once they said their goodbyes, Dani took a quick

shower, then threw on a pair of black yoga pants and a red T-shirt with the Chef-to-Go logo. Then she twisted her hair into a messy bun and applied bronzer and mascara. Almost ready to face the day, she ran downstairs straight to the coffee maker.

While the machine was working its caffeinated magic, Dani checked the newly installed dry-erase board on the wall next to the fridge. Technically, her renters didn't have to keep her informed of their comings and goings, but she'd asked them to indicate whether they were in the mansion or not just so she'd know if they needed to be evacuated in case of an emergency like a fire or tornado.

Studying the board, it appeared Ivy and Starr had already left and Tippi either hadn't woken up yet or had forgotten to sign out. Either of which were a possibility for her.

While Ivy and Starr generally followed the house rules to the letter, Tippi always pushed until Dani was forced to come down on her. Mrs. Epstein was a judge, and Tippi was pre-law, making Dani wonder sometimes if the girl had seen so many defendants wiggle out of a conviction due to a technicality that she used those same concepts to avoid her own obligations.

Giving her the benefit of the doubt, Dani assumed Tippi was still upstairs asleep or at least hadn't left the mansion.

After pouring herself a cup of coffee, Dani grabbed

a legal pad and began to make her list of supplies. Four hundred guests was a huge number and she checked and rechecked her figures, afraid that she'd miscalculate the amount she needed.

Vicki was true to her word and rang the bell at precisely nine o'clock. She approved the desserts, signed the contract, and gave Dani a certified check, then quickly left saying she had other vendors to see.

An hour later, Dani put her phone aside and rubbed her eyes. She'd placed the food and other supply orders, secured eight servers in addition to Tippi, Ivy, and Starr, and hired her friend Gray as sous-chef.

He'd wanted to work for free, but Dani insisted on paying him the going rate. Thankfully, there hadn't been any high-profile murder cases in a while, so he wasn't busy with his real job as chief detective of the Normalton Police Department. Dani was fairly certain that Spencer would not approve, but if he didn't like it, he could always come and help out too.

Chapter 5

D ANI WAS ANTSY. AT THE MOMENT, THERE WASN'T anything else she could do to prepare for next Saturday's engagement party, but it felt like she should be working on it.

She'd received a text from Spencer that he'd pick her up at 6:00 p.m. and it wasn't even noon. She wasn't one to sit around. What would she do with herself for the next half-dozen hours?

Gazing around the kitchen, she searched for something that needed her attention. Except for her dirty spoon near the coffee maker, the room was spic and span.

Saturdays, her boarders were on their own for meals and everything was already set to go for tomorrow afternoon's birthday party. For once the guests had no dietary restrictions, and the five-year-old's parents only specifications were that the food should be fun, not totally unhealthy, and cater to the birthday boy's obsession with trucks, trains, and heavy moving equipment.

Both the menu and the prep had been relatively easy. Dani had created veggie dip appetizers in small plastic glasses printed with trucks. She had also had skewers of fruit cut out to spell the child's name, as well as his favorite vehicle brands.

The main course was pizza wheels and mac-and-cheese bites. They were both ready to pop in the oven once Dani arrived at the boy's house. She'd found serving platters printed with construction equipment on which she'd place the finished entrées before putting them on the table.

And the dump truck birthday cake and frosting were both made and waiting to be assembled when Dani got home from church. She had Ho Hos and mini chocolate doughnuts standing by for the tires and axels, as well as the white gumdrops for the headlights, red M&Ms for the taillights, and Twix bars for the bumpers.

Just as Dani rose from her seat at the table to pour herself another cup of coffee, Tippi stumbled into the kitchen and muttered, "Morning."

The young woman's eyes were red rimmed, her face was puffy, and her usually squared shoulders were drooping. Had she been crying all night?

"Good morning," Dani answered as she walked behind the counter. "I was thinking of making waffles. Can I interest you in a couple?"

Waffles were Tippi's favorite breakfast food. And like Ivy, for someone so petite, she ate like a farmhand. While Dani waited for her boarder to process her question through her not-quite-awake brain, she examined the girl.

There was no mistaking it. Tippi looked miserable. Evidently, she had feelings for Caleb that she'd never revealed. Dani would have sworn the two were only friends, but this degree of desolation over him inviting another girl to the dance implied that Tippi saw the pre-law student from Texas as something other than a pal.

Had Caleb been under the same impression as Dani? Or was he just not interested in Tippi as anything more than a study buddy?

Although Tippi still hadn't responded, Dani took the waffle maker out of the cupboard and plugged it in to preheat. While she mixed up the batter, her boarder trudged over to the Ninja Coffee Bar.

The machine had been a housewarming, or maybe a thank-you gift from the girls' parents. And although Dani hadn't had time to explore all its capabilities yet, Tippi, Ivy, and Starr had quickly mastered it.

Tippi's favorite was espresso con panna, a shot of espresso with a layer of whipped cream on top. She went to work brewing it and soon carried her steaming cup to the counter, where she took a seat on the middle stool.

Finally, Tippi looked up, seemed to notice Dani

cooking, and said, "I'm not really hungry. I might have a stomach bug or something."

"That's fine." Dani poured the batter onto the hot waffle iron. "I'll put whatever is left in the fridge. They reheat pretty well."

After she had made four waffles, she put them, an empty plate, a bottle of maple syrup, and the butter in front of Tippi. Then grabbing her own dish, Dani helped herself to a waffle.

She hid her smile when, even before she'd finished slathering her waffle with butter, Tippi was pouring syrup on her own golden square of deliciousness.

Determined to cheer up the girl and knowing her weakness for fashion, Dani said, "So, I'm wondering if you can help me pick out an outfit for tonight."

Around a mouthful of the fluffy goodness, Tippi mumbled, "Where are you going?"

"Reapers Supper Club. And I hear it's pretty dressy." Dani took a bite.

"Mmm." Tippi half closed her eyes. "You don't have anything for that place."

"So?" Dani didn't have to ask how Tippi knew the contents of her wardrobe. At one point or another, all the girls had explored her closet.

"You're going with Spence, right?" Tippi tilted her head. "Cuz I'm not helping you if it's that detective."

"Of course it's Spencer." Dani rolled her eyes. The girls had taken sides even though there were no sides to take. "I'm not dating Gray. We're just friends."

"Right." The sarcasm dripped from Tippi's voice as thickly as the maple syrup did from the bite of waffle halfway to her lips.

"Believe me, I do not get any kind of I'm-interested-in-you-as-a-woman vibe from him," Dani stated firmly. "I really think he likes my kitchen and cooking equipment more than he likes me."

"Good." Tippi chewed thoughtfully. "In that case, we need to go shopping."

"Oh?" Dani wasn't crazy about the idea, but she did need a new outfit, and as an added bonus, Tippi was looking perkier by the minute. "Where would you suggest?"

"Von Maur." Tippi had already finished the waffle on her plate and speared a second one with her fork. "They'll have the perfect dress."

An hour later, Dani unlocked the driver's side door of the Chef-to-Go van and watched as Tippi zipped out of mansion. Instead of the bedraggled girl who had appeared in the kitchen earlier that morning, her hair and makeup were perfect. She wore slim-fitting dark jeans, a white silk T-shirt, and a long navy vest. Her designer purse matched her navy loafers.

She hopped into the passenger seat and said, "I hope you have your credit card."

Dani mentally checked her wallet. "Yep." She didn't usually carry her personal Visa. She didn't want to be tempted to buy something she didn't need. "I grabbed it when I went upstairs to change into my sneakers."

"Great." Tippi nodded, then in an imperial tone ordered, "Onward."

Dani was busy backing the huge vehicle out of the long driveway but spared a quick glance to make sure Tippi had fastened her seat belt.

"We're only going to Van Maur's, right, not the mall?" Dani asked once she'd assured herself that her passenger was safe and she was headed in the store's direction.

She hated the mall.

"Probably." Tippi chewed the inside of her cheek. "But we might have to go to another place for shoes if they don't have what you need."

"I own plenty of dress shoes." Dani mentally crossed her fingers. From her previous life working in human resources, she had sensible pumps in brown, black, and bone, as well as a couple pairs of dressy sandals, which should match anything she bought. Although none with heels high enough to earn Tippi's approval.

During the short drive, Dani and the girl chatted about Tippi's current issue with Caleb. Nothing had been resolved by the time they turned into the entrance of the parking lot that was shared by the row of upscale stores known as The Shoppes of University Knolls. It was crowded and Dani took the first space she spotted. The van was too large and unwieldy to be picky.

Before Dani even turned off the motor, Tippi

was out of her seat and heading toward Von Maur's entrance at a determined jog.

Dani had almost caught up to Tippi when she spotted Yvette Joubert pushing through the same door. Unwilling to be drawn into a long conversation about the woman's upcoming event, Dani slowed down until her client was out of sight.

Once Dani got inside the store, she found Tippi impatiently tapping her toe and asked, "Where shall we start?"

"Um." Tippi studied her feet, suddenly unable to meet Dani's eye.

"Yes?" Dani encouraged. What in the heck had gotten into the girl?

"The thing is," Tippi cleared her throat. "I'd suggest going into the contemporary department, which is my favorite, but most of the clothes there only go up to a size twelve and…"

"I wear sixteen, sometimes an eighteen," Dani said matter-of-factly, adjusting her cross-body purse and making sure she tucked her keys in one of the zippered compartments.

She might not be totally comfortable with her body, but the only way to lose weight would be to stop sampling her own cooking so much. And that would never happen. After all, she had to test her recipes to make sure they tasted right. At least, that was what she told herself.

"Then we should go into dresses," Tippi said leading Dani to her left.

"Nothing too fussy." Dani frowned at a rack of clothes that nearly blinded her with the amount of sequins and sparkly lace on display.

"Definitely." Tippi tapped her chin and scanned the aisle. "You need something sexy and cute." She pointed. "Let's look at those."

Dani followed as Tippi quickly darted over to the next aisle, held up a red high-low halter dress, and said, "What do you think of this one? I know you like red."

"Nope." Dani shook her head. "Nothing that I'd have to go braless."

"You know they do have strapless bras, not to mention this adhesive stuff."

"Sorry." Dani felt her eye start to twitch. She wanted the girls firmly ensconced in a sturdy bra, not a wisp of lace or some duct tape. "Not happening."

"Okay." Tippi blew out a frustrated sigh, then flipped through hangers for a few seconds.

Finally, she held up another dress, this one had a knee-length flowy tiered skirt of black-and-white polka-dot chiffon below a solid black sleeveless bodice with a sash at the waist that seemed to tie it all together.

"I like it." Dani fingered the material, which felt nice and light.

After rejecting several more dresses that were too short, too fitted, or too revealing, Dani ended up with three to try on.

When she and Tippi approached the dressing

room, a sales associate offered to help. The woman said she could bring different sizes or colors, but Tippi insisted she'd fetch anything that they needed.

Once Dani had stripped down to her underwear, she tried on her original choice first, but the length of the skirt was wrong. She really liked it, but there wasn't time to have it hemmed.

Next, she zipped up an off-white sheath. The color washed her out and she didn't want to look as if she were recovering from an illness, so she took it off and laid it aside.

She hadn't bothered showing either one of them to Tippi. She didn't need a second opinion to know that they weren't flattering.

As she pulled the final dress over her head, the white louvered doors burst open and Tippi strode inside the spacious fitting room. She looked at the two discarded options and let out a disappointed sigh.

Dani ignored her and finished putting on the remaining dress. The fit-and-flare skirt smoothly skimmed her hips and the bodice cupped her breasts. Dani twisted left and right admiring the black-and-ivory geometric print. The pattern gave the dress a nice polished look. She also liked the three sheer mesh bands above the hem. She thought that they added a modern element.

Noticing that Tippi was silently staring at her, Dani asked, "What do you think?"

"You look fabulous." Tippi beamed, then tilted

her head. "You know, I've never seen you spiffed up before. You're really pretty."

"Thanks." Dani wasn't sure if she should be flattered or offended. Clearly, the girl previously hadn't thought she was attractive. "Check the tag for the price. I can't spend too much."

Tippi's expression was stubborn. "You are getting that dress no matter what the cost. It's a classic that you can wear again and again."

"Mmm." Dani glanced back at her image in the mirror. "It is perfect."

Tippi's nose twitched slightly, evidently scenting victory. "You haven't bought anything new for yourself since I've known you."

"True." Dani twirled, admiring how the skirt moved around her legs. "And I do have a pair of black shoes that I could wear with it."

"High heels, right?" Tippi narrowed her eyes. "Not grandma pumps."

"Strappy sandals with a three-inch heel," Dani assured the girl.

"Sold." Tippi said, "I'll meet you in the makeup department. I need to pick up a tube of Bobbi Brown lipstick. I'm almost out of Retro Red and if I'm going to lure Caleb back, I need it."

"So you decided to fight for him?" Dani asked, not really surprised. Tippi was used to getting her own way and she went after what she wanted at full throttle. "It's too late for the Halloween dance,"

Dani warned. "He can't dump the girl he already asked."

"I realize that." Tippi stepped out of the dressing room. "But that doesn't mean I can't go with someone else and make him jealous. I'm going to fight fire with fire."

"Okay." Dani raised a brow. "But remember, the fire department usually uses water."

Tippi gave Dani a confused looked, reiterated that she'd be buying lipstick, and left.

After Dani re-dressed in her own clothes, she took a deep breath and looked at the price tag. The dress was a hundred and two dollars. A bit pricey, but she could swing it if she didn't buy the new Kamikoto utility knife that she'd been eyeing.

Dani pictured the knife versus Spencer's face when he saw her in the dress and resolutely headed to the register.

Once Dani had paid, she found Tippi trying on a new perfume. It only took a few sneezes from Dani before the girl gave up and they made their way toward the exit.

Von Maur was an upscale department store known for the large area near the escalators where sofas and chairs surrounded a baby grand. Today, instead of a pianist performing, Dani noticed a crowd lined up in front of three young men who were seated behind a long table.

Touching her young friend's arm, she asked, "Any idea what that's all about?"

Tippi turned her head, then pointed to a poster sitting on an easel. "Some of the Korn King's baseball players are signing autographs."

"Oh." Dani stopped to watch the event. "I didn't realize that anyone in the Middle America League was famous enough to draw that kind of crowd."

She studied the trio. They were all striking in their own way, but one player was getting a lot more attention than the others and Dani watched his pen glinting in the bright artificial light as he slashed signature after signature.

"See that guy with the long line?" Tippi jerked her chin at the guy Dani had been observing. "He's Marc Chandler. Rumor has it that he'll be called up in this year's Major League Baseball First-Year Player Draft. The one next to him with the freckles and curly red hair is Perry O'Toole and the big guy with the dreads is Udell Williams. They have a chance as well, but they say Chandler's a shoo-in."

"So he's good?"

Tippi shrugged. "I guess. They credit most of their wins to him."

"Then doesn't it seem odd that he's playing for the Korn Kings and didn't get drafted sooner?" Dani examined the man in question. "He has to be almost thirty. Isn't he a little old to just be making it now?"

Tippi shrugged. "Maybe he was injured in college or had to take a few years off because of some family problem or personal issue."

"I supposed that could be it." Dani continued to stare at the handsome man. What was his story?

Tugging Dani toward the exit, Tippi said, "Anyway, you've exhausted my knowledge of baseball so let's get going. I need time to do your hair and makeup and it's going on three o'clock."

As Dani hurried to keep up with the girl, she said, "I can do my own hair and makeup. You know, I have been out on a date before."

Truthfully, Dani was surprised at her offer. Of her three boarders, Tippi was the one that stayed the most aloof. She wasn't unfriendly; she just didn't seem to be that interested in becoming closer to Dani.

Still, she and Ivy and Starr had been friends forever. Maybe Dani had misjudged her or projected her own introverted tendency to hold back from making new friends onto Tippi. Had she been unfair to the young woman? Or had something happened to change the girl's attitude?

Chapter 6

SPENCER STRODE INTO THE MANSION, STOPPED AND stared at Dani, then said huskily, "You look spectacular. Like a work of art."

This was the first time he'd seen her in a dress and she reminded him of the sexy pinup girls on the World War II posters his father had collected. From her cute little scarlet-polished toenails to her shiny red lips, she was gorgeous.

"Aw. That's so sweet." Dani's beautiful whiskey-gold eyes lit up before she dropped her gaze to his chest and said, "You look pretty terrific yourself."

"Thank you, ma'am." It had taken Spencer longer than he'd ever admit to get ready. He'd finally settled on gray dress pants, a black button-down shirt with French cuffs so he could wear his favorite gun cartridge cufflinks, and a black-and-white tweed sports jacket.

"Just the facts, sir." Dani turned toward the

half-moon table against the foyer wall, picked up a black clutch purse and a white sweater, then turned back to him and said, "I'm ready to go if you are."

Spencer resisted the urge to sweep her into his arms. "I suppose we'd better. This place is so popular I bet they wouldn't hold our reservation. And it was too hard to get to risk losing it."

"That's what I thought too." She gave him a quick kiss on his cheek and winked. "Otherwise, I might have made you wait for me in the parlor like a proper gentleman."

Spencer put his palm on the small of Dani's back and guided her outside. "Doubtlessly, you'd have had the girls serving me tea and politely inquiring about my intentions while I waited."

"Definitely." Dani smirked. "Just like in *Pride and Prejudice*."

As they walked down the porch steps, he glimpsed the headlights of a shiny Mercedes-Benz backing out and asked, "Did you see that car?"

"What car?"

"That one." Spencer pointed as the Benz pulled away. "It doesn't belong to Tippi or Starr or Laz."

"It must have been someone turning around." Dani walked toward Spencer's pickup. "We get a fair amount of that because of the long, wide driveway."

"You're probably right." Spencer opened the door and assisted Dani into the truck, allowing himself to be momentarily distracted by the sight of her cute heart-shaped backside as she stepped up onto the running board.

Once Dani was safely settled in the passenger seat, Spencer closed the door, jogged around the pickup's hood, and climbed behind the wheel.

"I'm sorry that I took so long to answer your message yesterday." Dani tucked her purse beside her leg, then fastened her seat belt. "Between meeting with a high-profile client and the girls' crises, I lost track of my phone." She shook her head. "I never do that."

"Crises with the girls?" Spencer reversed onto the street and headed toward the restaurant.

As he drove, Dani explained Ivy's missing boyfriend, Starr's last-minute date cancelation, and Tippi's unhappiness with Caleb's interest in another girl. She finished with, "It took all my ice cream and expensive hot fudge to settle the girls down, and by then I was exhausted."

"Better you than me dealing with those kinds of issues." Spencer smiled. "Although, if it was Robert who bailed on Starr, I could have assured her that he had a good excuse."

"Oh?" Dani raised an eyebrow. "Can you tell me or is it top secret?"

Spencer summarized his Friday night, then added, "At least I was able to talk the administration into letting me rotate my security team through pig-watch duty or our date might have been a picnic in the ag barn."

"Sounds fun. I like adventures." Dani shrugged. "At least those kind."

Shoot!

Spencer gripped the wheel. He'd meant to play some romantic music on their short drive, not talk about swine and student pranks. But they were already pulling up to the restaurant and a valet dressed in a zoot suit was reaching for Dani's door.

He quickly exited the truck, handed the valet the keys, and helped Dani climb down from the cab and onto the sidewalk. If anyone was going to touch Miss Cupcake, it was him.

"This place looks amazing." Dani took his arm and they walked under the green-and-white-striped canopy.

They entered through glass doors with scythes etched in them and as soon as Spencer stepped over the threshold, he scanned the lobby. It was crowded with people waiting to be shown to their tables and he carefully guided Dani toward the hostess stand, where he gave the woman behind the podium his name. While she checked on their reservation, he examined the surroundings.

Round tables ringed a large dance floor, with booths lining both sides of the room. An impressive mahogany bar presided over an area to the right and a bandstand took up most of the rear.

Spencer could hear the strains of "As Time Goes By" and he noticed that Dani was swaying to the music. The expression on her pretty face was soft and her smile almost blinding.

As he opened his mouth to tell her again how beautiful she looked, the hostess said, "Your table's ready."

An aroma of sizzling steak enticed them as they walked into the dining room and were shown to a corner booth partially shielded by a huge brass urn filled with white-and-black ostrich feathers. His benefactors had really come through for him and Spencer was thrilled with the privacy the setting offered. He planned to take full advantage of it to steal a few kisses.

Dani gestured to the round tables surrounding a stage where a quartet was playing and clapped her hands. "This is so perfect."

"It is, isn't it?" Spencer nodded and helped Dani slide into the booth, then sat next to her on the red leather banquette.

Dani smiled, slipped her hand into Spencer's, and asked, "Is that for us?"

She tipped her head at a waitress heading toward them carrying a silver wine bucket on a floor stand and Spencer said, "Yes, I recalled that you said you didn't like champagne but enjoyed the taste of Lambrusco."

Dani gazed at him like he had hung the moon. "I can't believe you remembered that," she breathed. "I only told you that once. I must have told Kipp ten times and he still always ordered champagne."

"I remember everything you've ever said to me."

Spencer raised his hand and ran the back of his knuckles down Dani's soft cheek, then nodded to the waitress who began the ritual of the uncorking.

When the server left with their appetizer orders, Dani raised her glass and clinked against his. "To our first real date."

Spencer echoed her toast, then there was a brief, awkward silence. He wasn't sure if Dani preferred to forget business altogether and talk about something else or wanted to share her experience with her new client.

Finally, he squeezed her fingers and asked, "How was your day off?"

At the same time Dani said, "Did you get your motorcycle ride in today?"

They both started to answer at once, but Spencer insisted Dani go first.

"My day was weird." Dani chuckled. "I woke up to a panicky wedding planner calling me at the crack of dawn. She begged me to move up the engagement party to next Saturday."

"And did you agree?" Spencer let go of Dani's hand and held out the bread basket toward her.

She shook her head to his offer of rolls and said, "I did. But I tripled my rate and insisted that they sign the contract by 10:00 a.m. Then I spent the rest of the morning ordering food and hiring servers for the event."

"How many guests will there be?" Spencer asked, buttering the slice of pumpernickel that he'd selected.

"Four hundred." Dani's voice was a bit breathless. "It'll be my biggest catering job since I opened up the business."

"Did you hire anyone to help with the cooking?" Spencer asked taking a sip of wine. "I know you can do a lot ahead of time, but there's still got to be a lot to do on site."

"I did." Dani picked up the menu and opened it in front of her face.

"Who?" Spencer nearly choked on a bubble and he put down his glass.

He had a good idea as to the identity of Dani's sous-chef. He didn't like it one little bit but planned to play it cool.

"Gray Christensen," Dani answered from behind the large leather menu.

Before Spencer could respond, the waitress approached the table with their appetizers. Once the plates were in front of them, the server took their entrée orders, refilled their wineglasses, collected the menus, then left them alone.

Fighting his first reaction to Dani's announcement that the detective would be working with her, Spencer stalled for time and ate a spoonful of his clam chowder. It was very good. He could taste pieces of crab and scallops, as well as crispy bits of bacon. Their saltiness was a nice complement to the sweetness of the seafood.

Finally, Spencer forced a casual tone and said, "I

hope Christensen doesn't get called away to work on a case and leave you without any help."

Intellectually, Spencer knew his reaction to the police detective was pure jealousy. From everything he'd heard about the man, he was a stand-up guy. But Spencer had also learned that Christensen wasn't married or engaged or even dating anyone, which was worrisome.

Dani stiffened and said, "He promised that unless it was a multiple homicide, he'd be there." Then she smiled and touched his arm. "I was hoping you might be free to lend a hand that night too."

"Count on it." Spencer's chest tightened. She was just so sweet. "I might not be as good a cook as Christensen, but I can follow directions with the best of them and my knife skills are A1."

Dani cutely wrinkled her forehead in confusion and asked, "How did you learn to chop and dice?"

"I didn't mean those kinds of knife skills." Spencer winked and touched the case hanging from his belt.

"Oh!" Dani's eyes rounded. "I didn't realize you were armed."

"Yep. Always." Spencer didn't want to go into too many details, but added, "It's a habit I picked up when I worked undercover."

"Good to know." Dani nodded.

As they finished their appetizers, they chatted about the weather and the upcoming Halloween celebration at the college, then once their salads had been served, Dani said, "So tell me more about the guy pinned to the wall at Fox Hall."

"Unfortunately, there's not much more to tell. The security cameras didn't show anything. It was almost as if whoever did it knew exactly where the blind spots were located." Spencer ate a bite of blue cheese dressing drenched lettuce. "And there wasn't anything at the scene that pointed to a specific suspect."

"Hmm." Dani's pretty, pink lips pursed in thought.

"But it was darn hard to get the vic down. Those hatchets were embedded in the cinder block all the way up to the handles."

"And the guy on the wall stuck to the story about the disappearing Native American chief?"

"Emphatically." Spencer took a sip of water while he considered his answer. "He seemed to really believe what he was saying was true. He also claimed that he had no idea how he ended up dressed in the breechcloth and deer-hide shirt he was wearing. He said the last thing he remembered putting on were jeans and a polo."

"Do you think he was roofied?" Dani's mouth twisted with concern.

"Or passed out drunk." Spencer shrugged. "If it was a prank, a lot of kids had to be involved. At least two to lift him, and others to use whatever tool it would take to drive a tomahawk into a concrete wall."

"To quote Alice, curiouser and curiouser." Dani ate her salad silently, then said, "Maybe there's some type of saw that could make a slit like that and super glue to hold the hatchet in place." She giggled, then added, "Or it could be a poltergeist. After all, they do say that Fox Hall was built on an old Native American burial site and that's why the university's department of paranormal and psychic phenomena is housed there."

Spencer chuckled, "Right. But I think I'll still go take a closer look at the wall tomorrow before classes resume on Monday. It's too bad I don't have a forensic team to go over the place."

Spencer had briefly considered asking the Normalton Police to lend him a crime scene tech, but no one had gotten hurt, so he couldn't really justify the request. The victim had refused to have his blood tested, so they couldn't even prove he'd been drugged.

Pushing aside his salad plate, Spencer asked, "Did Laz ever contact Ivy?"

"Not as far as I know, but my guess would be no." Dani frowned. "Ivy was gone when I got up this morning, and by the time she came home, I was already in my suite getting dressed. When I knocked on her door and asked if she wanted to talk, she said she was busy studying. I think if everything was okay with Laz, she would have told me."

"Maybe I should call her and…" Spencer started to say as he caught sight of someone he'd hoped never to see again walking by their booth.

The woman stopped and stared with an exaggerated look of surprise. Then with a feline smirk on her collagen lips, she turned and strode around the decorative arrangement secluding their table from the rest of the restaurant. Brushing aside the feathers, she stepped up to Spencer and folded her arms.

Her action pushed her boobs up so far they almost overflowed her low-cut dress and Spencer jerked backward to avoid brushing against his ex's cleavage.

Sneering at Spencer's avoidance maneuvers, she drawled, "The people you run into when you don't have a gun on you."

"Yvi?" Spencer scowled. What in the world was his ex-wife doing in Normalton?

Dani glanced at him and then at his ex before she said, "Yvette?"

"You know her?" Dani and Spencer turned to each other and said simultaneously.

Dani's gaze bounced between Spencer and the woman. "She's my new client."

"Shit!" Spencer swore. "She's also my cheating, lying ex-wife."

"Oh." Dani's little puff of air and unhappy expression gutted him.

"Naughty, naughty." Yvette waved her finger in front of Spencer.

"Stop it!" Spencer snapped, thrusting the annoying digit away. The witch was lucky he wasn't the kind of man who hurt women or he'd break that wagging finger off at the knuckle. "What in the holy hell are you doing here?"

Yvette gave a tiny shrug and pointed a bloodred claw at Dani, "Like she said, I'm her new client. Your girlfriend is catering my engagement party."

"Engagement?" Spencer was confused. "I thought you and Brock were already married?" He'd been certain Yvi intended to march down the aisle with his ex–best friend before the ink had even dried on Spencer's and her divorce papers.

"No. We never enjoyed wedded bliss." Yvette put her hand to her chest and her expression turned pitiful. "Poor Brock lost his arm fighting a fire and he understood that I couldn't be with an amputee."

Dani winced and Spencer glanced at her. Her expression revealed her repugnance with Yvette's pronouncement and he was sure his showed the same disgust. He watched as Dani opened her mouth, then bit her bottom lip and met his gaze. She raised a questioning eyebrow, lobbing his ex's revolting bombshell back into his lap.

Although Spencer wanted nothing more than for Yvette to leave, there was one thing he had to know first. "Why are you holding your party in Normalton?"

His ex's high-pitched, fake baby-girl voice scratched along his last nerve when she said, "Didn't Dani tell you? I'm marrying Franklin Whittaker."

"And he lives here?" Spencer tried to recall why that name seemed familiar, but he couldn't quite place it.

"Where else would he live?" Yvette preened. "He

owns the Korn Kings baseball team." She tittered. "Along with most of Normalton and a lot of the rest of Illinois."

That explained it. Yvette had finally found someone rich enough to satisfy her.

"Congratulations." Spencer ignored the ice-pick-like pain stabbing his left eye. "I guess you didn't have to steal my money after all."

For the first time since she had appeared, Yvette looked a little uncomfortable, then she gave a phony laugh and said, "Well, a girl can never have enough cash. It's always good to have one's own little nest egg in case something unexpected happens."

"Translated, Franklin is a lot smarter than I was and made you sign a prenup."

"Only for the first year and I got a cool million just for accepting his proposal," Yvette blurted out, then put her left hand over her mouth.

Even in the dim light, the huge rock set on a diamond-encrusted platinum band sparkled. Spencer glanced at Dani, who didn't seem all that impressed with the pricey engagement ring.

Spencer grinned, happy at her lack of interest in the expensive piece of jewelry.

Dani shot him a puzzled look before she focused her attention on Yvette and said, "What I don't understand is when you saw Spencer's picture on my phone, why didn't you tell me he was your ex-husband?"

"I don't routinely share my personal history with

the help." Yvette waved as if she were chasing away a fly.

Spencer growled at her insulting tone and rose to his feet. "It's time for you to leave."

"Fine." Yvette rolled her eyes, then skewered Dani with a look. "Just remember you signed a contract so you better not be thinking about backing out of our agreement."

"I wouldn't dream of it." Dani's voice was stony.

Spencer could see the wheels turning in Yvette's head, and it was clear the gerbils running on them weren't gaining any ground. Finally, his ex nodded and stomped away.

Their waitress had been hovering, waiting to serve their main course, and Spencer gestured for her to come forward. She hurried over and placed Dani's lamb chops in front of her and Spencer's steak between his silverware.

After the server withdrew, Dani said, "That was awkward. I hope you don't mind me catering your ex's party."

"Not at all." Spencer sliced off a bite of steak and raised it to his mouth. "In fact, I'll still help you out."

"You don't have to do that," Dani protested.

"Nah." Spencer chuckled. "It'll be interesting seeing another guy get stuck with Yvette."

"You must have felt differently when you asked her to marry you," Dani chided gently.

"Well…" Spencer paused. Dani's expression held

nothing but concern. "When I first met Yvi, she seemed so alone and vulnerable. Her parents had moved back to France and she told me that the last man she dated was stalking her. I guess she brought out my protective instinct."

"But after everything that happened with your friend, you think she might have played you."

"To a certain extent," Spencer admitted. "She didn't have any family and the guy she'd been seeing was still calling her, but considering what I know now, he was probably just trying to get the things back that she'd taken with her when she left him."

Dani was quiet for a while, then smiled brightly. "Enough about Yvette. Let's enjoy the rest of this yummy meal."

They finished their entrées, and after lingering over their coffees, they moved to the bar for an after-dinner drink and listened to the music for another half hour. Finally, they left the supper club and drove home.

When Spencer parked in front of Dani's house, she turned and said, "It's been a fabulous evening."

"I'm glad Yvette didn't spoil it for you." Spence said, relieved.

He quickly got out of the truck and walked around the hood. Opening the passenger door, he helped Dani out onto the ground, then guided her up the steps to the porch. Pausing, he cupped her chin in his hand and kissed her until they both were breathless.

Dani unlocked the door and stepped inside. "I'll talk to you tomorrow after church."

"I'll count on it." Spencer ran down the steps. "Good night."

His cell vibrated as he climbed behind the wheel of his pickup. He dug it out of his pocket, frowning when he saw the call was from the campus security number.

Swiping the screen, he answered, "Drake here."

"Sir, we have another break-in at Area 51," the dispatcher reported. "And this time it's a girl pinned to the wall wearing an animal skin skirt and leggings."

Chapter 7

THE FOLLOWING SATURDAY MORNING, DANI WOKE up with a start, convinced that she had slept in and was already behind schedule for Yvette's engagement party's preparations. Her heart racing, she checked the clock.

It was only 6:00 a.m. She had plenty of time.

Collapsing back onto her pillow, she thought about the previous week. She was shocked how fast it had flown by. The seven days since Dani's wonderful date with Spencer had rushed past in the blink of an eye.

Between her usual tasks involving her Chef-to-Go business and the preparation for Yvette's event, Dani was lucky if she'd had the energy to send Spencer a hurried text before she fell into bed. She'd managed to squeeze in an occasional quick chat as she ate a hasty meal, but often he was working and unavailable when she called.

Now that the big day had arrived, Dani was worried that she might doze off while she was cooking the entrées. She needed caffeine stat.

For the next several hours, Dani worked steadily preparing ingredients and packing food and equipment in the van. Finally, it was time to leave for the baseball stadium.

Although she'd been mainlining coffee all morning, as she walked from the designated vendor parking area toward the massive white tent set up on the grassy area to the right of the stadium, she cradled a double-shot espresso from the Java Kat, her favorite shop.

This was by far the fanciest party tent Dani had ever seen and her stomach clenched. Its sidewalls featured cathedral-like windows and an immaculate white linen runner led up to the canopy covered entrance. She prayed that she was prepared for the evening's festivities.

Dani had planned to arrive early so that she would have time to reconnoiter the setting before everyone got there, and the area appeared deserted. There was no sign of anyone else and the quiet was a little unnerving.

Afraid she'd leave footprints, Dani avoided walking on the runner's pristine fabric. Instead, she took a huge step across the threshold and had to pause for a second to regain her balance.

From the entrance, Dani assessed the venue.

Forty round tables were arranged in a half circle around the dance floor with a long rectangular head table completing the ring.

The decorations were just as extravagant as Dani had expected. It was clear that no expense had been spared. The chairs weren't the normal flimsy plastic folding ones. They were sturdy white enameled wood with padded seats and their white-fabric-covered backs were adorned with huge black and silver bows.

The guest tables had black cloths with silver runners and matching napkins. Glass containers filled with silver and black balls alternated with vases holding black tulips, silver-gray roses, and black irises. Silver chargers held the black salad and bread plates, while place cards were displayed in tiny silver frames beside the cut-glass water goblets.

Coordinating with that color scheme, black and silver netting had been draped in a swirl pattern behind the head table, and white twinkle lights had been twisted through the loops.

The pièce de résistance was a huge black-and-white painting of Yvette resting on an easel in the middle of the dance floor. No matter where her guests stood, sat, or twirled, Yvette would always be the center of attention.

The tent suddenly darkened and Dani's gaze flew to the plastic windows. The earlier sunshine had disappeared and clouds were rolling across the sky.

The meteorologists had been predicting storms

in Central Illinois and she crossed her fingers that they would miss Normalton. She had a feeling that if anything negatively affected the party, Yvette would find a way to blame everyone involved.

Dani glanced upward at the crystal chandeliers hanging from the beams crisscrossing the tent's ceiling. Who was in charge of throwing the switch to illuminate them?

She'd like the light fixtures turned on sooner rather than later. Her servers would need them lit when they walked around with the trays of appetizers.

Feeling a bit overwhelmed with all the moving parts of this event, Dani started to exit the tent. However, the sound of sobbing stopped her.

She scanned the interior until she saw someone sitting at the baby grand piano set up in a corner off to the side of the main dining area and cautiously moved closer.

As she approached the shadowy figure, she called out, "Are you all right?"

A woman sniffed. "Yes. I'm fine."

A few seconds later, she stood and Dani recognized Vicki Troemel. She was wearing an elegant black dress and carrying a clipboard.

The wedding planner's eyes were puffy, but she smiled tremulously. "Oh, Dani. I'm glad I caught you. I need to give you the keys to the mobile kitchen." She reached into her pocket and handed them over, then said, "The plates for the entrée and desserts are already in there and the final listing of which entrée goes to which table and guest. Please start serving the appetizers at six thirty."

"Okay." Dani nodded, then glanced upward and asked, "Will the lights be on by then?"

"Definitely." Vicki's voice was nasal and it was obvious that she was still on the verge of tears.

Not sure how to approach the situation but unable to ignore the woman's distress, Dani said, "You've really done an amazing job pulling this all together on such short notice."

With that Vicki whimpered, "Except the pianist just called to say he can't make it. And that's all Yvette needs to ruin me."

"Really?" Dani's heart thudded at Vicki's confirmation of her own thoughts about the bride-to-be. What if she didn't like the food?

"Really. Yvette's fiancé owns the company that employs me and I'll be fired if she isn't completely satisfied." Vicki blew out a dejected breath. "If we were in Chicago, I'd at least have half a chance to find another musician in the next few hours. But down here, I just don't have the connections to get someone that quickly."

Thinking over the contacts she had made since she'd begun catering large events, Dani chewed her bottom lip, then snapped her fingers and dug out her cell phone.

She pointed it toward Vicki and asked, "How

about a student? I know a girl in the college orchestra, and for the right amount of money, I bet Jeanne-Marie would drop everything and perform here."

"Oh my gosh!" Vicki threw her arms around Dani. "You might have just saved a life." She paused in mid hug, then letting Dani go, muttered, "Although Yvette will still blame me for not getting the guy she told me to hire. And if your pianist doesn't know the songs on Yvette's playlist, that will be another thing she'll hold against me." Vicki sighed. "I'd better wait for Yvette in the parking lot, so that as soon as she gets here, I can plead my case, because if she finds out some other way, I'm doomed. I'd text her but this needs face-to-face supplication."

"Jeanne-Marie has an eidetic memory so I bet she'll know a lot, if not all of Yvette's requests." Dani comforted Vicki, then after giving her the pianist's number, left the tent and walked around back toward the mobile kitchen.

It was 2:55. She only had three hours to get the appetizers ready to go out on time. They needed to make sure the cocktail hour started according to schedule, so that the guests could be seated at seven thirty for dinner.

When Dani approached the long, silver trailer, she found Gray sitting on the steps. He was an attractive man in his thirties and wore a starched chef's jacket and crisply creased, black dress pants. His sandy hair was neatly combed and his cheeks appeared freshly shaven.

"I took a look through the window." Gray jumped up and gestured behind him. "This kitchen is amazing."

Giving him a quick hug, Dani said, "Nice jacket."

"Is it okay for me to wear it since I'm only the sous-chef?" Gray's cheeks reddened and he fingered the buttons. "After I bought it, I wondered."

"It's great." Dani beamed. "I hope this means you'll be available for me to hire for future large catering jobs."

"Absolutely!"

Dani had already briefed him on the menu and his duties, and she just hoped he and Spencer would play nice. With Gray's experience, he would be her second-in-command, leaving Spencer to follow both their orders, and she wasn't sure how that would go over with such an alpha male.

"Is the kitchen large enough for what we need to do?" Dani asked, unlocking the door.

"Should be," Gray answered as he followed her inside.

The interior was dark, but once she flipped on the lights it was well illuminated. Two huge ranges took up the entire rear wall, with stainless-steel counters and sinks lining the longer sides. An enormous glass-fronted refrigerator stood next to the entrance.

Blowing out a relieved breath, Dani said, "Yep, this will do nicely." Smiling, she gestured to the door. "Let's start bringing in the supplies. Spencer should be here soon to help. He had to work until noon because there was some weird stuff happening on campus."

"Oh?" Gray ran lightly down the steps, then trailed Dani as she walked to where she'd parked the van. "Anything the real cops should know about?"

Dani turned and shook her finger at him. "Do not say something like that to him."

Gray's hazel eyes crinkled. "Just kidding you. I know Drake would call if he needed us."

When Spencer showed up a few minutes later, Dani asked him to help Gray unload the van while she started on the appetizers. The preparations went smoothly and the men worked well together, so by the time the servers started arriving at five thirty, she was cautiously optimistic about the success of the evening.

Dani made sure the servers were all dressed in white shirts, black pants, and sturdy shoes, and that any long hair was secured in a ponytail or bun. After they passed inspection, she gave them their instructions and explained the food to them so that they could answer any of the guests' questions.

Once that was accomplished, she sent them into the tent with orders to find their tables, familiarize themselves with the setting, and report back to her at 6:25 sharp.

Checking the clock, she saw that she had just enough time to visit the mobile bathroom before starting to plate the trays of appetizers. Once they started to serve, Dani wouldn't have another chance to pee for several hours.

Accomplishing her mission, Dani was still drying her hands as she exited the restroom trailer, but stopped half in and half out when she spotted Yvette standing in the space between it and the kitchen.

The woman was poking someone who stood in the shadows and in a fierce whisper said, "You didn't see anything."

Dani froze. She definitely did not want to witness whatever was happening.

The shadowy figure said in a strident voice, "I may not have seen who it was, but I definitely saw you screwing a guy in the back seat of your fancy Mercedes, and when I tell Mr. Whittaker that will be the end of your engagement."

Retreating into the bathroom, Dani allowed five minutes to pass before she opened the door. The last thing she needed was Yvette to realize that Dani had overheard that particular conversation.

As soon as the coast was clear, Dani hurried back to the kitchen, plated the appetizers, and started sending them out to the hungry guests. The cocktail hour passed quickly, and once the servers reported that everyone was being seated, Dani turned her attention to the next course.

The servers had just left with the first round of salad bowls when lightning began to flash. Several minutes later, Ivy, Starr, Tippi, and the rest of the waitstaff returned for the remainder of the salads, but before they could leave the kitchen, there was a bright flash of lightning and almost immediately a loud clap of thunder.

Dani, Spencer, and Gray crowded into the doorway of the trailer. It was as dark as midnight outside and rain was pummeling the tent.

Wrinkling her brow, Dani asked, "Do either of you know how safe these kinds of party tents are in a storm?"

Before either man could respond, huge spiked balls of hail began pelting the vinyl fabric of the tent's sidewalls and Dani could see the frozen shards ripping through the plastic windows.

Suddenly a loud buzz sounded from Gray's cell phone.

He grabbed it from his pants pocket and explained, "That's the severe weather alert." After a glance at the device's screen, he announced, "We need to evacuate the tent. The storms are intensifying and there have been microbursts of up to sixty miles per hour as nearby as Towanda."

"You stay here with the servers!" Spencer shouted to Dani as he and Gray ran for the party tent.

She ignored his order and followed the men. There was no way she was staying tucked away in a protected environment while four hundred people were at risk. She was grateful that the servers were all out of harm's way or at least in the safest place readily available, but Jeanne-Marie wasn't. And Dani was responsible for the pianist being in this dangerous situation.

Dani had nearly caught up with the men as they neared the mobile bathroom, but before she could ask about their evacuation plan, a gust of wind pushed her to the ground. Spencer must have noticed her from the corner of his eye because he whirled around, snatched her arm, and hauled her upright.

He seized the trailer's railing and wrapped himself around her, trying to shield her from the debris shooting at them like buckshot from a shotgun. With nothing to hold on to, Gray was swept into the metal side.

In between bursts of wind, Gray struggled to his feet and the three of them linked elbows. The struggled to move forward, but they hadn't gone more than a couple of steps when the wind lifted the party tent into the air.

An instant later, it was slammed back into the ground. Dani and the men stumbled to a stop and stared at the horrific sight in front of them.

Dani watched in horror as anchoring plates were tugged from the dirt and metal support beams and poles toppled like trees under a chainsaw. Screams from those trapped beneath the tent tore through the night.

When the wind suddenly stopped, it caught Dani by surprise. Noticing that Gray and Spencer were already on their cell phones calling for assistance, she ran over to the collapsed tent to try to help get people out from under it.

As Dani reached the edged of the destruction, she

could see that the tent wasn't completely flattened. She dropped to her knees and crawled into a tunnel that had formed between several tables. A bloody hand shot out of the darkness and grabbed her wrist.

It took a second for her brain to translate the words "help me" and react.

There was a moment, as if someone had hit the Pause button on a DVD, then other voices yelled out. Dani worked blindly to free the woman from the debris pinning her down. She sent her out through the makeshift passageway, then crawled to the next victim.

As Dani moved among pockets of survivors, she began to breathe a little easier. So far, although there were some injuries, everyone was alive.

Little by little, she became aware that other people had joined her in the rescue attempt. Dim light began to creep into the darkness as more and more escape paths opened up.

Dani had been heading to where she thought the baby grand was located, when Vicki crawled toward her. The skirt of the wedding planner's stylish dress was ripped nearly off and her face was smeared with dirt. Her eyes were wide with shock and she stared past Dani as if she didn't know her.

Dani touched the woman's shoulder and said, "Vicki, it's me. The chef. Did the pianist that I suggest agree to come here to play?"

"What?" Vicki blinked. "Oh, right. Yes. She got

here about an hour ago." With that the wedding planner pushed Dani's hand away and hurried past her.

Shoot! Dani had been hoping that Jeanne-Marie hadn't been available.

Moving as quickly as her torn-up hands and knees could take her, Dani crawled on. When she finally saw the baby grand, she breathed a sigh of relief.

The huge piano was still on its legs and Jeanne-Marie was underneath it. The girl appeared unharmed and Dani blew out a sigh of relief.

Jeanne-Marie caught sight of Dani and asked, "Is it okay to come out? I figured sheltering in place like they taught us in school was the safest bet."

"That was smart thinking." Dani motioned to the girl. "But now you need to follow me. I'll lead you to an exit."

Dani watched Jeanne-Marie scoot from underneath the baby grand, then shook her head as the girl gathered up her sheet music, tucked it into a carrying case, and clutched it to her chest.

Once she and Jeanne-Marie emerged from the wreckage, Dani realized that most of the guests had now been evacuated, and there were plenty of first responders helping those that still needed to be extracted.

With the adrenaline wearing off, the cuts on Dani's palms and legs were starting to hurt. It was time to pack it in and get out of there.

She and Jeanne-Marie were directed to a triage

area where a line of ambulances was parked. Both women tried to tell the first responders that they were fine, but the paramedics insisted on checking them for injuries.

Normalton police and fire departments were on the scene along with several from neighboring communities. Flashing lights, sirens, and agitated voices filled the chilly night air. Evidently, the storm had pushed out the autumn heat wave and temps felt like they were now closer to fifty than the previous eighties.

A firefighter came up to Dani and demanded, "Did you see anyone else inside that needed assistance?"

"No." She pushed her hair from her eyes. "Everyone I saw was being helped."

Before she could ask any questions, the paramedic working on her cuts dabbed them with something that stung and she gulped down a squeak.

Catching her breath, Dani anxiously looked at the firefighter and asked, "Have there been any fatalities?"

The man shrugged and started to walk away.

Dani called after him, "The wedding planner should have the list of attendees."

"Thanks." He turned and asked, "Where is she?"

Dani looked around. "I don't see her." Dani bit her lip, then remembered that she had a list too. The one pairing the entrées with the guests. "But I have a record of the names in the mobile kitchen."

"Come with me." The firefighter jerked his chin at her to follow him.

"Am I good to go?" Dani asked the paramedic.

He taped the last of the gauze pads to Dani's hands and knees and nodded.

"Thanks." Dani jumped from her seat and caught up with the firefighter. "This way."

She breathed a sigh of relief when all the servers were still in the kitchen where she'd left them. Tearing off the sheets of paper that she'd taped to the counter, she handed them to the firefighter.

"This is all the guests who were expected, but some may not have actually shown up." Dani rechecked the servers and said, "All my employees are here, but there were three bartenders and I don't have their names."

"Is that all the people who should have been in the tent?"

"Maybe a DJ, but I believe he or she was scheduled to arrive after dinner. The pianist was supposed to entertain during the cocktail hour and the meal and she's safe."

"Thanks." The firefighter nodded. "I'll get this to the person in charge."

"Let me know if I can do anything else." Dani watched him leave, then said to the servers, "Why don't you go home? Come by the mansion tomorrow and I'll pay everyone then."

With the exception of her boarders, the servers gathered their belongings and headed out. Ivy, Tippi, and Starr lingered and Dani observed some silent communication going on between the three girls.

Finally Starr said, "We'll help you get the unused food and equipment to the van."

As they began packing up, Ivy asked, "Where's Uncle Spence? He texted me a while ago to say he was fine and to see if I was okay, but it's been a long time."

"We texted a few times too, so I know he's all right. He's probably still helping the first responders, but before I leave, I'll find him and have him text you again."

Dani waited until the girls headed to the van with the first load, then allowed herself to flop into a chair. She was dangerously near a total breakdown. She bit the inside of her cheek until it bled. The coppery taste shocked her back into focus. She didn't have the luxury of giving in to her feelings. She had things to do, but what first?

She knew that Gray was working with the police. Like Spencer, he'd texted her. He'd asked if she needed help and when she assured him she didn't, he said he'd stop by the next day.

What she wanted—no, needed—was to find Spencer. Intellectually she knew he was safe, but she wanted to see it with her own eyes.

Dani sent him a text asking where he was, then struggled to her feet. Having rested a bit, her legs were stiff and she felt about a hundred years old.

A second later, Spencer answered her text and said he would meet her at the ambulances. Dani left the girls a note and headed to that area.

She'd just arrived when an older man staggered past her. Dani glanced at the woman he was carrying in his arms and gasped.

It was Yvette. And Dani was pretty sure she was dead.

Chapter 8

Dani sat in the Korn Kings' locker room wondering when she'd be allowed to go home. She tried to figure out how she had gotten there, but the past couple of hours felt like a bad dream. In fact, since seeing the tent collapse, it was almost as if she was in a nightmare and couldn't wake up.

After Franklin had walked into the triage area carrying his fiancée and Yvette had been declared dead, the police were summoned. Due to the disaster, they were already on-site and arrived within seconds.

Moments later, Gray was sent for, and as soon as he appeared, the original responding officers pulled him aside. They held a lengthy whispered conversation, Gray made a quick call, and he took over the scene.

He directed the officers to secure the area. Several people, including Dani and Spencer, were ushered into the stadium where they were ordered not to talk to each other while they waited to be interviewed by an officer.

The witnesses, or whatever the police thought they were, had all been soaked from the rain, and one of Whittaker's minions had brought in a stack of clothes from the concession stands. They'd been allowed to use the restroom to change out of their wet things, but again cautioned not to discuss anything among themselves.

Then, wearing sweatpants that were too big and a T-shirt that was too small, Dani had been assigned a seat at the opposite end of the row from Spencer. They were separated by half a dozen other detainees and, beyond raised eyebrows and pointed looks, had no way to communicate.

Perched on the edge of her chair, sipping really bad coffee, Dani was surprised that the locker room was so comfortable. Not only didn't it stink of sweat, it had nice leather chairs rather than wooden benches. She had expected it to look and smell like the ones in her high school.

Out of boredom, she watched several bigwigs embroiled in an animated conversation on the other side of the room. Gray seemed to be the center of the discussion, with the mayor, the police chief, and a couple of people Dani didn't recognize lecturing him about something.

Dani's eyes kept drifting closed, only to jerk open as her head sagged forward onto her chest. It was going on 11:00 p.m., her head throbbed, and she needed food. To make matters worse, her cell phone had been confiscated and she had no idea what was going on.

Gray had gotten her purse from the mobile kitchen, and when he'd handed it to her, he'd assured her that he'd let Ivy, Starr, and Tippi know that she was fine. He'd also informed her that the girls would finish packing up the van and once that was done, they would return the keys to him before going home.

While Dani had been grateful for both her purse and the assurances, what she would have really liked was to be told why she and the others were being detained—an inquiry that the detective completely ignored.

In the hours she'd been waiting, Dani mulled over what she knew. If Yvette had been killed when the tent collapsed, what did the police need to talk to Dani about?

As far as Dani could tell from her quick glance at the bride-to-be's injury, it had looked as if it were made by one of the support poles hitting her in the head. But if that was the cause of death, what possible information could Dani share with the police?

In her earlier interview, Dani had been asked to explain why she'd been inside the collapsed tent. The officer had seemed especially interested in who she'd encountered and where the people were located while she was trying to rescue the trapped guests.

Dani kept attempting to recreate the situation in her mind. Had she'd forgotten anything important? She was still going over it again and again when Gray startled her back into the present.

Blinking, Dani looked around. The folks Gray had been arguing with were gone, as were Dani's fellow detainees, including Spencer. They all must have been questioned and dismissed while Dani was lost in her thoughts. Now she noticed that she was the only one left.

Gray took the chair next to her, but before he could open his mouth, she demanded, "What's going on? Why am I being held here? Can I go home now?"

"Not yet, but soon." He pulled his seat closer and said, "What can you tell me about Ms. Joubert?"

"She wanted what she wanted and she was willing to pay for it." Dani shrugged. "She had expensive tastes, demanded perfection, and wasn't interested in hearing excuses."

"Oh?" Gray had a notebook out of his pocket, flipped it open, and said, "For instance?"

Dani closed her eyes trying to think. "For instance, the pianist canceled at the last minute and the wedding planner freaked out. She said that Yvette would destroy her career if she didn't find a replacement."

"Anything else?"

"When I spoke to the florist earlier in the week to check on the size of the centerpieces, she mentioned something about a hissy fit Yvette threw when a certain black iris called Before the Storm wasn't available. Now that this happened, the name is pretty ironic, right?"

Ignoring her digression, Gray asked, "Did Yvette threaten all her vendors? I remember you saying that when she changed the date of the party, no one really felt they could refuse."

"Before I answer any more of your questions"—Dani crossed her arms—"how about you tell me why the police are interviewing people about what seems like an accidental death?"

Gray fingered the crease in his pants. "I'm not at liberty to say at this time."

"I completely understand." Dani got up and stretched. "But then it's a shame that I'm just too tired to remember anything else."

"Hmm." Gray rotated his neck; furrows of exhaustion were etched in his handsome face. "I could charge you with obstruction and interfering with an investigation."

"But I know you won't." Dani shot him a tiny smile. "Maybe we should do this tomorrow once we've both had some rest."

"I was thinking along those lines too." Gray agreed. "But if there's anything that I might need to know immediately, I'd appreciate it."

"How in the blazes should I know what information might be important?" Dani's head was splitting, she was starving, and she was beyond cranky. "You won't tell me what's going on or why you're asking questions. What do you want me to do, read my crystal ball to figure out if there's something I should tell you?"

"Just try a stream of consciousness." Gray took her hand and tugged her back down onto her chair.

"Let's see." Dani scrunched up her face and tried to remember everything she'd heard about Yvette. "I didn't deal with many of the vendors in person, and I only talked to Yvette about the party once, the day she interviewed me. Everything went through the wedding planner."

"How about today?" Gray leaned forward, his palms on his knees. "Did you see Yvette or hear anything about her?"

"No." Dani bit her lip. "Wait." She had run into the bride-to-be. "I just remembered. I did see her. Remember right before we started to serve the appetizers when I went to the washroom?" Gray nodded. "Yvette was standing between the two trailers arguing with someone."

"Who?" Gray's shoulders tensed and he added, "What were they saying?"

"I don't know who. That person was in the shadows." Dani tapped the arms of her chair. "And all I heard was Yvette saying that they didn't see anything. They replied, 'I did too and I'm telling Mr. Whittaker.' Or words to that effect."

"Would you recognize the voice?" Gray pressed.

"I doubt it, but I truly am too tired to think." Dani glanced down. "Maybe if I had a shower, a good night's sleep, and some food, I'd be more helpful, or at least more coherent."

"You're right." Gray sighed, dug into his pocket, handed her the van keys, and said, "I'll come over to the mansion to talk to you tomorrow morning."

Dani glanced at her watch and saw that it was a few minutes past midnight. "It is tomorrow morning." Dani stood, picked up the plastic bag holding her wet clothes, and moved toward the door. "After church, I'll be home the rest of the day. I'll even cook you brunch."

"It's a deal." Gray guided Dani out the door. "Around ten okay?"

"Sure."

Gray walked Dani to her van, and she saw him watching her as she drove away. She wasn't sure if it was the exhaustion or what, but the more she thought about the people being interviewed and Gray's questions, the more she was convinced that Yvette's death hadn't been accidental.

Chapter 9

WHEN DANI ARRIVED HOME, THE FRONT OF THE mansion was dark, but light poured from the family room windows in the rear. And if that wasn't enough of a hint she had company, the vehicles crowding the driveway making it difficult to find a place to park the van would have clued her in to the fact.

She could identify the visitors by their vehicles. The gleaming red Maserati belonged to Laz and he had been the first to arrive. Caleb's beat-up Dodge Charger with its primer and Bondo exterior was pulled up right behind the expensive sports car, and Robert's practical Jeep was next to Starr's cute little aqua MINI Cooper. That left the spot by the carriage house for Tippi's' beige Volvo.

Ivy didn't own a car, but her Uncle Spencer's pickup rounded out the herd. His truck had obviously been the last to arrive and the wheels on his passenger side were off the pavement.

Dani narrowed her eyes. It was a good thing she didn't really care about the landscaping or he'd be in trouble for leaving tire prints in her lawn.

With her limited choices, Dani had to drive partly on the grass herself in order to get to the last remaining opening, a spot near the carriage house. It was the farthest space from the kitchen door and she vowed to make her uninvited guests help her unload the van.

Blowing out an exasperated breath, Dani hiked to the back entrance. Between the lights and the no-guys-allowed-above-the-ground-floor rule that Spencer would surely enforce, she figured everyone would be either in the family room or the kitchen.

And she'd bet a good amount of money that they'd all be hungry.

Like Dani, Spencer, Ivy, Starr, and Tippi would have expected to eat the leftovers after the engagement party dinner had been served. None of them would have had a meal before coming to work and by now would be ravenous. Then there were the three bottomless pits: Laz, Robert, and Caleb, who were always starving.

Dani usually loved cooking for her friends, but she was dog-tired. She just wanted to nuke a can of soup and go to bed. She paused with her fingers barely resting on the doorknob. *What would happen if instead of going inside, I turn around and head to a hotel?*

Immediately the image of Spencer's panic if she went missing made her turn the handle and open the door. Stepping over the threshold, Dani was greeted with a cacophony of snores. She rolled her eyes, then continued through the kitchen and followed the sound into the family room.

Sleeping bodies littered the furniture and the floor. She'd furnished this room by shopping at the secondhand stores and Spencer, who had clearly been home and changed clothes, occupied her best find: a comfy brown leather recliner.

It had only had a miniscule rip on the arm, which Dani had been able to patch with a leather repair kit that she found online. She'd gotten the lounger for a couple hundred dollars and after she mended the tear, it looked brand new. That tiny slit and quick fix had saved her over a thousand bucks.

Ivy and Laz shared the cocoa nailhead-on-velvet sofa that Dani had discovered on the curb of Normalton's ritziest suburb. It had been put out for the trash collector, but the owner had been happy to let her haul it away. The small wine stain on the back was easily covered by an afghan. She'd seen that same couch for sale for three Gs and change.

Tippi had the remaining chair, another perfectly nice and comfortable thrift shop acquisition. Her feet were propped up on the coffee table and Caleb's head rested against her leg.

Starr and Robert had clearly lost the coin toss and lay on cushions scattered across the rug. Starr's cheek was on Robert's chest and his arm was around her waist.

When Dani snickered at the scene before her, Spencer's eyes popped open. He leaped to his feet and reached down toward his leg, then noticed Dani and casually slipped his hand into his pocket. She figured he'd been going for his gun and was glad he hadn't accidentally shot her.

Note to self: Between the weapon on his ankle and the knife on his belt, startling Spencer awake or trying to jump out and scare him is a suicide move.

Spencer's actions had jerked Ivy awake, and when she spotted Dani, she rocketed off the couch. Crying, she pushed past her uncle and swept Dani into a hug. Ivy clutched her as if she might never let Dani go again.

Through her sobs, Ivy asked, "Are you all right? Why did they keep you so long? Was it because you witnessed the tent collapse?"

Ah! That was interesting! The authorities must not have released the fact that Yvette was dead and Spencer hadn't informed the girls either.

Dani stood still and waited for her friend's tidal wave of questions to recede, then said, "I'm not sure why they kept me, but I'm fine."

The others gathered around them in various stages of wakefulness, and Laz awkwardly patted Dani's shoulder. "Glad you're okay. Knowing Ivy and all of you were working that event, I really freaked out when I heard about the bad weather and the tent collapsing."

Laz was slim with broad shoulders and refined features. His blue eyes shone with intelligence. And even in this situation, he was dressed in pressed khakis and a crisp button-down blue oxford shirt.

"Right." Robert moved closer. "Me and Caleb too. We were at our study group." He stopped and added, "We're in the same constitutional law class." Then he continued his explanation. "When the alert came though on our phones, Caleb wanted to go to the stadium, but I knew they wouldn't let us anywhere near the place. So I suggested we text the girls that we'd meet them here."

Robert was a muscular six foot with tanned skin and chiseled cheekbones. His cargo pants and camo T-shirt were a reflection of his stint in the military.

"That must have been awful for all of you." Dani gave each of the three young men a quick hug and kissed their cheeks. Not something she'd usually do, but considering what they'd all been through, the affectionate gesture felt right.

She stepped back and studied the group. Had the trio of couples settled their various issues, or were they just put aside until after the crisis? She was about to ask, but realized that doubtlessly she'd hear all about it once the guys left and the girls got her alone.

Spencer pushed his way through the crowd until he was next to Dani, then he slipped an arm around her waist and whispered into her ear, "We need to talk. Alone."

She nodded, then looked at the guys and girls around her and said, "I don't know about you all, but I'm starving."

There was a split second of silence while they processed her words, and then everyone started talking at once about how hungry they were. Satisfied, Dani turned to go to the kitchen.

Starr followed and put a hand on Dani's shoulder. "Why don't you go take a quick shower while just this once Ivy, Tippi, and I cook for you?"

Robert, Caleb, and Laz frowned, clearly aware of their girlfriends' lack of culinary skills. Ignoring the guys' doubtful expression, the three girls walked with Dani to the kitchen.

Once they were behind the counter, they looked at each other questioningly, until Dani said, "What did you do with the perishable leftovers from the party?" She sure hoped they weren't all sitting in the back of the van spoiling.

"We loaded them all into Tippi's Volvo, brought them home, and put them in the big refrigerator." Ivy pointed over her shoulder.

"Good thinking." Dani praised them, then added, "While you girls cook, the guys can unload the rest of the stuff from the van."

"Sure thing," Caleb said, while Robert and Laz nodded their agreement.

"Thanks." Dani smiled at them, then turned to the girls. "I can't imagine Mr. Whittaker wanting the food back, and if he does, I'll pay for what we use. Heat up eight portions of the pappardelle and grill three lamb chops per person."

"Like, cook outside?" Tippi squeaked. "Do we even have a grill?"

"Okay. Forget the lamb, we'll use eight of the red snapper filets instead," Dani said quickly, not wanting the expensive meat to be ruined when she could freeze it and maybe use it for another event or a personal chef gig. "We can have the bomboloni for dessert since they don't keep well. They'll be too stale to eat in a day or two."

"What do we do with the fish?" Ivy asked, opening various cabinets in what seemed to be a random pattern.

Dani took a deep breath as she combed her memory for an easy recipe.

Finally she said, "Preheat the oven to 350 degrees, coat a couple of the nine-by-thirteen pans with cooking spray, and sprinkle chopped red bell pepper and onions on the bottom of them. Season the red snapper with salt and pepper, put them on the bed of peppers and onions, and completely cover the filets with pats of butter. Add more butter to the bottom of the pan, then put it in the oven for about twenty to twenty-five minutes."

"We've got it." Ivy gave Dani a thumbs-up, then shooed her away.

When Spencer took Dani's hand and the two

began to walk away, Starr called out, "Remember the rule. No men above the ground floor."

Starr was by far the most empathetic of Dani's boarders, but she had a playful side. Tonight, her brown eyes sparkled with mischief and her round face was wreathed in a smile. Like Ivy and Tippi, she still wore the black slacks and white shirt Dani required of her servers.

"Grownups' exception." Spencer's voice was firm. "We'll be back in twenty."

Robert leaned down and whispered in Starr's ear, then gave her a meaningful look.

Her cheeks flushed, then she said, "Of course. Sorry. I was just teasing."

As Dani and Spencer climbed the stairs, Dani murmured, "I wonder what Robert said to Starr? She doesn't usually back down that fast."

Spencer chuckled, "He probably reminded her that not making a fuss about me going up with you might clear the way for future exceptions."

"Poor guy. He couldn't be more wrong about that if he tried." Dani giggled. Then as they reached the sitting room of her suite, she asked, "What did you need to talk to me about in private?"

Instead of answering her question, Spencer asked one of his own. "What happened after the police let me go?" He sat on one end of the overstuffed loveseat looking out of place on the pastel floral upholstery. "I wanted to stick around until you could leave too, but an officer escorted me to my truck and made sure that I drove away. I thought about waiting just outside the perimeter that they'd established, but I didn't want to make the cops any more nervous than they already were. They were already wired pretty darn tight."

"Gray kept me until last, then questioned me about Yvette's relationships with the vendors." Dani couldn't suppress a yawn. "And he also wanted to know if I'd seen her with anyone."

Dani hesitated. She'd forgotten about Spencer and Yvette's encounter at Reapers. Well, not exactly forgotten, but pushed it so far back in her psyche that she hadn't thought to mention it to Gray.

"What did you tell him?" Spencer asked, tugging her downward, clearly wanting her to sit beside him.

Dani resisted, and as she recapped her conversation with the detective, she moved into her bedroom. "Let me shower and change, then we can talk more. I don't want to leave the girls alone in my kitchen too long. Last time they managed to set the toaster on fire."

"Okay!" Spencer shouted through the closed door as she started to undress. "But we need to discuss one more thing before we go downstairs."

Grateful to shed her borrowed clothes, Dani hurried into the bathroom and turned on the shower. The warm water felt wonderful, but the stinging spray found every bruise, cut, and scrape she had sustained. And when she went to wash her hair, she discovered unidentifiable chunks of debris tangled in the strands.

The hot shower helped loosen the kinks in her back and revitalized her. She felt less tired as she toweled off and looked forward to getting some food in her growling stomach. She hurriedly put on a pair of black yoga pants and an oversized red sweater.

Then, not bothering to dry her hair, she secured it in a messy bun on top of her head. But as she started to leave the bathroom, she glanced in the mirror and skidded to a halt. She looked like crap.

Make that crap scraped off the bottom of a shoe. She wasn't ready to let Spencer see her like that. Heck, they hadn't even slept together. No way were they at the relationship level where she could be this casual about her appearance with him.

A few minutes later, after applying concealer, mascara, and lip gloss, she returned to the sitting room. Spencer was staring at his phone and when he noticed her, he shoved it into his pocket.

"Feeling better?" Spencer tilted his head and scanned her from top to bottom.

The concern in his voice was soothing and she smiled. "I'm fine. A little stiff and sore, but considering what could have happened, I'm doing okay." Dani sat next to him. "How about you?"

Spencer hesitated, then took Dani's hand and said, "By the end of our marriage, I really hated Yvi, but while I'm not grief stricken, I am sorry that she's dead."

"She was a difficult woman, and not a very nice

one, but she didn't deserve to die." Dani gently squeezed his fingers. "Did you tell Gray that she was your ex-wife? I didn't mention it."

"That's good because neither did I." With his free hand, Spencer rubbed the back of his neck. "I'm meeting Christensen first thing tomorrow morning to come clean about it. I just wanted to figure out what was going on first."

"What do you mean?" Dani had a good idea but wanted to hear his thoughts.

"The police response was not the way they typically behave when presented with an accidental death."

"Oh?" Dani perked up. That was what she'd thought too. "How so?"

"If they believed Yvette had died due to the tent's collapse, they wouldn't have acted the way they did." Spencer frowned. "They may have wanted to talk to all of us at some point, but it wouldn't have been right then with everything else that was going on as a result of the disaster."

"So did you figure out what got them all in a flutter?" Dani asked.

"I think so." Spencer fished out his phone and swiped the screen, then handed it to Dani with a social media site showing. "I was certain that some of the bystanders would have managed to get photos of Yvette's body when her fiancé brought it into the triage area."

"Ghouls," Dani muttered. "How in the world is

your first instinct to take pictures when people around you are hurt and need help?"

Spencer shrugged, then enlarged the photo on the screen and said, "Can you see the wound on Yvette's head?" When Dani nodded, he continued, "Something definitely hit her, maybe even a tent pole, but I don't think that was what killed her. Look at her left eye."

Dani squinted. She could barely make out the end of an object protruding from the socket. She wouldn't have noticed it at all if Spencer hadn't pointed it out.

Gesturing to it with the tip of her pinkie, she asked, "What's that?"

"I'm not sure." Spencer rubbed the stubble on his cheeks. "But whatever it is, I'm guessing it penetrated the ocular cavity and passed into the frontal lobe of her brain, causing intracranial bleeding."

"Ew!" Dani's expression twisted in disgust. "How do you know stuff like that?"

"Sorry." Spencer put his arm around Dani. "It's a popular execution method in prisons. Sharpen a tooth-brush and shove it into your enemy's eye. Preferably when he's asleep or in the shower."

"Could it have happened during the tent collapse?" Dani was doubtful but really didn't want her suspicions to be true.

"Anything is possible, but that would be highly unlikely." Spencer sighed. "And it seems that the police feel the same way."

"Because they interviewed us?" Dani asked feeling more and more anxious.

She did not want to be accused of another homicide. Once in a lifetime was enough. Actually, it was too much. Never would have been perfect.

"Us and everyone else who crawled under the tent to rescue people."

"What?" Dani had wondered how the police had selected the people they'd isolated. "How do you know that? You couldn't possibly have recognized them while we were all sitting around waiting."

"I was trying to figure out what all of us seques-tered in the locker room had in common, but until I got my phone back and started looking through what people had posted on social media sites, I didn't tie it all together."

"How did you know what to look for and where to find it?" Dani couldn't imagine combing all the sites for specific postings.

"Campus security is testing out a new app that allows us to search most social media using hashtags and keywords." Spencer grinned. "It was developed by an NU student who's dating one of my staff, so we got first dibs at trying it out."

"That's awesome, but the staff member isn't Robert, right?"

"No." Spencer gave Dani an odd look and added, "With all that's going on, you're concerned about Starr's love life?"

"Hey." Dani pulled away from him and thwacked his bicep. "You wouldn't have to live with a young woman going through a breakup. I would."

"That hurt," Spencer teased and melodramatically rubbed his arm. When Dani didn't respond he shrugged and swiped through several screens on his cell, then handed it to her. "See, here are photos of those who helped get folks out from under the tent and here are photos of the police leading you, me, and the others into the stadium. Both groups contain the same people."

"Shoot!" Dani buried her face in her hands. "So we're suspects?"

"More like persons of interest right now." Spencer stroked Dani's back.

"How about the people who were already under the tent?" Dan demanded. "They had the same opportunity to kill her as we did."

"True." Spencer nodded. "But we're more suspicious because we entered a dangerous situation with no good reason. Police do not trust altruism as a motive."

"Great." Dani would still have helped rescue people, but it really was true that no good deed went unpunished.

"The cops will get around to the guests who were already under the tent once they confirm it was a murder and start looking for a someone who wanted Yvette dead."

"You mean like an ex-husband who was taken to

the cleaners financially in the divorce?" Dani tensed. "Or like someone dating that ex-husband?"

"Don't worry." Spencer hugged Dani. "Christensen won't suspect you. He knows you have no reason to kill my ex. Why would you be jealous when she was marrying someone else? And you were catering her party, which suggests that you didn't have any negative feelings toward her."

"How about you?" Dani shuddered. "You and Gray aren't exactly pals."

"No. But he's an honest cop and I have nothing to gain from Yvi's death. Her dying won't get me my money back, and I've never made threats, so I should be fine." Spencer blew out a breath. "Although, I do need to tell him first thing in the morning that she was my ex."

"Before he finds out on his own and wonders why you hid it from him."

"Exactly." Spencer rose from the love seat and helped Dani to her feet. "Now we'd better get downstairs because I think I smell smoke."

Chapter 10

THE FISH WAS CRISPY INSTEAD OF SOFT AND THE pasta was a tad over al dente, but the eight of them were so hungry they shoveled the food in their mouths with no complaints. Not even Dani's usually picky palate protested as she cleaned her plate.

She was happy that the girls hadn't needed to do anything to the desserts except put them on a tray and set them in the center of the table. At least that part of the meal would be delicious and not just filling.

When every scrap of the entrées was gone, the eight of them sat around with their dirty dishes pushed to the side and sipped coffee. Everyone seemed to be in a food coma and Dani was wishing they'd all leave so she could go to bed.

Unfortunately, as Ivy ate her second, okay, fifth bombolone, the sugar and caffeine roused her from her stupor, and when Spencer put down his cup, she speared him with a sharp look and said, "Although I'm positive you'd love to get Dani alone for some sexy times, my guess is that you followed her upstairs for a less fun reason."

Spencer and Dani were seated side by side and exchanged glances, then they both shrugged. It wasn't as if Yvette's cause of death would be a secret for long. It would probably be all over the internet as soon as the autopsy was completed and the medical examiners' results were filed.

"There's a good chance that the woman who hired Chef-to-Go to cater her party was murdered." Unwilling to caffeinate at this time of night, Dani had opted for tea and she dunked the bag of Black Cherry Berry repeatedly into her cup of hot water.

"How?"

"Why?"

"Seriously?"

A chorus of rising voices questioned Dani's statement and Spencer finally put his fingers into his mouth and whistled. Dani put her hands over her ears and glared at him, but he just shrugged unapologetically.

When everyone quieted down, Spencer outlined his suspicions and told them how he'd come to his conclusions. He held back a few choice tidbits of information, the ones about why he and Dani might end up as prime suspects, and stuck to a bare-bones explanation of the facts as he saw them.

Robert grinned, then leaned across Dani and thwacked Spencer's shoulder with the back of his hand. "You used AG's app, didn't you?"

"I did." Spencer gave Robert a fist bump. "I'll have to let her know how well it worked and thank her for providing it to us."

"She'll be stoked." Robert beamed and added, "Especially if you end up recommending it to other U.S. law enforcement agencies."

Despite Spencer's earlier assurances, Dani studied Robert as she sipped her tea. Was he the employee dating this AG person? And if so, was Starr aware of that relationship? Maybe that's why he stood her up.

No. There was no reason that Spencer would lie to her about his staff's love life. And Robert seemed devoted to Starr.

"So why all the need to talk to your girlfriend in private?" Tippi's deceptively sweet voice broke into Dani's thoughts. "It's not as if that woman's cause of death will be a big secret for very long. At least not once the autopsy is done."

It wasn't surprising that out of all of them, Tippi was the one to figure that out first. Her mother was a judge and Tippi was studying to become a lawyer. She'd grown up seeing how criminal investigations and cases worked and was fully aware what the police could and couldn't keep confidential.

"I wasn't sure it was appropriate to share my conjectures with too many people until the police released the news," Spencer hedged, then popped an entire Baileys Irish Cream–filled bombolone in his mouth.

Dani could tell he didn't want to talk about Yvette being his ex, but she doubted the girls or guys would let him get away with dodging the issue. She nibbled on a bombolone stuffed with matcha custard as she waited to see who would be the first to try to wheedle more info from him.

Although he'd been quiet throughout the discussion, Caleb had obviously been listening intently to what everyone had said because he was the one to ask, "What changed your mind?"

Caleb was a true Texas gentleman. His Stetson was never far from his reach and his boots were always polished. His skin was ruddy, as if he'd been out riding the range, and his jaw was square.

"Yeah." Laz had also been silent, but now he slowly finished his pumpkin-cream-filled bombolone, then licked his fingers and said thoughtfully, "If your real intention had been to wait for the police's conclusions, you wouldn't have told us so easily."

Dani hid her smile. Spencer should have realized that their young friends were all too smart to be satisfied with a partial truth. Who would prod him for more information next?

When Spencer didn't respond to either Caleb's or Laz's questions, Ivy narrowed her eyes. Dani had a good idea of what was coming. She should have realized that, as Spencer's niece, Ivy would have recognized Yvette as his ex-wife. She may not have encountered the bride-to-be before the event started, but

Ivy probably got a good look at her as she served the appetizers.

Dani was a little surprised that Spencer hadn't thought of that and said something to Ivy before the engagement party. No matter how short the marriage, surely his niece would have at least seen pictures of the woman he married, if she didn't meet her in person.

Dani squeezed Spencer's leg in warning. He flicked a questioning glance at her and she jerked her chin in Ivy's direction. His niece ate the last bite of her bombolone with a smug expression, then lifted her brows as if to say *your move*.

Comprehension dawned in his eyes just as Ivy crossed her arms and smirked. "You know that I know the real reason, so spill it."

A stubborn look settled on Spencer's handsome face and he shook his head. Dani reacted by pinching his thigh harder. Surely he realized the benefit of being the one to tell the story?

He gave her an annoyed scowl, then defiantly put another bombolone in his mouth. His entire focus appeared to be on chewing.

"Dude," Ivy snorted. "Don't make me share with the class. You know it'll come out. There's no way to hide any skeletons in your closet with the internet around. You are the one with the superagent app that lets you spy on all students in your kingdom."

"Fine," Spencer mumbled, then swallowed and blew out a long, irritated breath. "But you all need to keep quiet about this for the next twenty-four hours so I have time to talk to the police. Which is why I was trying to keep it quiet." He glared at Ivy. "I forgot that there was a spy here who would be willing to sell me out."

"Oops." Ivy covered her mouth with her hand, then leveled a threatening stare at all of her friends. "If anyone blabs, you'll answer to me."

"Me too." Dani crossed her arms and met each of the guys' gazes. "No more free food for anyone who snitches." She turned and gazed on Tippi and Starr. "And if either of you let it slip, you'll be assigned to baby shower duty on a permanent basis."

None of them liked serving at baby showers. The high-pitched screams and oohing and ahhing over diaper disposal machines, not to mention the embarrassing games like pin the sperm on the uterus, made the girls do almost anything to get out of working them.

When everyone had promised their silence, Spencer said, "Dani's client, Yvette Joubert, was my ex-wife. We were married for less than a month, but the divorce proceedings took years."

Dani studied the various expressions around the table. Tippi and Starr exchanged troubled looks while Robert's swarthy skin paled.

With the exception of Starr and Ivy, the others were all either pre-law or in law school, but Robert's mother was the Normalton Police Chief and his father was a colonel in the army. While the rest had an idea of Spencer's problematic position as Yvette's ex,

Robert doubtlessly had firsthand knowledge that his boss might be in big trouble when Spencer's relationship with the victim was revealed.

No one had much to say after Spencer's disclosure, and once the kitchen had been cleaned and the dishes washed and put away, the guys headed to their cars. And after their boyfriends were gone, the girls said their good-nights and went upstairs.

Spencer was the last to leave, and as he and Dani stood at the door, he took her in his arms and gave her a lingering kiss. The satiny feel of his lips moving over hers was intoxicating, but even that couldn't stop Dani from yawning. She was beat.

With a resigned chuckle, Spencer brushed his mouth against hers one more time, then turned to go.

Placing a hand on his back, Dani stopped him and said, "Call me after you talk to Gray."

Spencer turned and, although his smile seemed a little forced, he brought two fingers to his forehead in a mock salute and said, "Will do."

Dani kissed his cheek. "Just don't forget that I'll be waiting to hear how he takes the news."

"It'll be fine." Spencer gave her a hug.

She squeezed him back, then gently shoved him out the door. Once she was sure the mansion was locked up tight, Dani trudged up the three flights of stairs to bed. She loved having a floor all to herself, but when she was this exhausted, she sure wished that it wasn't the top one.

Chapter 11

SPENCER WAS HALFWAY HOME WHEN HE REALIZED that he should be with Dani when Christensen came by the next day to talk to her. No way was he allowing her to be interviewed alone for a second time. Spencer knew exactly the kind of tricks the detective might use to make her blurt out something she didn't want to say.

Without considering that she might have already gone to bed, Spencer swung his truck around and returned to the mansion. He'd only been gone a little while, but it was clear by how long it took her to answer the doorbell that she'd been upstairs. He could see the exhaustion etched into her pretty face and he felt guilty for dragging her all the way down from the third floor.

He should have just texted or called her. And he probably would have chosen that option, but after everything they'd been through, he really needed one more kiss to assure himself that she was safe and sound.

For an instant, when Dani had disappeared under the collapsed tent, Spencer thought his heart had stopped. He couldn't even call for her to come back because when his heart started beating again, it jumped into his throat, choking off any words he might have tried to utter.

In the few seconds it had taken him to follow Dani inside the disaster area, she'd vanished. The chaos had completely swallowed her up.

Then, before he could look for Dani, an elderly woman had cried out for help, and by the time he'd freed the octogenarian, another victim needed his assistance. Then another and another.

Now, as Dani stepped aside to let him into the foyer, the memory of almost losing her overwhelmed him and Spencer could only hug her. They stood silently for several seconds before he could bear to release her.

Her brow wrinkled in concern and she asked, "Are you okay? What happened? Why did you come back?"

Instead of telling her how he felt, Spencer blurted out, "I don't think you should see Christensen alone tomorrow. I should be here with you."

"Seriously?" A beat went by, then Dani narrowed those pretty whiskey-gold eyes of hers and huffed in an I-can't-believe-you-said-that-to-me tone, "I'm an adult and I can handle the detective's visit without supervision."

Spencer persisted. "But he might—"

"Stop!" Dani interrupted him, then she put her hands on her lush hips, stuck out her cute little chin, and drawled, "Do I need to remind you that I am better able to deal with Gray than you are? That he and I are actually friends? And considering we have no idea how he'll react to your revelation about your relationship with Yvette, you being here could be like pouring water on a grease fire."

"You win." Blowing out a defeated breath, Spencer gave up, admitting to himself that if he had thought the matter over and not acted on impulse, he would never have made the suggestion. What was it about Dani that turned his mind to mush?

"Of course I do." Dani's smile was smug, but she allowed Spencer to steal that extra kiss he'd been craving, so he forgave her for it.

"Sorry I dragged you back downstairs." He opened the door and headed for his truck.

Before he got inside the pickup, Dani called out, "Be careful tomorrow with Gray. I doubt that he's going to take the news that you're Yvette's ex very well."

Spencer grunted his agreement, then backed out of the mansion's driveway. As he drove down the college town's mostly deserted streets, he wished that Dani was in the passenger seat beside him.

No. Not just next to him, but still in his arms. He loved the feel of her soft curves and the smell of her lemony vanilla scent as it wrapped around him.

He needed to have Ivy find out the name of Dani's perfume so he could surprise her with a bottle.

Spencer's smile faded and he smacked the steering wheel with the heel of his hand. This was not at all how he had planned for the evening to end, and he was sick of things getting in the way of him spending time with Dani.

Yes. He shouldn't be worried about his own happiness when so many people were banged up and Yvette was dead, but, if he was brutally honest with himself, that's how he felt. All the injuries had been slight and Yvette, well, she was a lot like the criminals he'd encountered. It wasn't *if* she would come to a bad ending; it was *when*, and how many people she'd bring down with her.

When he'd first met Yvi, she'd seemed so vulnerable. She'd aroused all his protective instincts and it had felt so good finally to have someone sweet and good in his life. Too bad most of that persona had been an act. Yvi had seemed like the Little Mermaid and turned out to be a lot more like the Sea Witch.

Shaking his head at having ever become involved with the evil woman, he returned his thoughts to Dani and smiled. He'd been hoping to take her out for a drink and a bite to eat after she finished working. He knew she'd be tired and hungry, and he'd found the perfect little restaurant where she could relax.

Once he'd given up fighting his attraction to his sweet caramel-haired Miss Cupcake, he couldn't get her out of his mind and spent hours thinking of ways to make her happy. It was just too bad that she was so damn independent and stubborn.

From the little that she'd shared about her childhood, he understood that she wasn't used to being anyone's priority. Her father had punched massive holes in her self-esteem, then her asshole ex had come along and added a few blows of his own.

Spencer intended to change all that. He would be the one man in her life who appreciated her beauty, intelligence, and strength. He would never let her down or do anything to make her think less of herself.

This business of her insisting on meeting with Christensen alone drove him nuts. On one hand, he could see that she was perfectly capable of handling the detective on her own and probably in a better position with the man to do so. She was probably right about Spencer not being the best person to have around just a few hours after he confessed that Yvette was his ex-wife. But what if things went south?

Spencer wanted to be there to look after her. Even if she didn't need it.

Thumping his head against the back of the pickup's seat, Spencer stared out the windshield at the empty street. It was a good thing that he was only a few miles from his town house. He was nearly as tired as Dani and his eyes kept trying to close without his permission.

Spencer rolled down the window, hoping the

cold air would keep him awake. Why was everything always so damn complicated?

He'd been so happy that things with Yvette were finally settled. He'd been thrilled she was out of his life for good. Why had karma allowed her to turn up in his new hometown and end up dead?

That night when Yvi had shown up during his date with Dani, he'd come closer to losing his temper than in all the times he'd dealt with her during their marriage and divorce. The minute he saw her smirking face, he'd wanted to hit something. Her standing there, as if she belonged, had nearly ripped away his famous self-control.

Spencer had been seconds from allowing his emotions to take over when Dani had touched his arm and a sense of contentment settled over his shoulders like a warm sweater. Then Dani had once again surprised him when she calmly accepted the news that her new client was his ex-wife.

Instead of melting down, Dani had shown such grace that Spencer felt blessed to have someone like her in his life. And at that moment, he vowed to do everything in his power to keep her by his side.

A year ago, Spencer would have said he wasn't interested in a serious relationship. Hell, six months ago, his fondest desire had been to keep all women at arm's length. Then he met Little Miss Cupcake, and now she was always in his thoughts.

Spencer inhaled sharply. No woman had ever

affected him this way. Was it crazy to think that he might have actually met the right one? The one who was meant for him?

He was pretty sure he knew the answer to that question, but she wasn't ready to hear how he felt about her so he'd keep quiet for a while. But sooner rather than later, he planned to tell her and find out if she felt the same way.

As Spencer neared his town house, he thought again about the moment Dani disappeared under that collapsed tent. It had been horrifying to see her in such a dangerous situation, but it also warmed his heart and confirmed his opinion about her strength of character.

She was such a strange mixture of tough business-woman and caring individual. She rarely did what he expected her to, and although he normally hated being caught by surprise, he found that he didn't mind it so much with her. Maybe that was the real test of true love.

Spencer shook his head. It was too late at night to deal with something this important, and he was relieved to turn in to his driveway. He'd get some rack time and think about it all in the morning.

Spencer was surprised that there were no lights in the windows of the adjoining town houses. Most of his neighbors weren't exactly early-to-bed kind of people, so it wasn't often he returned to total darkness, but he guessed that even the most dedicated party animals had to sleep sometime.

After pulling into the attached garage, Spencer climbed out of the pickup's cab and winced as he walked toward the door. He'd already been stiff from his time crawling around under the collapsed tent, and dozing off in the chair at Dani's hadn't helped. Another sign that it was good he'd come out from undercover. Being a UC was a young man's game, and his thirtieth birthday was long past.

Ignoring the aches and pains, Spencer went inside and headed to the kitchen. Despite his exhaustion and longing for his bed, he was all stirred up and needed a beer if he had a hope in hell of falling asleep anytime soon.

Grabbing a bottle from the fridge, he opened it, walked into the living room, and flopped down on the couch. The wood frame creaked under his weight and the faux leather crackled as he wiggled into a comfortable position.

He took a swig and his thoughts skittered back to Dani's last words. Spencer knew she was worried that he would be a prime suspect in his ex's murder, and although he'd played down the probability of that, he was concerned that Christensen would take this opportunity to give him a hard time and keep him under the microscope.

Spencer's stomach churned. That would be bad on so many levels. First, the threat of bad publicity could cause the university administrators to consider cutting him loose.

Like all other university employees, his contract had a morals clause. And being accused of murder could certainly violate it.

Second, Spencer needed to keep a low profile to remain off the motorcycle gang's radar. He paid a hacker friend to keep his name out of social media and off the internet, but he doubted even his pal could erase everything fast enough if he were accused of murder.

All he needed was a member of Satan's Posse to see his face and realize that he had been the Tin Man. A guy who was supposed to have been dead for a couple of years.

Spencer kicked off his shoes, put his stocking feet on the coffee table and balanced his beer bottle on his stomach. If the gang found him, Dani and Ivy would be in danger. Satan's Posse had a scorched-earth policy that included destroying their enemy's loved ones.

Should he suggest to Ivy's father that she needed to take a semester off from college? Maybe she could study abroad. Spencer's family may not know the details of his previous career, but they knew it was dangerous and his brother would definitely take his warning seriously.

Of course, thinking that way meant that he should back away from Dani too. Without Ivy living with her, it would be easy enough to keep his distance and keep her safe from the gang's reprisals.

Spencer thought about it awhile longer, then

abruptly sat up, barely catching his bottle before it went flying across the room.

Hell no!

Christensen had proven himself a reasonable guy. In fact, if the detective didn't insist on hanging around Dani, they'd probably be friends. Spencer would just have to make him see reason. And if worse came to worst, he'd approach Christensen's superior.

While Chief Cleary didn't know everything about Spencer's undercover work, she knew enough to understand why his being named a suspect would be almost as bad for citizens she was sworn to protect as it was for him.

After leaving the stadium without telling the detective that Yvette was his ex-wife, Spencer had had second thoughts. Withholding that information from the police probably hadn't been one of his best ideas.

He definitely needed to catch Christensen and explain the situation before the guy found out on his own about Spencer's past relationship with the victim. The detective had agreed to meet Spencer at the police station downtown at seven sharp. Surely he wouldn't have a chance to research Yvette too deeply before morning.

Still unsettled, Spencer paced the short length of his living room looking around the place as if seeing it for the first time. All he had was furniture and a TV. Undercover, it was dangerous to have pictures or any other mementos, and he was still in the habit of maintaining that type of Spartan surroundings.

What would Dani think of that? The mansion was full of warm touches and personal possessions. Would she think they were too different to get along?

Spencer rubbed the back of his neck. No woman before Dani had ever been in his thoughts so much. Even during his brief marriage, he could go days without thinking about Yvi.

He chuckled darkly at himself. Maybe that was why Yvette had cheated on him. She was a woman who had craved attention and he sure hadn't given it to her.

Shaking his head at all his past mistakes, Spencer thought of the myriad of ways he had screwed up his personal life. He was determined not to do that again. This time he would take things slowly with Dani. And he would be a lot more honest with her than he'd ever been with his ex.

He would work regular hours that allowed him to concentrate on really getting to know Dani. Only then would he attempt to take their relationship to the next level.

While she was always in the back of his mind, and just before going to sleep at night, he'd fantasize that she was beside him, he would wait. It would be torture, but for now her hugs and kisses would have to be enough. Especially until Yvette's murder was solved.

Chugging the last of his beer, he walked into the kitchen and put the empty bottle in the recycle bin.

Then, instead of going to bed as he had intended, he pulled out a chair and sat at the table. There was something else bothering him. Something he'd tried hard to convince himself couldn't possibly be true.

What if the murderer wasn't someone with a grudge against Yvette? What if he or she was someone from Spencer's past? The gang hadn't been the first criminal enterprise that Spencer had infiltrated or the only group of creeps who had a grudge against him.

It was a little farfetched, and Spencer wasn't sold on it, but if it was some perp who had just gotten out of prison, he might not know that Yvette wasn't someone that Spencer cared about anymore. Or if he did, he might have killed her hoping to set up Spencer for the fall.

Which meant Dani could be in danger. Spencer's gut clenched.

Maybe he should take a look at the case. After all, the local cops could probably use some help. They might have their fair share of murders in Normalton, but most of the homicides they dealt with were due to domestic violence, robbery, or drugs.

A true whodunit would be difficult for them to investigate. Especially one with a prominent citizen like Franklin Whittaker at the epicenter.

As Spencer finally headed to bed, he had a plan beginning to form. After he'd come clean to Christensen about his relationship to Yvette, he'd be free to reach out to some of his old pals and see what his ex had been up to since their divorce.

Once Spencer and Yvette had parted ways, the only contact he'd had with her was through their lawyers. He hadn't really had anything to do with her or his friends since he'd left Chicago. Maybe it was time to rectify that situation.

Chapter 12

ON SUNDAY MORNING, AS DANI GOT READY FOR church, the thought of Spencer's upcoming conversation with Gray nibbled at her as if it were a mosquito that refused to die no matter how much she swatted it. If both men remained calm and reasonable, there shouldn't be a problem. But she had a hunch that a single wrong word by either of them would set the other one off, and that could be the Jenga piece that toppled the tower of trust they had been slowly building.

Maybe her apprehension was due to a lack of rest. Dani couldn't remember a time anymore when she wasn't at least a little tired.

She'd been tempted to skip Mass and sleep a few more hours, but church was probably a good idea. Not only for her soul, but also to hear the chatter about last night's disaster.

Normalton wasn't exactly a small town, but it

wasn't the big city either. The tent collapse would have been big news and there was usually someone who had heard something about any momentous event that happened in the immediate area. And, more important, was willing to gossip about it.

Slipping on a simple blue sheath with three-quarter-length bell sleeves and navy pumps, Dani studied her reflection in the mirror. She'd pulled her hair into a low ponytail and covered the dark circles under her eyes with makeup. She wouldn't win any beauty contests, but she was vertical and dressed. That had to count for something, right?

Hurrying downstairs, Dani went out the kitchen door and retrieved her van from its spot near the carriage house, then drove the few minutes to St. Sebastian's. She lucked into a parking space along the side of the building and dashed inside, slipping into a seat moments before the entrance procession began.

As always, the service was both soothing and uplifting. Dani loved the simplicity of the church's interior. It was plain, with cream walls, oak pews, and simple statues of Mary and Joseph. There were no gilt or gaudy ornaments, and even the cross was made of wood, not gold or silver.

In his homily, Father Allam achieved a perfect balance between concern for the people who had been harmed during the tent collapse and confidence that everything that happened was God's plan.

After the Apostle's Creed, Father Allam started

off the Prayer of the Faithful by saying, "For our wonderful chorus who allows the rest of the flock to lip-synch."

Dani snickered as she murmured, "Hear our prayer."

The rest of the service flew by, and before she knew it the recessional played. Dani followed the others as they made their way down the aisle, but before she got to the exit, she noticed a knot of people at the back.

As she neared them, she realized that they were exchanging opinions about the tent collapse. Stepping out of the aisle, she lingered at the edge of the group.

A man dressed in shiny navy pants, a white shirt, and a pumpkin-print tie said, "Junior told us it was raining sideways and the wind tore into that fancy tent like a herd of drunken buffalos."

One of the women shivered. "Your son was lucky to get out alive."

"Yeah." The man wiped his forehead with a starched white handkerchief. "Thank goodness the drinks tables were along the sides of the tent so he and the other bartenders were able to crawl away pretty easily."

Dani saw her opportunity and interjected, "Did the police talk to him?" When she saw the man frown, she hastily added, "I mean about his experience. You know, for the insurance reports and all."

A woman standing next to the bartender's father patted her hair, which was arranged in a towering structure of curls, and said, "My son was too shaken up to give any kind of statement. We want him to talk to our attorney before he says anything to anyone. He needs to be compensated for the emotional trauma of almost being killed."

The pack murmured their agreement, then a man in an expensive gray suit and polished black shoes said, "That big shot Whittaker better have a lot of insurance coverage because everyone will be suing his rich butt."

"Well, not the lady who was killed," snickered a bald man near Dani. Then with a malicious look in his porcine eyes, he added, "A woman who looked like her would have really taken him to the cleaners."

"They were getting married," the bartender's mother protested. "She wouldn't be bringing a claim against her own husband now, would she?"

"Maybe not," Mr. Gray Suit allowed. "But she would have still eventually cost the guy a pile of cash, if not everything he owned." He put his thumb in his breast pocket. "My friend's wife's cousin works at the law firm that represents Whittaker, and she said the prenup was the stupidest thing she ever saw. It started the moment the woman said yes to his proposal and she got a million dollars just for accepting his ring. After the formal announcement at the engagement party, that amount doubled."

Voices rose as everyone in the group offered their views as to whether Yvette was a gold digger or not.

Opinions were leaning heavily on the yes-she-was-definitely-marrying-him-for-his-money side when Dani slunk away.

As she passed the bulletin board, she glanced at a bright-blue poster that read: DON'T LET WORRY KILL YOU OFF—LET THE CHURCH HELP.

Chuckling, she vowed not to let worry or the church kill her, then headed for the parking lot. It was time to get home and cook Gray a brunch that would make him think twice about suspecting either her or Spencer.

And while Gray ate her amazing food, she'd also feed him an alternative theory to the ex-husband-is-always-the-killer philosophy. He would definitely want to know about Franklin Whittaker's prenup agreement.

~

"So, the general consensus is that Franklin killed her to save himself a million dollars." Dani finished telling Gray what she'd heard at church as she slid a lemon-blueberry crumb-cake waffle in front of him.

As Gray reached for the pitcher of Dani's best pure Vermont maple syrup, he said, "Interesting that Mr. Whittaker never mentioned that to us."

"I'm not surprised." Before the detective could pour the precious nectar, Dani quickly sprinkled a brown-sugar crumb topping on his waffle, then motioned him to continue with the flow of gooey goodness.

"Me either." As Gray picked up his fork, he shot her a pointed look. "It seems like a lot of people didn't share what they knew last night. Both you and Drake failed to inform me of an important fact."

"Very funny." Dani scowled. "I didn't think of it at the time."

Dani was concerned at how ticked off Gray sounded. He sure wasn't his usual sweet self and it scared her. She searched her thoughts, trying to come up with another lead to cheer him up, but nothing popped into her head.

"You don't expect me to really believe that, do you?" Gray's tone was curt, but his expression brightened as he demolished a crisp slice of bacon.

"It's true." Dani crossed her heart. Then deciding it was time to turn the tables on Gray, she said, "Maybe if you'd have mentioned that Yvette's death wasn't an accident, I would have thought of it."

"So you think Drake has a motive to kill his ex?" Gray pounced.

"No! What?" Dani's pulse raced. "Wait!"

Had she really just said that?

"Why else would the fact that Ms. Joubert had been murdered make you remember that Drake was her ex-husband?" Gray continued to eat, a tiny smile playing along his lips as he watched her squirm.

"Fine." Dani finished making her own waffle and walked around the counter. She took the stool next to the detective and continued, "Yes, that information would have then caused me to make the connection with Spencer, but not because I think he killed her, but due to the fact that I knew the police would suspect him."

"Good catch. I can understand why you were good at your career in HR." Gray ate in silence for a few minutes. Finally, he seemed to relent and admitted, "Although I have to consider Drake as a possibility, I can't see him having any motive other than pure revenge, which doesn't match his character at all."

"You're right, it doesn't." The anvil that had been sitting on Dani's chest lifted and she was able to take a bite of her waffle. It was a new recipe that she was considering for the Dog Park fundraiser brunch she'd been hired to cater in December. "Yes, Yvette cost Spencer some money, but my impression is that he was more relieved to be rid of her than upset about the cash."

"Of course that's what he'd want you to think." Gray's tone was teasing, or at least Dani hoped that was the intention of his comment.

"So do you suspect me?" Dani crossed her fingers, hoping Gray would reassure her that she wasn't on his list of possible killers.

"Well…" Gray picked up another piece of bacon from the platter next to him. He pointed it at Dani before he took a bite. "I suppose you could have murdered her in a jealous rage."

Dani felt bile rise in the back of her throat. Was he serious?

Gray must have noticed her distress because he asked, "Are you okay?"

She nodded, not trusting herself to speak.

He wrinkled his brow, clearly not believing her, but continued his thought. "Although since there's no evidence that Drake had any interest in his ex and is obviously head over heels for you, there's no logical reason that you'd be jealous."

"That's right." Dani took a deep breath and hid a smile. Was Spencer really head over heels for her? Mentally shaking her head at how easily she was distracted from the important conversation at hand, she quickly asked, "So who is on your list of suspects?"

"Someone who owns a custom-designed, green-and-gold Mont d'Eau fountain pen. And who was willing to sacrifice something that cost twenty-five hundred dollars in order to shove it into Ms. Joubert's eye socket." Gray paused, then added, "And who knew that he or she could kill the vic using that method."

"Did you get prints from it?" Dani asked, crossing her fingers. If there were prints, she and Spencer could be totally eliminated.

"There was only one, which was on the ink cartridge. The outside of the pen was wiped clean." Gray blew out a frustrated breath. "And that print isn't in the system."

Chapter 13

MONDAY MORNING, AS SPENCER DROVE ONTO the Normalton University campus, he noticed the changing colors of the leaves on the trees that lined the road. At last, fall was making an appearance in central Illinois, and the chill in the air confirmed that the weather was finally catching up with the calendar.

He was relieved that the local meteorologists were predicting a cold and wet Halloween. If it was warm and dry, more students would celebrate on the streets and outdoors in the quad. The frosty winds and rain would drive most of the college kids inside, where any rowdy situations were easier to contain.

That was a good thing, since Spencer had had to cancel his morning plan to go over tactics and strategies with his security guards and push it back to the next day. His team needed some guidance regarding use of force during the often out-of-control upcoming holiday and he didn't want to wait until the last minute to spot any potential problems among his staff.

With Halloween falling on a Friday, the students had three days to party, and a lot of them would be steeped in alcohol for the duration. College kids acting as if they'd been smacked upside of the head by a Ouija board was always a PITA for campus security, and there were several new hires, as well as seasoned officers, who could use a review of the basics.

Now, instead of working with his team, Spencer was headed to an appointment with the vice president in charge of university safety. He needed to tell her about his weekend activities, in case she got a telephone call or visit from the police. Having the cops show up at the VP's office without any explanation or warning was a career-ending move.

Christensen had taken the news about Spencer's previous relationship with Yvette as well as could be expected. Actually, his attitude had been better than Spencer anticipated. The detective hadn't given him a hard time about withholding information or threatened him or tried to intimidate him.

In fact, during their early Sunday morning meeting, Christensen had acted as if he believed Spencer when he said that he didn't have any reason to want his ex-wife dead. The detective's behavior had been puzzling and even a little weird.

After Christensen had confirmed that the police were officially treating Yvette's death as a homicide, he had asked Spencer some reasonable questions, taken a few notes, and then, as if they were friends, he'd walked Spencer out of the police station and waved goodbye.

Maybe Dani's assertion that Christensen only saw her as a friend with a mutual interest in cooking was true. Spencer had observed them carefully as they worked together preparing food at the engagement party, and he had to admit there didn't appear to be any sexual tension between them. The man treated Dani like a sister.

Still, there was always the off chance that Christensen was playing it cool, both with Dani and the murder investigation. He could be targeting Spencer as a suspect while pretending he believed him. That was exactly what Spencer would do if their positions were reversed.

With that in mind, Spencer knew he had to keep ahead of the curve and inform the university about his situation. He was reasonably sure his boss wouldn't be too disturbed by the news, but she certainly would be ticked off if the cops broke it to her instead of him.

Spencer carefully kept his speedometer at twenty-five miles per hour, the campus speed limit. Not only did he want to set a good example, going slowly gave him a chance to collect his thoughts and figure out the best approach to use on the vice president.

The first time he'd met her, he recognized her as a tough cookie, and while he wasn't afraid she'd fire him, he didn't think she would welcome the information he might be a murder suspect either. University bigwigs weren't known to be happy campers about anything that might bring bad publicity to their schools—especially anything that could make parents uneasy enough to withdraw their children from the college.

Even driving at a crawl, his truck ate up the few miles from his town house to the administration offices and he arrived at 7:50 for his eight o'clock appointment. It was the newest structure on the college grounds and unlike the other more classical buildings, it reminded Spencer of a huge cement cardboard box that had been squeezed in the middle by some giant.

The multi-angle edifice held an auditorium, administration offices, IT facilities, and a café. It was touted as a state-of-the-art addition to Normalton University's largely traditional campus, but Spencer didn't see the appeal. He preferred red brick and ivy to concrete and metal.

As he crossed the sidewalk and went through the entrance, Spencer inhaled deeply. The lobby smelled of pine-scented disinfectant. The long counter that ran the length of the back wall had tidy stacks of papers in boxes lining the stainless-steel surface, and oddly enough, an old-fashioned brass desk bell, which he tapped lightly.

There was no response, but a few minutes later a teenager bobbing to whatever he heard through his earbuds leisurely strolled out from behind a group of shelves and file cabinets. When the teen zeroed in on Spencer, he frowned.

"We don't open until eight." The kid's voice was loud, probably because he hadn't bothered taking out his earbuds.

"I have an appointment with Dr. Kayley." Spencer bit back a lecture about being more aware of one's surroundings. Anyone could come in here with a weapon and the kid wouldn't know it until the first bullet hit him. "Is she in?"

"Yeah." The teen pointed up. "She's in her office. Do you know the way?"

"I do," Spencer said, then asked, "Are you a student at the college?"

"Yeah." The teenager leaned his hip against the counter. "Why?"

"Just wondering." Spencer narrowed his eyes. The kid looked familiar, but he couldn't place him. "What's your major?"

The teenager peered at him for a long moment, then muttered, "Parapsychology." Before Spencer could comment, the kid thrust out his chin. "Don't bother telling me that I'm not studying a real science or that I'm wasting my parents' money on a useless degree or hum the *Ghostbusters* theme."

"Whoa, dude." Spencer held up his palm. "I would never do that."

"Yeah?" The teenager's tone was skeptical. "Well,

everyone else does." He shook his head. "Especially with Halloween coming up."

"That's a shame." Spencer put out his hand. "By the way, I'm Spencer Drake, head of campus security and I promise to take you seriously."

The young man tentatively shook Spencer's hand and muttered, "I'm Will Luder."

"Good to meet you, Will." Spencer smiled. "I think I've seen you around Fox Hall in the evenings when I've done walk-throughs."

"Yeah." Will shrugged. "I help Professor Anderson with her research."

The young man wore a black T-shirt with a pair of dark jeans and an army jacket. His brown hair was short and he had spiky bangs.

"That must be it." Spencer's mind immediately went to the poor young woman they'd rescued the Saturday before last. Like the previous student, she'd had no memory of how she got to Fox Hall dressed in animal skin clothing and pinned to the wall by two hatchets. She did admit to drinking heavily at several parties but couldn't remember where she'd been last. "Have you noticed anything unusual going on in that building? People who shouldn't be there?"

Will opened his mouth, then seemed to reconsider and said, "Nope. Not really."

Spencer considered pressing the teenager, but glanced at the wall clock and saw that it was 7:59. This was not an appointment he could afford to arrive at late. Tucking the kid's name into his mental rolodex, Spencer kept his expression genial as he said goodbye to Will and hurried to the stairs.

A minute later, Dr. Kayley greeted him from behind her desk. "Mr. Drake, please come in and take a seat. I'll be with you in a second."

The vice president was a middle-aged woman with a blond bob and a serious expression. She wore a tan jacket over a print dress, and Spencer watched as she fingered a heavy gold necklace while she talked on the phone.

Dr. Kayley concluded her conversation, hung up, then turned her attention to Spencer. "I was surprised to get your text. What's so urgent? I hope nothing's wrong in your department."

"No. I'm afraid this has to do with a personal matter." Spencer sat stiffly in his chair. "My ex-wife was killed yesterday."

"Do you need time off to handle the arrangements?" Dr. Kayley asked. "We certainly can arrange for a couple of bereavement days."

"Thank you, but that won't be necessary." Spencer shook his head. "I'm sure her fiancé will take care of that sort of thing."

"So?" Hitting her palm with the pen she'd been using to take notes while she was on the phone, Dr. Kayley stared at him for a moment before saying, "Then what can I do for you?"

Spencer asked, "Did you hear about the tent

collapse at the baseball stadium during the storm on Saturday night?"

She frowned. "Was the woman who died in that accident your ex-wife?"

"Yes." Spencer nervously smoothed his fingers over the arm of the chair. "But it is highly probable that the pole that hit her wasn't the cause of her death."

"Really?" Dr. Kayley's expression was difficult to read. "Then how did she die?"

"It's not official yet." Spencer took a breath, then continued, "But once the autopsy is complete, I believe the police will announce that she was murdered."

"Oh my." Dr. Kayley crossed her arms. "And you know this how?"

"I was at the event." Spencer straightened the crease in his suit pants to avoid making eye contact. "And I spoke with the investigating officer yesterday morning."

"Because?" Dr. Kayley prompted, then didn't wait for his answer. "Because as the woman's ex-husband, you would be a suspect."

"That's possible." Spencer folded his hands in his lap to stop his fidgeting. "But Sunday's conversation was to inform the detective of my prior relationship with Yvette and explain why he shouldn't waste his time on me since I had nothing to gain from her death."

"Did the officer believe you?" Dr. Kayley demanded, worry crawling across her attractive features.

"Detective Christensen stated that he couldn't see

a viable motive for me." Spencer's voice was somber. "But I'm sure I will come under a certain amount of scrutiny until the real killer is caught."

"Shoot!" Dr. Kayley slumped. "How long do you think that will be?"

"I have no idea." Spencer rubbed his chin. "But I'm hoping that it will be soon."

"Are you planning to call in some favors to see if there's anyone in her past, besides you, that might have a grudge against her?"

Spencer nodded. "I thought I might be able to provide some insight."

"Just don't dig yourself a hole," Dr. Kayley warned. "Make sure the police want your help and don't view it as interference with their investigation."

"Something to consider." Spencer agreed, then asked, "Do you need any more from me?"

"No." Dr. Kayley pinched her nose. "You've given me quite enough to worry about first thing Monday morning. But do keep me informed."

Spencer rose, leaned over the desk, and shook his boss's hand. "Definitely."

Hurrying down the stairs, Spencer decided to take a few extra minutes and talk with Will Luder. He wanted to see if he could get the kid to reveal whatever he'd considered telling him earlier about Fox Hall. Unfortunately, when Spencer got to the lobby, there was a handwritten sign on the counter that said: CLOSED. INFORMATION WILL REOPEN AT NOON.

Hmm! That was unusual. Had Will left suddenly in order to avoid Spencer?

Returning to his truck, Spencer's mind went over his lengthy to-do list. He was tempted to push it aside and stop over at the mansion to see Dani.

Although he'd texted her yesterday that his meeting with Christensen had gone fine, her response seemed less than convinced that everything was okay. At least her own text after speaking to the detective had seemed more upbeat.

Spencer would have suggested that he take Dani for a bite to eat Sunday night so they could go over their experiences with Christensen in person, but as usual, one of them had to work. Dani had a personal chef gig that evening and didn't expect to be done much before midnight.

Spencer was halfway to the mansion when he realized Dani would be knee deep in lunch-to-go preparation. Pulling over to the side of the street, Spencer sent her a message suggesting they get together at his town house that night and order a pizza for supper. Then, before putting his phone away, he had an inspiration and dialed a number he knew by heart.

His friend Hiram answered on the first ring and agreed to meet him for an early lunch at his favorite hangout, the Down's Diner.

Hiram Heller had been Spencer's mentor since the police academy and he needed the older man's advice as to how to approach investigating Yvette's murder. With a few rare exceptions, since living in Normalton, Spencer had mostly kept his nose out of police business. However, his ex being killed in his own backyard wasn't something he could trust to someone else.

Hiram usually had an opinion and wasn't shy about sharing it. He also had some of the best connections and sources outside of Homeland Security.

With a couple of hours before his lunch appointment, Spencer headed to his office and buckled down to draw up plans for how campus security would be deployed and manage the Halloween crowds. Once they were completed, he printed out the information and put it in each of his officer's mailboxes with orders to memorize the information, as there would be a test the next day.

At 11:15 Spencer alerted the dispatcher that he was leaving the building and drove to the café. The familiar double doors with their cloudy glass and fading red paint welcomed him. The notices taped to the window informed him of an upcoming Halloween party for ages three through twelve, a new neighborhood daycare with openings, and someone looking for jobs raking leaves.

When Spencer entered the diner, the wonderful combined scent of grilling hamburgers, french fries, and coffee made his stomach growl. Breakfast had been a bowl of cold cereal at the crack of dawn.

The café consisted of six booths against the wall,

three tables for two down the center of the room, and a row of eight stools lined the counter. Spencer greeted Uriah, the café's owner, as he walked by him on the way to Hiram's usual end booth.

True to form, Hiram was already there and Spencer slid onto the bench across from his mentor. Before he was fully seated, Uriah approached the table and wordlessly cocked a brow at Spencer.

Not even bothering to open the laminated menu, Spencer said, "I'll have a Reuben and fries."

"Meatloaf, mashed potatoes, and green beans for me," Hiram added.

Uriah grunted and headed back to the kitchen. The owner of the diner was well over six feet, with a broad chest and thickly muscled arms. No matter the season or temperature outside, Spencer had never seen him in anything but a pair of white cotton pants, a T-shirt, and an apron.

Uriah's ethnicity was anybody's guess. His bronzed complexion and unusual light-green eyes could be Greek or Middle Eastern or one of a hundred possibilities. He never had much to say, and although in his sixties, he handled the cooking and serving without any hired help.

His only employee was a cleaning lady. He spoke to her in a language Spencer didn't recognize, but it almost sounded like Latin.

Hiram looked over his glances at Spencer and asked, "What's the emergency?"

His mentor had the rough voice of a two-packs-a-day smoker, but Spencer knew he had never had that habit. Hiram was barely five foot eight and a hundred and forty pounds at the most. But his unimposing build hadn't kept him from being one of the best agents in his agency.

"Hi." Spencer smiled. "I'm fine. Glad the weather's cooler. How about you?"

"Get on with it," Hiram growled.

The old man had never been one to tolerate a lot of chitchat. He had guided Spencer's career since Spencer was a raw recruit, and he had never given him a bad piece of advice. Including the suggestion to cut his losses when Yvette cheated on him, get out from undercover, and have a life.

Hiram had taught Spencer how to navigate the politics of the law enforcement profession, how to be a good officer, and how to be a good man. In return, Spencer had shared his hopes, dreams, and troubles.

He'd talked over his concern that, while he was ready to quit the agency, he would never be happy if he was completely out of the protect-and-serve business. Hiram had nodded, thought about it for a moment, and then recommended that Spencer apply for the head of security job at Normalton University.

"Yvi's dead," Spencer said to Hiram, then paused when Uriah returned with their food.

Hiram set aside his newspaper, took off his

glasses, and said, "Yep. Saw that in the headline of the *Normalton News*. Didn't shed a tear. Did you?"

Ignoring his mentor's jibe, Spencer asked, "Did it mention it wasn't an accident?" He rose and walked to the coffee machine on the counter. Cups were on the tables and everyone was expected to serve themselves. "Want a refill?"

"Don't mind if I do." Hiram nodded. "So Yvette finally double-crossed the wrong person." He narrowed his eyes. "Why do you care? That woman was a lying, cheating bimbo who wore enough makeup to scare a drag queen back into jeans."

Spencer shook his head at his mentor's political incorrectness but didn't bother trying to reform him. The world had changed, but Hiram wasn't someone who would change with it.

Grabbing the carafe, Spencer poured a cup for himself and topped off Hiram's white crockery mug, then answered his mentor's question. "Because I was at the event and might be a suspect."

"I see." Hiram leaned back, and without flinching at the scalding hot liquid, he took a long sip, then asked, "Why were you at your ex's engagement party?"

"It's kind of complicated." Spencer stared over Hiram's shoulder. "You remember my niece's friend? The one who runs the catering company and inherited the mansion and rents rooms to the girls?"

"Dani Sloan." He wiped his mouth with the back of his hand.

"We've been sort of..." Spencer removed the napkin from around his silverware and put it in his lap. "Seeing each other."

"I knew you were sweet on her."

"The thing is"—Spencer focused on pouring ketchup on his plate for his fries—"there's this other guy and he helps her sometimes with her catering jobs, so I've been helping her too."

"Is that a fact?" Hiram tilted his head and examined his protégé. "And she was the one Yvette hired to cater her engagement party?"

Spencer nodded. "I don't think Yvi was aware I was seeing Dani, but who knows?"

"So you helped your current girlfriend cater your ex-wife's engagement party?" Hiram's lips quirked. "That had to be awkward."

"Dani took the news well." Spencer squirmed on the uncomfortable wooden bench, uneasy with his thoughts. "And Yvi had no idea I was in the kitchen with Dani."

"Interesting." Hiram took another sip of his coffee.

"At first it looked as if Yvi's death was an accident caused by the tent's collapsing in the high winds." After Spencer ate a bite of his Ruben, he continued, "But then it turned out to be murder and although the lead detective says I'm not a suspect, he'd be a fool not to include me in his investigations."

"And you're afraid if he doesn't find the real killer soon, he might poke into your past and stir up the hornets' nest of your undercover work."

"Right." Spencer tested his coffee and found it cool enough to take a drink. "So I thought I'd give the police a hand."

"What do you need from me?"

"I'd like a background check on Yvi. Say for the period since our divorce." Spencer tilted his head. "Something like our old agency would do if they were investigating her."

"That shouldn't be a problem." Hiram took a small red notebook from his shirt pocket and jotted down a note.

"And my name can't be associated with it."

"Ah." Hiram pinched his bottom lip between his index finger and thumb and pulled it out. "A little more difficult, but doable."

"How soon?" Spencer slid his cup in circles on the cracked plastic top of the table.

"Depends how much you're willing to pay to grease the pertinent wheels," Hiram said.

"Five hundred?" Spencer asked.

Hiram nodded, then said, "Is the detective handling the case someone reasonable?"

"He seems so." Spencer ate a french fry. "But he's the guy who helps out Dani."

"So he might see you as a rival for her affections?" Hiram leaned back in his seat and extended his arms across the back.

"I'm beginning to think not." Between bites, Spencer filled his mentor in on his observations. "However, he could be fooling me."

"True." Hiram nodded approvingly. "That's smart."

Clearing his throat, Spencer said, "Getting back to the possibility that my undercover identity might be revealed, any suggestions?"

"Find Yvette's killer ASAP."

Chapter 14

SHOOT! DANI TOOK OFF HER YOGA PANTS AND STARED into the mirror on the back of her bathroom door. She was wearing only her red Chef-to-Go T-shirt, and absentmindedly she noticed that her underwear had a huge hole near the crotch.

However, the deplorable state of her panties wasn't the cause of her distress. It was the realization that she'd promised to help cook the meal at the food pantry that evening. She regularly volunteered at the pantry's monthly free hot dinner for the poor, but she'd forgotten to add it to her calendar and had already told Spencer that she was free to meet him for pizza. In addition to having a yen for some crispy crust, gooey cheese, and spicy tomato sauce, she really wanted to hear the details of his meeting with Gray. His brief message had been more frustrating than informative.

Great! Now she would have to wait until Thursday. Tuesday night was Spencer's turn to guard Oinkphelia and Hamlet, and Dani was booked for a personal chef gig on Wednesday evening.

It might be possible for them to squeeze in a late lunch tomorrow. Or…Dani picked up her cell from the bathroom counter. Maybe Spencer would be willing to volunteer at the food pantry with her, and then they could go to his place for a late pizza supper afterward.

Dani tapped out a quick text, put the phone back on the counter, and stripped off her shirt, bra, and panties. Stepping into the shower stall, she was thankful that the water had been running long enough that it was nice and hot.

For a few seconds, she just stood there and let it massage the knots from her shoulders and back. There was one Monday a month that none of her three workers were available to assist her with preparing and selling the lunch-to-go bags and this had been it.

She'd tried to get as much done ahead of time as possible, but a huge selling point for her product was freshly prepared food, rather than precooked fare. This meant a lot of the items had to be made that morning, and as far as she could figure out, there just wasn't any way around that.

Thankfully, the decline in demand for her lunches had indeed been due to the three-day school break. With the students back on campus, the sales were greater than ever. If this trend continued, it might be time to think about hiring an additional employee.

Someone who could work weekday mornings, as well as be available to help with catering jobs.

Dani shampooed her hair and rinsed the suds from her scalp, then grabbed her body wash and poured it on the net bath pouf. As she washed away the morning's sweat, she frowned remembering her afternoon appointment.

She was getting together with Vicki Troemel to wrap up the loose threads of the disastrous engagement party. She wasn't sure what to expect from the meeting. She'd never had a client die during an event before.

After one, sadly yes, but Dani's contractual obligation had already been fulfilled at that point. At best, she'd only satisfied a third of what she'd promised to do for Yvette's engagement celebration.

It had briefly crossed Dani's mind that Franklin Whittaker might contact her yesterday. But once she thought about it, she realized that the poor man was probably so overwhelmed with both the legal implications of the tent collapsing and his fiancée's murder, he couldn't care less about the leftover food currently residing in Dani's freezer.

Besides, Mr. Whittaker was doubtlessly used to delegating tasks to his employees. And Vicki would be a lot more aware of the contract's fine print.

Dani turned off the water, stepped from the stall, and grabbed a towel. After drying off and dressing in black straight-leg wool pants and a white blouse with ebony piping on the collar and cuffs, she clipped her hair into a low ponytail with an onyx barrette, then applied concealer and mascara.

Retrieving her cell phone from the bathroom, she went downstairs and grabbed one of the two leftover lunch-to-go sacks. She had an hour and a half before Vicki was due, and she was hungry.

Dani browsed recipes on her tablet as she ate. There were so many intriguing dishes that she wanted to try. She'd never run out of inspirations.

A knock on the kitchen door startled her and she jerked her head toward the sound. Standing there with a huge grin, Frannie Ryan waved her reporter's notebook and gestured for Dani to unlock the door.

Sighing, Dani got up and walked over. She wasn't surprised to see the journalist. Actually, she was shocked it had taken the young woman so long to show up at the mansion. In the past, Frannie had arrived almost before the body was cold.

A little taller than average and a lot curvier than was fashionable, Frannie radiated a confidence not often seen in someone her age who lived in a college town surrounded by a plethora of young, beautiful, thin females. It was a self-assurance that Dani greatly admired and needed to emulate more often.

The abundance of size-four young women in Normalton often made Dani feel like a moose among the gazelles. Although Spencer's constantly voiced admiration was helping, between Kipp and her father sniping at her figure, Dani's body image was at an all-time low.

After twisting the lock and waving Frannie inside, Dani said, "I expected to see you yesterday morning. What took you so long?"

Frannie's nose twitched in annoyance. "Of all weekends I decided to go to Scumble River with my boyfriend. Justin's mom isn't in too good a shape mentally and his dad has lots of physical problems, so he needs to go and take care of stuff for them at least once a month. I figured that I'd drive up with him this time so we could tell my dad our news in person."

"Your news?" Dani perked up. She had an idea about the nature of Frannie's news and Dani was a sucker for a happy ending.

"Uh-huh." Frannie beamed and held out her left hand. "Justin popped the question and I said yes."

Dani admired the modest solitaire, mentally comparing it to Yvette's huge diamond. This ring was sweet, and Dani would bet there was a lot more love behind it than the gigantic rock her client had sported.

"Was your father happy for you?" Dani snagged the remaining sack lunch and gestured for Frannie to take a seat at the table. "Would you like something to drink? Coffee, soda, water?"

"Water would be great, thanks." Frannie chose the chair opposite the one Dani had been sitting on, then said, "And yes, Dad was thrilled and immediately wanted to start planning the wedding. But we're not sure what we want yet so we had to slow his roll."

"Still, you had a nice time, right?"

"We did." Frannie frowned. "But not good enough to make up for missing the story of the century."

"Did they assign the murder to someone else?" Dani asked. She'd seen the headline in the *Normalton News* but hadn't had time to read the article or notice whose byline was credited with it.

"Yeah." Frannie opened the red-and-white-striped bag and pulled out the Full Monty, a beef, turkey, Swiss, and cheddar sandwich with lettuce, tomatoes, and mustard sauce. "Yum."

"That was the indulgent choice for the day." Dani nodded to her plate. "I'm having the healthy one. Thinly sliced roasted zucchini sprinkled with oregano, mozzarella cheese, sautéed sweet peppers, baby arugula, and extra virgin olive oil with an olive tapenade spread on whole grain bread."

"That sounds yum too," Frannie said, accepting the bottle of water.

Dani resumed her seat and asked, "If another reporter is covering the murder, to what do I owe the pleasure of your company?"

Frannie had taken a huge bite and held up a finger indicating she'd answer in a second. While the young woman chewed, Dani picked up her own sandwich and started to eat it again.

Frannie swallowed, then took a sip of water

and said, "I talked my editor into letting me do the human-interest angle. He knows that's my specialty. I'm going to look into the victim's past."

Crap! Dani kept her expression bland as her mind raced. Should she tell Frannie about Spencer's relationship with Yvette? The journalist would doubtlessly discover it, and if Dani told her, maybe she could control the way he was portrayed in the story.

"How did you find out that I catered the party?" Dani asked, buying time to consider the pros and cons of revealing that Yvette was Spencer's ex-wife and that he was present during the incident.

"The original article mentioned that you were among those helping rescue people. It also mentioned that detective who cooks with you and your boyfriend." Frannie's head popped up from her sandwich like a jack-in-the-box. "Don't you read the paper?"

"Normally." Dani shrugged. "But I was too busy this morning."

"Oh." Frannie disappeared back into her meal and Dani relaxed.

After a few seconds, Frannie's silence started to make Dani nervous and she said, "Where's Justin? Don't you and he generally work as a team? You for the physical paper and him for the website?"

"He's still in Scumble River helping out his folks. Some of the stuff he has to do for them can only be done during business hours." Frannie wiped her mouth with a napkin. "We were supposed to be off until Wednesday, but when I saw the story about the tent collapse, I borrowed my dad's spare car and drove down here first thing this morning. I'll return later in the week, drop it off, and ride back with Justin."

"Oh. I see." Dani nodded as she took another bite.

She wondered exactly what was wrong with the young man's parents. She admired him for taking care of them. A lot of twentysomethings wouldn't put their families ahead of their careers. *Heck.* A lot of people of any age wouldn't. Look at her own father.

"I hope I can get back to Scumble River in time to poke around a little." Frannie tapped a fingernail on her reporter's notebook. "I think the mayor is up to something again and I'm afraid it's something that will put my friend Skye's husband in a bind."

"What's he doing?" Dani recalled that Skye's husband, Wally, was the Scumble River chief of police and a friend of Spencer's.

"Sorry." Frannie winked. "I never talk about my stories before I write them in case I get scooped."

"Alrighty then." Dani made a mental note to mention this conversation to Spencer so he could give Wally a heads-up.

Frannie finished her lunch, deposited her trash in the empty sack, and after taking a swig of water said, "That was great. Thanks."

"You are very welcome." Dani pushed a plate of deviled eggs toward Frannie. "Try these. I put a little horseradish in them to give them some zing."

Frannie selected an egg but before eating it said, "I wonder who watched a white thing come out of a chicken's butt and thought, wow, I bet that would be tasty."

"Good question." Dani laughed, then got up, cleared the table, and ran water in the sink to wash up the last of the lunch-to-go dishes.

"So, tell me everything you know about Yvette," Frannie ordered, her fingers poised over her tablet. "What was she like as a client?"

Dani noticed that Frannie used both a paper pad and the digital device and wondered why, but instead of asking said, "Particular. She knew what she wanted, which is a good thing, and she was willing to spend whatever was necessary to get it."

"Also a good thing, right?" Frannie winked. "Speaking of money…"

"Do we have to?" Dani asked, pretty sure what was coming next.

"Yes." Frannie shot Dani a look. "How much was this engagement party of hers costing? Was she paying or was her fiancée?"

There was nothing in the contract that prohibited Dani from revealing that information to Frannie. And Dani's rates were available on her website, so the young woman could get a ballpark idea once she got a copy of the menu, which had been featured on several easels around the tent. All it took was one guest to have snapped a photo and posted it on social media for Frannie to find.

Again, deciding that it was better to control the info, Dani said, "The check was drawn from an account dedicated to the wedding, so I have no idea who provided the original funds. And my portion of the party was thirty-five thousand to feed the four hundred guests."

"Wow!" Frannie stopped typing and sat with her mouth hanging open.

Dani chuckled. It was clear that Frannie hadn't had a lot of experience with the cost of high-end events. She watched as the young woman regained her professional composure.

"Off the record." Frannie pushed her tablet aside. "What percentage of that amount is profit for your company? Three-quarters?"

"I wish." Dani washed a huge bowl that had contained the rice pilaf salad for the healthy option. "Usually about ten percent after I pay for the food and workers. Probably closer to fifteen percent this time. Because of the short notice, I had to up my prices." Before Frannie could respond, Dani held up a soapy hand. "But I had to turn down several personal chef gigs in order to use those evenings to prep ingredients in order to be ready for it on time."

"Why was there short notice?" Frannie joined Dani at the sink and asked, "Was the engagement a surprise and she wanted a party right away?"

"No." Dani finished the last sheet pan and wiped her hands on a towel.

"Then, why?" Frannie persisted as she picked up a large spoon and dried it.

"Because her original date was the Saturday after Halloween and she didn't realize that until after she had booked everything."

"So?" Frannie frowned, then added, "By the way, we're back on the record."

"I'm not entirely clear. It could have had something to do with her being afraid people would come in costume, or maybe she thought it was unlucky."

"It couldn't have been worse than the day she ended up picking."

"True." Dani rolled her eyes. "However, since Yvette wasn't clairvoyant, there's no way she could have known that when she decided."

"Maybe she should have spent some of the money earmarked for the party on a psychic," Frannie said with a serious look on her face.

Before Dani could respond, the doorbell rang and she realized that she needed to get rid of Frannie before the young woman found out the person at the door was Yvette's wedding planner.

"Oops!" Dani snatched the dishcloth from Frannie and said, "That must be my afternoon appointment." She herded the young woman toward the kitchen exit. "And I really don't know much else about Yvette."

Frannie stopped by the table, picked up her tablet and reporter's notebook, then raised a brow and said, "Not even that she's your boyfriend's ex-wife?"

Shoot! Dani forced herself to keep her expression impassive.

"Yes. I knew that, but Spencer's relationship with Yvette was over long ago."

"Still, he would know a lot about her past." Frannie's tone was thoughtful.

"Probably, but I doubt he'd be willing to share any of it with you."

"Exactly." Frannie narrowed her eyes. "And I'd hate to write anything negative about him, but if others talk and he doesn't…"

The doorbell rang again and Dani sighed, "Fine. What do you want from me?"

"Explain the situation to Spencer and get him to meet with me." Frannie walked to the back door. "You can be there and I promise to only ask reasonable questions."

"I'll try, but no promises." Dani waved Frannie away and rushed off to let the wedding planner in before Frannie could see her.

Frannie probably wouldn't recognize Vicki, but the young woman had a nose for news and just might have looked up pictures of everyone who worked on the engagement party.

Chapter 15

As Dani hurried down the hallway clutching the Joubert/Whittaker folder to her chest, she noticed that the floor was scuffed and needed to be polished. Evidently, all the foot traffic from Saturday night had taken a toll on the hardwood finish.

Glancing around, she noticed the sunlight pouring from the foyer's windows illuminated the dust on the stairway banister. That needed to be taken care of as well.

It was a good thing that the girls owed her some time—their rental agreement included a certain number of employee hours. Once they got home from class this afternoon, she'd put them to work cleaning.

Thinking of her boarders reminded Dani that, with the exception of a brief mention by Starr Sunday as she was hurrying out the door, the girls had acted as if the catastrophe Saturday night hadn't happed. Dani wasn't sure if they were really that unaffected by the tragic incident or were choosing to ignore their feelings.

Maybe she should try to talk to them about it. She certainly was still shaken up.

Then again, Dani wasn't a therapist or their mother, so it might be best to let the girls decide when, or if, they wanted to discuss it.

Dani also hadn't had a chance to chat with the girls about their love lives. She had no idea if they'd made up with their boyfriends or whether the various problems among the couples still existed. But that should probably be a topic of conversation that only came up if the girls chose to confide in her about it.

Pushing all those worries out of her mind, Dani opened the door, then just stood and stared at the wedding planner's changed appearance. Instead of the attractive, put-together, professional woman that Dani remembered, Vicki looked as if she'd just gotten out of the hospital. Or should still be in one.

The wedding planner's cheeks were sunken, she had dark circles under eyes, and her fair skin was almost translucent. She wore a track suit rather than an outfit suitable for a professional meeting, and her beautifully manicured nails had been chewed to the quick.

As Dani greeted Vicki and ushered her inside, she quickly revised her plan of holding the meeting in the parlor and guided the wedding planner down the corridor and into the kitchen. This woman needed to be fed.

Once Dani got Vicki seated, she said, "Would you like something to drink?"

"Uh…" Vicki shoved her hair off her face. "If it's not too much trouble."

"Not at all." Dani put the folder she'd been holding on the table, then grabbed the kettle, filled it with water, and put it on the stove to boil. "In fact, I missed lunch." She mentally crossed her fingers at the fib. "How about we have afternoon tea?"

"I'm not very hungry." Vicki shook her head. "I haven't been since…"

"Of course," Dani said. She totally understood that losing someone was hard to handle at the best of times, but Yvette had been young and her death unexpected. "I'll put a few things out and you can just nibble."

Dani quickly put together a platter with finger sandwiches, scones, and petit fours. She brought them to the table along with dishes, napkins, and utensils. Then after preparing a pot of gunpowder green tea, she placed it, cups, a bowl of sugar, a pitcher of cream, and a plate of lemon slices between her chair and Vicki's.

Once Dani sat down and poured the tea, she asked, "Have you been home to Chicago?"

"No." Vicki added sugar to her cup and stirred. "Mr. Whittaker asked me to stay and work for him. He's provided a nice condo and had someone in Chicago pack up the things I needed and drive them down to me. I've spent the last couple of days trying to settle all the loose ends from the event for him."

"How's Mr. Whittaker holding up?" Dani asked.

While she waited for an answer, she filled a small dish from the tray and put it in front of the wedding planner. Vicki's nose twitched as if she'd scented the enticing food. Slowly, she selected a watercress–egg salad sandwich and lifted it to her mouth.

Before taking a bite, Vicki responded to Dani's question. "That poor man. As if losing the woman you love isn't enough, people are attacking him like a flock of vultures. You wouldn't believe the lawsuits that have already been filed."

So the woman at church was right.

"Oh?" Dani prodded, then sipped her tea.

"The vendors, the guests, heck, even the videographer has jumped on the bandwagon." Vicki finished the tiny sandwich and picked up a blueberry scone. "Only you and your servers haven't come after him."

"Well, we weren't anywhere near the tent when it collapsed," Dani said happy to see the woman eating. "So no need to worry about us."

"That's good to hear." Vicki spread lemon curd on her scone. "But I swear some of the people suing weren't in the tent either."

"Really?" Dani wasn't at all surprised. How many times after a bus or train accident did people try to claim they'd been injured when they hadn't even been a passenger?

"Mr. Whittaker's attorneys and his insurance carrier's representatives are going over the official video and social media with a fine-tooth comb to weed out the phonies." Vicki twirled a strand of hair around a finger. "I hope they throw the book at those fakes."

Hmm! Dani studied the wedding planner. Was her vehement defense of Franklin Whittaker more than just the response of a loyal employee? Her body language and the way she said his name made Dani wonder if Vicki was in love with the man. If that were the case, Vicki might have seen Yvette as an obstacle to be removed in order for her to pursue a relationship with him. That should be a tidbit Gray would want to hear.

Tucking that piece of info away in her mental file, the one marked GRAY, Dani watched the wedding planner finish her third scone and lick her fingers. Evidently, once she'd started eating, Vicki's appetite had returned in full force. She'd polished off what Dani had put out and was eyeing the single cookie remaining on Dani's plate.

Finally, as Vicki sipped her second cup of tea, she said, "We've looked over your contract and although it doesn't specify what happens to any unused food, Mr. Whittaker would like an inventory."

Dani had suspected that there would need to be some kind of accounting for the remaining ingredients so she'd taken stock of them on Sunday and printed up a list. Flipping open the file, she slid a sheet of paper toward Vicki and kept a duplicate for herself.

The wedding planner took a pen from her purse and ran her finger down the row ticking off items as she read. Dani glanced over and saw that she had put a mark next to the lamb, red snapper, desserts, as well as items that obviously weren't fresh fruit or produce, like the bottled capers and cans of black olives.

Looking up, Vicki said, "I assume you froze the meat, fish, and desserts?"

"Except for a few portions of snapper that my servers and I ate that night." Dani put a tiny check by those items on her own list. "Oh. And not the bomboloni. They don't handle freezing very well."

"What did you do with the rest?" Vicki asked her pen poised over the paper.

"Anything that would spoil in a day or two, I donated to the food pantry." Dani tapped several items. "We're cooking a meal for those in need tonight, and the menu was planned around those ingredients."

"Mr. Whittaker will want a receipt for his taxes with the amount."

"Here you go." Dani had organized that list Sunday before dropping off the food at the pantry on her way to a personal chef job. "Both the director and I have signed it."

"Excellent. You seem well prepared," Vicki said. "Has this happened before?"

"Not to this extent," Dani answered cautiously, unwilling to share her other clients' stories. "But it's not uncommon to have leftovers." She shrugged. "As you know, even guests who RSVP their acceptance don't always show up."

"Sure." Vicki smoothed the sheet of paper in front of her, then took a deep breath and said, "Mr. Whittaker wondered if you would be willing to prepare the unused food for the luncheon he's hosting after the memorial service." Before Dani could answer, she hurriedly added, "Of course, he would pay for your time and that of your employees, as well as any ingredients you needed to purchase to complete the dishes."

"Does he want the same entrées?" Dani asked. "The desserts are obviously already finished, and depending on the number of people he expects, there might not be a need to substitute something for the bomboloni."

"Whatever you want to do with the lamb and fish for the entrées is fine." Vicki placed her tablet on the table and tapped the screen a couple of times. "We're planning for two hundred."

"That many?" Dani swiftly calculated the portions remaining. "With no appetizers, the entrées will need to be larger."

"Personally"—Vicki leaned forward—"I think there will be far fewer."

"Why is that?" Dani had a good idea, but wanted to hear the woman's explanation.

"Yvette was not well liked." Vicki's lips twisted as if she'd drank sour milk. "With her dead, her sycophants will have already moved on to the next big thing. The people who come will only be there for Mr. Whittaker."

Again Dani noticed the wedding planner's voice soften at her boss's name.

"Well, I'm sure he has a lot of friends and business associates that will attend to offer him support." Privately, Dani figured the man probably had his own entourage of parasites.

"True." Vicki giggled. "Just the employees and players for the Korn Kings would make up half the number." She paused. "Or more."

"Okay." Dani started making notes. "I'll plan for two hundred and supplement the entrée with a hardier side to make up for the lack of appetizers. The cake and pie should be adequate for that number, but I may add ice cream so I can slice the cake into smaller pieces but still have a generous dessert."

"Good idea." Vicki glanced at her watch. "So you can do the memorial luncheon?"

"As long as I have the slot available." Dani opened up the calendar app on her cell phone. "What date and time is the service going to happen?"

"The mayor assured Mr. Whittaker that the body would be released by the end of the week, so we're planning for the service to be Sunday afternoon at the Pinnacle Country Club." Vicki looked at Dani. "However, if you're busy, we can push it out a few days, say Monday or Tuesday."

"Nope." Dani entered the date. "Sunday works for me as long you're not worried the police might change their mind about the timeline."

"The autopsy is obviously already complete since the cops have announced that Ms. Joubert was murdered." Vicki grimaced. "Why else could they need to keep the body?"

"Who knows?" Being a huge fan of mystery novels and television police dramas, Dani actually had a couple of ideas, but she didn't think it was wise to share them with the wedding planner.

"If that's all." Vicki checked her watch again and stood. "You can call me when you have the contract ready for signature."

Dani got to her feet too. "I'll have it ready by tomorrow morning." She escorted the wedding planner out of the kitchen. "My fees will be double, as once more it is a last-minute booking. And like before, with such short notice, I'll need payment in full with the signed contract. I'll subtract the portions my employees and I ate from the total."

"Don't be silly. It's understood that the catering staff will be fed." Vicki stopped in the foyer. "It is a pleasure working with you again, even under these circumstances."

"You as well." Dani shook Vicki's hand, then as she opened the front door for her guest, she said, "Please extend my sympathy to Mr. Whittaker."

"What do you mean?" For a nanosecond, Vicki appeared confused.

"For his loss." Dani prompted the woman. "You know, of his fiancée."

"Right. Sorry about that." Vicki's expression smoothed. "Between the sharks suing us, and the cops harassing us, so much has happened over the weekend, it took me a moment to remember."

"Oh." Dani noted that the woman said *us*, not *me* or *him*, then she kept her tone casual and asked, "Have the police questioned you?"

Vicki snapped, "Three freaking times. Do they think our answers will change?"

"They probably hope to catch you or Mr. Whittaker in an inconsistency," Dani said, then asked, "What kind of things are they asking you?"

"Oh, you know." Vicki shrugged. "Where was I when the tent came down? What did I see once it had collapsed? Was there any reason I wanted to see Ms. Joubert dead? Did I know anyone who did?"

"Where were you when it happened?" Dani blurted out before she thought better.

"I was over by the piano, talking to the pianist." Vicki gave Dani an odd look. "You saw me when you rescued her."

"No. Remember, I was on my way toward her. You were already crawling toward an exit." Dani shrugged. "I couldn't see where you were before I ran into you because it was so dark."

"That's what I told the cops." Vicki stepped over the threshold. "But they sure didn't seem to believe me. I wish they'd been there, trapped like a fish in a net, and seen how they would've reacted."

"Yeah." Dani agreed. "Me too, and they didn't seem too happy with my answers either," she said, omitting the fact that once Gray questioned her, the other police officers had backed off. "I should have used the flashlight app on my cell phone but I didn't think about it."

"My phone was back at the head table." Vicki took a few steps onto the porch. "And I sprained my knee when a chair slammed into me."

"Is it okay now?" Dani felt bad that she hadn't asked earlier how the wedding planner had fared being caught in the disaster.

"As long as I have the brace, it's not too bad." Vicki indicated her sweatpants. "Which is why I'm stuck wearing these."

"Were you able to tell the police about anyone who wanted Yvette dead?"

"I gave them a list." Vicki's smile was cold. "A long, long list."

Chapter 16

AFTER CHECKING HER CELL PHONE AND DEALING with the voicemails and texts, Dani settled down to plan the menu for the memorial dinner. Although Yvette's funeral luncheon wasn't a pleasant occasion to cater, as she worked, Dani couldn't keep a tiny smile off her face.

Spencer's message agreeing to help out at the food pantry meal warmed her heart. He'd said that spending time with her was what mattered, not where they were or what they were doing. Being together was what counted.

An hour later, when the doorbell rang, Dani had just finished placing an order for the ingredients that she would need to supplement the unused food from the engagement party. She considered ignoring whoever was pressing the button. There wasn't anyone she particularly wanted to see at the moment, at least no one who didn't either have a key or who wouldn't come to the back entrance.

Still, although clients rarely stopped by without an appointment, she wasn't in a financial position to risk losing a booking. She really needed to look into one of those doorbells with a camera so she could see who was ringing and decide whether to answer it or pretend no one was home. If they were under a hundred bucks and she could install it herself, she was getting one next week.

Muttering to herself, Dani stood, smoothed her hair, and hurried down the hallway.

Before reaching for the doorknob, she checked the foyer's window and gasped. Her hand on her chest, she backed away from the glass.

What was her father doing standing on the porch? It had been five months since she'd moved into the mansion and he'd never visited before.

Heck! She'd lived in her apartment seven years and he'd only been there twice. Once the day she graduated from college and once when he had an early flight out of Normalton Airport and decided to spend the night rather than drive in from Towanda.

After nearly a year of excuses as to why they couldn't get together, her dad's sudden appearance was just what she needed to add to her already über stressful day. There was no reason she should rearrange her plans, even if they only included a long, hot bath and a book, to be at his beck and call.

She'd pretend not to be home and he could text her. That way she could prepare herself for whatever reason he finally wanted to see her. After all, electronic messages had been his preferred method of communication since she moved away from home at age seventeen.

Unfortunately, before she could get out of the foyer, her father's impatient tenor came through the solid wood door, "I know you're there, Danielle."

Her father's familiar, irritated tone sent a stab of dread through Dani's heart and her stomach felt as if a rhino had stepped on it. Forget next week. She was getting one of those doorbells tomorrow.

Dani had a good idea why he'd shown up. He read the *Normalton News* from cover to cover and had doubtlessly seen her name in the article and wanted to know what she was doing at the engagement party. But she really didn't want to see her dad or hear how she'd disappoint him once again.

"You know you're being childish." Her father raised his voice. "And I don't have all day."

Dani stepped forward, but stopped with her hand on the knob. Why should she obey him? Why should everything run on his schedule?

"Open the damn door!" A thump followed Dani's father's order. "I'm leaving on an extended business trip and I need to be at the airport by four. I've already had to reschedule an important meeting because of you. Don't make me late for my flight too."

Dani groaned as he pounded on the door again. It was probably better to get it over with today than worry about it until he returned to town. If she talked to him now, at least she knew he'd be gone in half an hour.

Still, her stomach clenched. Facing him was worse than being a contestant on *Survivor*. Heaven only knew what horrible things he'd say to her before he voted her out of the tribe.

Forcing her hand to turn the deadbolt, she took a deep breath and eased the door open. Jonas Sloan stood with his fist raised, evidently ready to keep knocking until he got his way.

Her chest tightened at how much older he looked than the last time she'd seen him. His gray-blond hair had receded even more, leaving a large expanse of forehead, and the wrinkles around his mouth were etched so deeply they looked worse than the cracks in her driveway.

But what really concerned her was the color of his face. It was redder than the paprika she used in her goulash recipe. He really needed to get his blood pressure checked before he had a stroke.

Without acknowledging Dani, her father brushed past her into the foyer. He scanned the area, clearly taking in the sweeping staircase and rich woods. He turned and looked into the parlor for a long time.

Then nodding to the antiques, he said, "So that old lady who went to college with my mother left you this? Free and clear? Didn't her heirs object or try to sue?"

"Nope." Dani crossed her arms. "Mrs. Cook didn't have any family and her will was ironclad." She added, "Plus, she was Grandma's Alpha Sigma Alpha sorority sister, not just a college friend. That relationship is for life."

Jonas scowled. "Why didn't you sell it? You don't need all this room."

"I thought about it." Dani cleared her throat. For some time, she had intended to tell her father about her change in career, but she'd wanted to do so in person. She'd tried to visit him on several occasions, but he'd always had an excuse not to see her. This was her chance.

"What stopped you?" he asked in a tone that didn't convey curiosity as much as displeasure.

"The kitchen. Once I saw it, I knew it would be perfect for a catering business."

"So that was why you were at that fancy party?" Jonas snapped. "How do you have time for that? I hope you're not slacking off on your real job."

As Dani started to speak, her father pinned her with an enraged glare. For a moment she was distracted by his resemblance to Ming the Merciless and forgot what she was about to say.

Jonas prompted her: "You know, the profession you went to college to learn."

"Ah, well, the thing is, you know I've always wanted to be a chef." Dani battled to stand firm when what she really wanted to do was run.

Jonas exhaled noisily, an angry expression twisting his face.

"So, a few months ago"—Dani forced herself to continue despite her father's obvious hostility—"I quit my job and opened up Chef-to-Go."

"You resigned from a well-paying position with benefits and a good chance of promotion?" Jonas clarified as if he couldn't believe it.

"Yes." Dani was getting worried. Her father was way too calm.

Suddenly Jonas sputtered, "You're telling me you've thrown away your education, an education for which I shelled out a lot of money, and now you are, for all intents and purposes, nothing more than a glorified—"

Without thinking, Dani cut him off. "Cooking has been my passion since seventh grade. You know I wanted to go to culinary school, but you refused to pay for anything other than what you termed a real degree." She tensed. Now she was in for it. Her father was not a man who tolerated interruptions, especially from women. "I mean…"

"You mean you deliberately went behind my back and flushed your career down the toilet to cook for rich people and be treated like a servant?" Jonas shouted, his complexion now closer to eggplant. "You always did test the water by jumping in with both feet rather than doing something sensible like dipping in a toe first."

Dani's shoulders drooped. Her father was all about appearance. He would never understand that doing what made her happy was more important than having a prestigious career and lots of money.

Her silence seemed to enrage him and he thundered, "What do you have to say for yourself, Danielle? Why am I not surprised that you didn't think this out? It was the same thing when you didn't give poor Kipp a chance to explain and just dumped the man."

"Poor Kipp?" Dani's head jerked up and she straightened her spine. "Are you freaking kidding me? He had a fiancée, and it wasn't me."

"Kipp told me that he was waiting for the right time to end his engagement." Jonas tsked. "His fiancée had some mental health issues and he couldn't break up with her until he was sure she wouldn't harm herself. You wouldn't have wanted that, would you?"

"Of course not." Dani rolled her eyes. "But if that was really true, and I seriously doubt it, he shouldn't have started dating again until he was free from his obligation to her. Or at the least, he should have been honest with me about his situation so I could have made an informed decision as to whether I was willing to date him or not."

"He fell in love with you at first sight," Jonas protested. "Just like I did with your mother. He was afraid you wouldn't give him a chance."

"He was right." Dani raised a brow. "Come on,

Dad. Would you have deceived Mom like that? Made her nothing but a side chick?"

Pain flickered across Jonas's face and he slowly shook his head.

"Because you really loved her." Dani put her hand on her father's arm. "Kipp was only after what he could get. Be it free satellite TV, home-cooked meals, or se…" she stuttered, unwilling to go down that path with her father. Besides, she hadn't slept with her ex, much to his frustration.

"But he…" Jonas trailed off, clearly unable to come up with an adequate defense of the man he'd been endorsing.

Sensing a weakening in her father's approval of her ex, Dani said, "Kipp approached me a few months ago, supposedly to make amends, but his real reason was because he was in trouble and needed money."

"Oh?" Jonas conveyed his doubt regarding Dani's truthfulness with that single word. "Why would he need cash? He's got to make a good living. For crying out loud, he's a doctor after all."

Dani explained her ex-boyfriend's problems and what had happened to her because of them, then demanded, "So now do you understand?"

"How could I have been so wrong about Kipp?" Jonas sagged against the wall.

Feeling sorry for her father, even though she knew she shouldn't, Dani led him into the kitchen and said, "Do you have time for a cup of coffee or something?"

Jonas checked his watch. "Coffee would be great." He took a seat on a counter stool and looked around. "This is really nice. Modern."

"Yep." Dani poured a cup of java from the already brewed pot and handed it to him. Remembering his sweet tooth, she got out the sugar bowl and put it in front of him. "Mrs. Cook had it all remodeled and brought up to code."

"What do you do with the rest of the house?" Jonas added several teaspoons of sugar, stirred, then took a sip from his mug.

"Right now, I have three college girls who rent rooms from me, but when I get some capital together, I plan to renovate the remaining rooms and take in a few more boarders. I also want to create a couple of apartments out of the old carriage house." Dani hesitated, then took a slice of chocolate-pecan tart out of the fridge and slid it in front of her father.

It was left over from her Sunday night personal chef gig. Her employers had raved about the pastry, but since they were leaving on a trip the next day, they'd told her to take the rest of the dessert home with her. They had said that it was too scrumptious to go waste.

"How is your business doing?" Jonas picked up the fork she'd put next to his plate and dug into the dessert. "Are you in the black?"

"I am." Dani watched her father taste the tart and when he ate another bite, she smiled. "With the girls' rent and not having a mortgage, I've been able to operate at a profit from the beginning."

She crossed her fingers. She was telling the truth, but the profit margin was a lot slimmer than she, or her father, would like.

"That's impressive." Jonas finished his piece of tart and licked the fork clean. "Let me know when you're ready to renovate, I can give you the name of some reliable construction companies."

"That would be great." Dani's heart lightened. "From what I made from the disaster engagement party and what Mr. Whittaker is paying me to do the memorial luncheon for his deceased fiancée, I should be able to start right after Christmas."

Her father seemed to have accepted her decisions to quit her HR job and open a catering business. He was finally treating her like an adult. Maybe they could finally have a positive relationship.

They chatted amicably for a while about the plumbing and electrical considerations of adding rooms and occupants to the mansion, then he drained his coffee cup and said, "I should probably get going. I can't miss this plane or I'll have to wait until Wednesday for the next one. Either that or drive to the city to catch one from there."

That was the problem with a small airport; the flight schedules were sparse and often inconvenient. Still, it was usually better than going into Chicago and taking off from the disaster known as O'Hare.

Midway was a little better, but still crowded.

Jonas stood up and headed down the hallway with Dani following him. When they got to the foyer, he paused and cleared his throat. Then he ran his hand over his hair and twisted his expression into a grimace.

"What's up?" Dani knew her father well enough to see that there was something he wanted to say, but didn't know how to start.

"In addition to checking on you after reading in the paper about that unfortunate woman's death, I wondered if, that is…" Jonas licked his lips. "How did you come to cater Franklin Whittaker's event?"

"One of my clients recommended my company to his fiancée. Then after interviewing me, Yvette and their wedding planner hired me."

"So you don't know Whittaker?" Jonas asked, his disappointment evident.

"Not really." Dani wondered what her father was getting at. "I suppose that I'll see him Sunday at Yvette's memorial since, as I mentioned, he hired me to cater the dinner after the service. Why do you ask?"

"My company would like to supply the equipment for the food stands at his ballparks." Jonas shoved his hands in his pockets, not meeting her eyes.

"Ballparks?" Dani asked, surprised at the plural. "He has more than one?"

"Whittaker already has controlling interest in several smaller stadiums across the Midwest. Now he's venturing into the major leagues." Jonas beamed. "And he has plans to enlarge the concession areas in all of them."

"Which is why you finally made time to see me." Dani closed her eyes to halt the sudden threat of tears.

She had thought for one brief, shining moment that she and her father could get past all of the hurts and disappointments, but he only wanted to see her because of business. Her chest hurt and she absently rubbed the spot over her breaking heart. Would she ever learn not to get her hopes up?

"Of course not." Jonas's denial didn't ring true and he awkwardly patted her shoulder. "I'm sorry it's taken me so long. I just…" He shook his head. "It's just hard for me to do much that isn't work. I think about it, but then I'm overwhelmed."

"You should see a therapist." Dani had always suspected her father was clinically depressed. "He or she might be able to help you feel better. To get over Mom's death and move on."

"Like you did?" Jonas barked. "Laughing with your friends the day of her funeral?"

"I was only fourteen years old." Guilt choked her. "It seemed unreal."

She'd been heartbroken when her beautiful mother died, and certain memories or events could still trigger a bout of crying, but she hadn't felt anywhere near the depth of her father's grief. Should she have?

"Well, I don't want to get over it, as you so casually put it."

"It's been sixteen years, Dad." Dani got between her father and the door. "Do you really think Mom would want you to live like this?"

"I refuse to discuss this with you." Jonas pushed Dani aside, opened the door, and marched outside onto the porch. "I'll allow you to make your own decisions and you let me make mine."

He was nearly to his car when Dani called after him, "If I see a chance, I'll mention your company to Mr. Whittaker on Sunday."

"Thanks." Jonas stopped and walked back to Dani. "Here's my card. Tell Whittaker that I can send some links for him to look at." His voice was rough when he said, "I'll be back in two weeks. Maybe we can have dinner."

"I'd like that." Dani wasn't sure, but she thought she saw something she hadn't seen in years in her father's gaze. Could it be affection?

Chapter 17

AFTER HER FATHER LEFT, DANI SAT IN THE PARLOR staring out the front window trying to absorb everything that had happened in the past few days. She'd been holding it together, but Jonas's visit had taken away the last of her emotional control.

It was difficult enough to come to terms with Yvette's death, let alone that she'd been murdered. Add to that, despite Gray assurances, Spencer might be a suspect in his ex's homicide, and it was just too much to handle.

Dani couldn't quite believe that the detective would truly ignore an ex-husband on the scene. He might give Spencer the benefit of the doubt, but he was probably keeping him on the back burner and still investigating him.

Then there was Dani's father. His arrival had been a shock. Although at first he'd acted exactly how she'd expected, toward the end he'd seemed almost to believe that she'd make a success of her business.

Or was their whole conversation an act on his part because he wanted Dani to help him get his foot in the door with Franklin Whittaker? Maybe instead of affection, that last gleam she'd seen in his eyes had been satisfaction that she was doing what he wanted.

She'd never been able to read her father very well. Could she be just interpreting his expression to be what she hoped to see?

Dani rested her head against the back of the settee and closed her eyes. There was something else bothering her. Something she'd tucked away to worry about when she had more time. What was it?

Yvette's death. Check. Her murder was never far from Dani's mind.

Spencer. Check. Concern for his situation in the case was right up there too.

Dani's business was fine. There was nothing she could do about her father. But there was definitely something niggling at her.

The girls' behavior!

It was odd that she'd seen so little of them since Saturday night. It was even odder that they hadn't talked to her about their boyfriends. Had Laz slipped off the wagon? Was Robert seeing someone else? Did Caleb like Tippi as more than just a friend?

Resolving to sit down with the three of them soon and get caught up on what was happening with her young friends, Dani made herself stand up. She was due at the food pantry in fifteen minutes and she still had to change clothes.

Dani's head was pounding as if a drummer had gotten into her skull and was beating out Queen's "Another One Bites the Dust" on her brain, but despite how she felt, she couldn't let the hungry people down. The organizers needed her to take the lead in cooking the meal. There were others who could help, but she was the one who knew how to produce the dishes in bulk quantities.

Once Dani got to her suite, she swallowed two ibuprofen capsules and stripped out of her business attire. After putting on a pair of jeans and a fresh chef's jacket, she selected a cowl-neck sweater to wear later in the evening and tucked it into her tote bag with her makeup case. Then she hurried downstairs and put a note on the whiteboard regarding her whereabouts.

With one last glance to make sure she wasn't forgetting anything, Dani picked up her purse and slung it over her shoulder along with the tote bag. Ready for the evening, she walked out to the van.

There was a definite chill in the air and she shivered as she hurried across the driveway. She almost went back to get a jacket, but decided not to bother. It wasn't as if she'd be outside any longer than it took to go from the parking lot to the building.

The food pantry was located in an old restaurant that some Good Samaritan had donated to the cause. Sadly, their benefactor hadn't left any money to fix it up and it looked as if it were leaning slightly to the left.

The shingles were mismatched and several were loose, with pieces of the asphalt roofing material lying in the weeds. At one time, the structure had been painted white, but that was a distant memory. Rusty streaks leaked down from the gutter and the rest of the siding was a faded gray. One of the cracks in the windows had been fixed with duct tape and it was already peeling away from the glass.

The food pantry manager had explained to Dani that they had used what funds they had available to bring the interior up to code and the health department had given them six months to repair the outside.

Even with the lack of curb appeal, when Dani arrived, the parking lot was already packed. Often those in need came hours early in order to get in line. Although they served until the food ran out, there were always some who didn't get the hot meal.

Those people were given whatever else was available. No one left hungry, but sadly some just got a peanut-butter-and-jelly sandwich and a small bag of chips.

At least there was always plenty of lemonade, coffee, and tea available. As well as a warm, safe place to relax and socialize.

Dani stepped through the entrance, but stopped in the area between the outer and inner doors to look at the poster sitting on an easel. She knew what was supposed to be served, but she wanted to make sure the menu was correct. She treated this just as she did any of her paid catering jobs, which meant everything had to be perfect.

With the supplies Dani had contributed from the doomed engagement party, they were offering a choice of pappardelle in a tomato sauce or lemon chicken with cauliflower. A nearby farmer had contributed the poultry and a couple of the local supermarkets had given them items whose expiration dates were fast approaching, as well as lettuce, carrots, and red cabbage that wouldn't last another day, which Dani planned on turning into salads.

It had been a challenge figuring out recipes that would use all the donated ingredients and produce a delicious dish, but Dani had poured over cookbooks— physical and online—until she found what she hoped were the perfect options for the food pantry meal.

She knew that the pappardelle would be a big hit; pasta was always popular. And she was confident that the chicken would win over diners if they would at least taste it before turning up their noses. Many of their clients preferred the basics, like meat and potatoes, but Dani strived for a healthier option.

To round out the meal, several neighborhood bakeries had given them all their day-old bread. Dani planned to slather the loaves with garlic and butter, then pop them into the oven to warm up. This would make good use of the not-quite-freshly-baked bread.

Thinking of all she needed to accomplish in the next hour, Dani opened the inner door and stepped across the threshold. She didn't get far before a trio of men crowded into the space behind her.

They were all big, well-built guys wearing designer jeans, hoodies, and sunglasses. They didn't quite push her aside, but if she hadn't moved quickly, they might have mowed her over.

As they hurried past her and headed toward the main office, they each muttered, "Excuse me," but none of them spared her a glance.

They weren't the type of volunteers Dani was used to seeing. She was squinting after them trying to figure out what they were doing at the food pantry, when a teenage girl ran up to her and shouted, "Emergency," then sprinted away without checking to see if Dani followed her.

Dani jogged forward and grabbed the girl's arm. "What's going on?"

"Rocky won't let any of us near the chicken." The girl tried to keep going, but Dani had a good grip and didn't let her go.

"You need to explain what you mean by that." Dani couldn't remember a volunteer named Rocky, and she wanted to be clear on what was happening.

"She's shouting something about conditions in the chicken farm and cruelty to animals." The girl shrugged. "I don't understand. It's not as if they'll reanimate if we don't cook them. They aren't zombie fowl. They'll just have died in vain."

Dani released the girl and counted to ten. As much as she wanted to, she couldn't march into the kitchen and slap Rocky silly. Someone would call the cops on her. Plus, although she'd had the urge a couple of times, she'd never hit anyone in her life.

It wasn't that she didn't understand the woman's concern, but this was not the time or place to stage some kind of protest. The hungry people expecting to be fed would be the ones to suffer, not whoever might be mistreating chickens somewhere in the vast agro business that Rocky was doubtlessly hoping this demonstration would influence.

Once Dani had her temper under control, she entered the kitchen. The girl who had raised the alarm trailed her though the path cleared by the other volunteers, but she kept her distance.

And Dani could see why. The woman holding the poultry hostage was waving a butcher knife approximately the size of a machete. Rocky stood in front of the refrigerator that Dani assumed held the hijacked hens, and was loudly threatening anyone who came within arm's length of her.

She wore a bright-pink dress that had a short full skirt. She had on equally-bright-blue knee-high socks and neon-green sneakers. Behind large round glasses her eyes were shining as if she was having a wonderful time.

With the hand not clutching the knife, she tucked a strand of magenta hair behind her ear, zeroed in on Dani, and said, "Are you the cook?"

"I'm the chef," Dani said in a firm voice. "And you must be Rocky."

"You've heard of me?" Rocky's voice rose in delight. "Has the TV crew arrived?"

"Why would they be here?" Dani edged closer. "I doubt the people who come to the food pantry for a hot meal would appreciate the publicity."

"They'll realize it's for the greater good." Rocky's expression morphed into that of a sulky two-year-old who had been denied an ice cream cone. "Michie"—she pointed to a young man who looked as if he wished he were somewhere else—"is filming for my vlog, but the whole point is to have a bigger audience."

"Well, you aren't getting it, so let's wrap this up." Dani crossed her arms.

"I will too." Rocky cocked her head. "In fact, I bet they'll be here any minute."

"Who called them?" Dani sent a death glare around the circle of onlookers.

A middle-aged man tapped Dani's shoulder and said, "They're coming for the members of the Korn Kings."

"Here?" Dani frowned. No one had mentioned anything about ballplayers to her. "Why?"

"In exchange for a photo op of the players helping in the kitchen and serving food," the man explained, "the team is covering the price of new siding, a new roof, and thermal windows."

"Wow!" Dani wondered how much that would cost Mr. Whittaker.

"But"—the man gave Dani a cynical look—"my guess is that since this is supposed to be a feel-good story to show the players in a good light, if this lunatic is still here shouting about chicken abuse, the players will skedaddle and the team won't give us the money."

"Crap!" She glared at the hen hijacker.

Dani's headache was now at epic proportions and she'd had enough. No one would interfere with either the hot meal or the funding that would help Normalton's neediest citizens.

The man glanced at his watch. "If you're going to do something, do it now."

"Here's the thing, Rocky." Dani advanced on the woman. "We are cooking those chickens and you are not using our guests to further your cause."

"Come any closer and I'll cut you." Rocky thrust the knife at Dani.

Dani put her hands on her hips. "Fine. We'll do it your way."

"I didn't think you'd risk that pretty face," Rocky gloated.

"I'm not the one at risk." Dani narrowed her eyes. "I'm having you removed."

"By who?" Rocky sneered. "No one around here is willing to sacrifice what I am."

Dani looked at the man by her side. "Please get whoever is doing security tonight." She paused. "Tell them to bring his stun gun."

No one spoke as the guy hurried away. The only

sound in the room as they waited for his return was the buzz of the overhead lights. Rocky leaned casually against the refrigerator and tested the edge of her knife against her finger as her cameraman continued to record.

A couple of minutes later, the kitchen door burst open and the three ballplayers Dani had seen entering the food pantry earlier rushed inside. Now that she could see their faces more clearly, she recognized them as the guys signing autographs at Von Maur's when she and Tippi had been there shopping for her date-night outfit.

She briefly wondered why these three were suddenly making so many appearances. She mentally shrugged. Maybe it wasn't all that unusual for them to be in the public eye and she was just hyperaware because she was working for the team's owner.

While Dani's mind had been wandering, the player who was a few steps ahead of his pals, Marc Something, the one Tippi had said was a shoo-in for the major leagues, advanced on Rocky. Then, in a move Dani couldn't follow, he had the protester flat on the ground.

His left knee held down Rocky's wrist, as he pried the knife from her grasp bending each finger back until she released the handle. While he got the weapon away from her and into his possession, he used his weight to pin the rest of her body to the floor.

The second player, the one Tippi had identified as Perry O'Toole, snickered and said, "Dude, I know you're into all that crazy survivalist crap, but if that's how you treat that chick you've been hooking up with, it's no wonder you haven't been getting any the past few days. Is that why you won't tell us her name?"

Growling at his friend, Marc tilted his chin toward the young man who had been filming Rocky's last stand, and said, "Perry, maybe you should worry about young Mr. Tarantino instead of my personal life."

Perry jerked his head around toward the videographer and then stomped over to the guy. He plucked the cell phone from his unresisting fingers and dropped the shiny, black rectangle to the dingy linoleum, crushing it under the heel of his expensive cowboy boots.

The third and largest player scrutinized the onlookers. He had to be six foot six and two hundred and fifty pounds. Dani guessed that the big guy was checking to see that no one else was using their phones to record the incident.

Seemingly satisfied, the big man leaned against the wall, crossed his legs at the ankles, took out his own cell, and started tapping away. Dani could hear the sounds of *Candy Crush* as he played the popular game.

With that, Dani had her first inkling as to why these three might need to improve their public images. They'd acted too quickly for this to be their first rodeo. She'd bet her prized Lodge cast-iron griddle that these three had been in more than one fight together.

Clearing her throat, she asked, "What happened to the security guard?"

"He's not here yet, but we told Ms. Milne that we'd handle the problem," Marc answered.

"I see." Dani looked at him and suggested, "Maybe you should let Rocky up now." When he didn't respond, she added, "You know, before the television crew gets here."

"Oh." He blinked. "Right." He got Rocky to her feet but didn't release his grip on her arm. "What do you want me to do with her?"

Dani inclined her head toward the woman and asked, "Will you leave peacefully on your own?"

Rocky didn't answer as much as make a weird growling sound, but Dani took that as a no.

She looked at the woman's friend and said, "Here's what we're going to do. Instead of calling the police and having you two arrested, these gentlemen will gently escort you and Rocky to your vehicle. They will buckle her in the back seat with her arms under the belt. You will drive away before you release her."

While the young man nodded, clearly eager to leave, Rocky snarled, "I'll just come back. You can't stop me from spreading my message."

"If you return, we will call the cops who will charge you and your friend with trespassing and aggravated assault," Dani said.

"What?" the young man yelped. "Rocky didn't hurt anyone and this is a public place."

"Wrong and wrong." Dani had been dating someone in law enforcement long enough to know some of the legalese. "Assault charges don't require physical harm. Just that you behave in a way intended to put someone in reasonable fear for their safety." She glanced at the onlookers and asked, "Was anyone here afraid she'd hurt you?"

Everyone's hand shot into the air. Well, everyone but the huge ballplayer who yawned.

"You all can't be serious," Rocky whined.

"So, police or leave?" Dani crossed her arms. "Which is it? I've got a dinner to cook, so whichever you choose, make it snappy."

Chapter 18

THE PHONE WAS RINGING WHEN SPENCER STEPPED into his office. Shortly after he left Hiram at the diner, he'd been summoned to the university's union to handle a physical altercation between two students. He'd been dealing with the fallout from that incident up until a few minutes ago, when he'd finally given up trying to talk the pair of stooges out of beating the crap out of each other and turned them over to the Normalton police.

The numbskulls would be held overnight. Then, in the morning, depending on their attitude and demeanor, the officers would make a judgment call as to whether the dipshit duo could be safely released.

Nothing Spencer had said had made the punks back off from pounding on each other. As far as he could tell, the fight had started when one of blockheads had told the other one's sister that she should sleep with him because if she died a virgin the terrorists who were expecting seventy-two untouched maidens would be up there waiting for her.

While he hadn't been surprised the bozos were fighting over a girl, Spencer had to admit that Romeo's approach had been unique. Horribly insensitive and extremely politically incorrect, but unique. He hoped that cooling their heels in jail for a while would help the two idiots come to their senses and agree not to beat each other up again. But he wasn't holding his breath.

Busy with the dueling doofuses, Spencer hadn't had a chance to call Dani, but he had sent her a short text agreeing to meet her at the food pantry dinner as soon as he was free. Although he'd been disappointed that they wouldn't have the whole evening alone together, at least they'd have a few hours at his town house, where they could talk in private. And maybe get in a few kisses without worrying about one of the girls wandering into the room.

Blinking back into the here and now, Spencer scooped up the receiver on the fourth ring, just before it went into voicemail, and said, "Drake here."

"Heller here," Hiram responded. "Where in tarnation have you been all afternoon? I've called your cell every fifteen minutes since three o'clock and it's nearly five now. I finally got fed up and decided to try your office."

Spencer could tell from the excitement in Hiram's tone that he'd found out something interesting. "Sorry.

I was knee deep in testosterone. You know the drill: two yo-yos, one in lust with the other's sister."

"Yep." Hiram chuckled. "That never ends well. What happened?"

"I couldn't get them to back down, so now they're in the local jail until morning." Spencer pulled out the chair behind his desk, sat down, took out his cell, and saw Hiram's missed calls. "But enough about that. I'm guessing you've found out something good about what Yvette's been up to since she and I parted company."

"Your BFF Brock Ortiz has gone off the grid," Hiram drawled. "He lost an arm while on duty and Yvette dropped him like a hot potato."

"Yeah, she told me that she couldn't be with an amputee." Spencer had forgotten his ex telling him about Brock, but now that Hiram mentioned it, a jilted lover was a great suspect. "By off the grid, you mean you can't find him or he's just laying low?"

"You know darn well there's no one I can't find." Hiram exhaled so loudly it sounded like he was blowing a raspberry at Spencer. "It just may take a day or two to track him down to his hidey-hole."

Spencer was well aware that his mentor had never failed to locate a suspect or witness or anyone else that he really wanted to find. "In that case, give me a holler when he turns up. Meanwhile, I'll let the detective working Yvette's case know about Brock."

"You do that." Hiram paused, then added, "Up until Ortiz screwed your wife, I really liked that boy.

I almost couldn't believe that he betrayed your friendship like that." Hiram paused again. "I just don't think he has it in him to have killed her like that."

"Like what?" Spencer definitely wanted to hear his mentor's thoughts on the subject.

"If Brock had shot her in the heat of the moment, or if he'd smacked her and she hit her head, I could believe that." Hiram sighed. "But to stab her through the eye while she was already unconscious doesn't fit his character." Hiram chuckled. "But then again, having an affair with his best-friend-since-grade-school's wife didn't seem like something he'd do either. So what do I know?"

"You know a lot. And you taught me to never disregard a gut feeling." Spencer opened his desk drawer, took out a Snickers, and tore off the wrapper. "Did I ever tell you that Brock cornered me shortly after I found about him and Yvette and tried to explain it to me?"

"No." Hiram's voice sharpened. "What did he have to say?"

"All I heard before I walked out was that Yvette was the love of his life, she'd put a spell on him, and he had no choice. That he felt like he'd die without her, and that he was pretty sure that I didn't feel the same way about her."

Spencer had been about to take a bite of the candy bar, but suddenly his stomach roiled, remembering the sense of betrayal he'd felt during that brief encounter with his ex-buddy. He hadn't examined his feelings at the time, but now he realized he'd actually been more upset with losing Brock's friendship than losing Yvette.

After the queasiness passed, Spencer said, "Maybe I should have listened to him back then."

"Nah. You weren't ready to hear what he had to say. If you had stuck around, you probably would have punched out his lights."

"Oh. I did that before I left." Spencer flexed his fingers, remembering the sting of his fist hitting his friend's cheekbone.

"Good." Hiram's voice shook with laughter. "He absolutely deserved it."

"That he did." Spencer didn't regret throwing that punch, but he was glad it had been only one and that he'd walked away after that.

There was a moment's silence, then Hiram said, "Do you know if Brock continued to feel that Yvette was the only one for him? I mean after he'd been with her awhile, did the shine wear off of her?"

"Well, I went back undercover shortly after that incident." Spencer suddenly remembered he was starving and he took huge a bite from the candy bar.

"Then you never saw them together again?" Hiram's tone was innocent. "Never slipped away and took a gander at the lovebirds?"

"Maybe once," Spencer mumbled around his mouthful of chocolate and nuts, "or twice." He recalled watching Yvette and Brock eating at a neighborhood restaurant, one that the three of them had frequented. Swallowing Spencer added, "Purely by accident of course."

Hiram made a noncommittal sound, then asked, "And was the luster still on the rose?"

"I guess you could say that." Spencer smiled. Hiram's way of putting things always amused him. "Although Brock certainly seemed like he was crazy about her, Yvette was a lot harder to read. She accepted his attentions, but she didn't appear to reciprocate."

"Most scam artists are like that." Hiram's words reminded Spencer that his mentor had never liked Yvette and had tried to warn him about her. "That painted woman always acted as if being worshipped was her due."

"I can see that now." Spencer still couldn't figure out how his ex had fooled him, but he thought it had to be that she had sensed his loneliness, as well as his ingrained need to protect those around him, and homed in on it like shark sensed chum in the water.

Hiram's voice broke in on Spencer's little trip down memory lane. "This all makes me even less convinced that Brock would kill Yvette."

"Or"—Spencer considered his next words—"he felt like he had to kill her, maybe thinking that if she were dead, he could forget about her."

"If he's turned psycho, that is a possibility." Hiram agreed, then added, "And another possibility is that the reason he's difficult to find is that her death didn't help and he offed himself later that night or the next day."

"Let's hope that isn't the case." Spencer's voice cracked.

Brock wouldn't have been the only first responder to eat his gun. Spencer knew of at least three personally and a few others who were friends of friends.

Men and women in the protect-and-serve professions were called to the scenes of incredibly graphic and traumatic events. Their jobs required them to run toward dangerous and life-threatening situations. And even now, a lot of them felt there was a stigma in seeking help with their emotions.

Hiram and Spencer said their goodbyes and Hiram hung up with a promise to continue searching for Brock. With that settled, Spencer went through the rest of the missed messages on his cell phone. He had turned it to vibrate while he'd been busy at the union trying to keep the students from hurting each other and hadn't felt it buzzing in its holster on his utility belt.

As he scrolled through the list he finished his Snickers, but nearly choked on a peanut when he read the last text, which was from Dani.

Dinner at the food pantry is running a bit late. Crazy woman tried to hold the chicken prisoner, but baseball players disarmed her and sent her on her way. Hopefully, she won't come back with a bigger knife.

As he read the words "bigger knife," Spencer leaped to his feet and checked his ankle holster. Once he had made sure his weapon was in place, he ran out of his office and shouldered open the door to the stairwell.

He took the steps two at a time, and as soon as he burst through the exit, he sprinted for his truck. Although he knew better, he read the rest of Dani's text while he drove.

If the TV crews stay out of our way, we should be serving around six. Try to get here by then because we could really use the help since some volunteers were too scared to stay.

It only took him a few minutes to drive from the security building to the food pantry, which was located just outside of the university's campus. Spencer hurriedly parked, but quickly scanned the area before jumping out of his truck. The last thing he needed was to have his image flash across America's television screens.

After assuring himself that there were no news cameras around, he rushed in the direction of the small structure that housed the pantry. Nearing the front, he saw a line of people snaking around the corner. The crowd wore clean if faded clothing and were well-behaved.

The folks who attended these dinners were those who lived on the fringes. It wasn't usually the homeless that showed up for a hot meal. Instead, it was the elderly who barely made ends meet with social security. The single mothers who were trying to supplement their food stamps. And the marginally employed who couldn't quite make their paychecks stretch to the end of the month.

Hastily detouring toward the rear, Spencer glanced at his watch. It was a few minutes before six. If the lunatic who had threatened the volunteers was going to return, mixing in with the hungry throng waiting to go inside would be a good way for her to gain entrance to the facility. And, if that happened, he wanted to be with Dani in case she was the nutjob's target.

Spencer was relieved to see an enormous young man leaning against the back door. He probably wasn't much more than eighteen or nineteen, but he was big enough to stop anyone that appeared to be a threat from entering.

When the guy spotted Spencer, he straightened and narrowed his eyes.

"Hey." Spencer raised his hands palm forward and said, "The chef's expecting me."

"Dani didn't mention that she was expecting anyone." The Hulk's tone was protective.

Spencer was caught by surprise at the tiny flicker of jealousy, but accepted it and decided to make his position clear. "I'm her boyfriend, Spencer Drake."

He took out his phone and showed the guy a picture of Dani. Best to get his status out in the open right now and avoid any misunderstanding with the ballplayers she mentioned in her text.

"Udell Williams." The big guy stuck out his hand and shook Spencer's, then jerked his thumb over his shoulder and said, "Go ahead."

As Spencer passed him, he read the notice taped to the outside wall and chuckled. DON'T THROW YOUR CIGARETTE BUTTS ON THE FLOOR. THE COCKROACHES ARE GETTING COPD.

Walking inside, Spencer found himself in a small storage alcove. The shelves were lined with nonperishables and off to the side a huge chest freezer hummed. A large calendar was pinned to a bulletin board, its squares holding notations in various colors.

Next to it was an industrial-size mixer with a sign stuck to it that read: THIS MACHINE HAS NO BRAIN. USE YOURS. It appeared that someone working at the food pantry had a sense of humor.

Moving past a pallet of generic paper products, Spencer stepped into the kitchen. His gaze immediately went to Dani, who was bending over a stove sticking a thermometer into a huge roasting pan.

It took less than a nanosecond to realize that he wasn't the only male admiring the view. Spencer scowled at the two men who had stopped what they were doing and were staring at Dani's rear end.

They must be the other two ballplayers that Dani had mentioned. Now that Spencer looked at them, he recognized the blond as Marc Chandler, an up-and-coming pitcher, and the other guy as Perry O'Toole, the Korn King's catcher. They, along with the man at the door, had been in the *Normalton News* quite a bit lately due to the rumors that they might be moving up to the majors soon.

Even as he was identifying the jerks who dared to look at Dani that way, Spencer moved to her side and said, "That smells great. If it's ready, can I get it out of the oven for you, honey?"

Clearly bemused at the endearment—he hadn't used one for her since they started dating—Dani's pretty eyes widened, then she must have figured it out and smiled. "That would be great, sweetie. Put it on the counter by the serving window and I'll let the director know we're ready."

Following Dani's instructions, he placed the hot pan next to a large bowl of salad and a tray of garlic bread. Volunteers were lined up, ready to start serving food as the diners picked up their plates and passed by the window.

Once the director made the announcement, it only took a few seconds before people were three deep, creating a human wall blocking any view to the rest of the area. The triple line snaked twice around the perimeter of the room.

As Dani walked the row of volunteers, directing them on the health department required methods of serving, she reiterated, "Stick to the portion size I've outlined. If we have any leftovers, we can allow diners to come through a second time, but we want to have enough for everyone."

Spencer peered out and saw a television crew aiming their camera at the baseball players as they served the first folks in line. He swiftly turned his head so his face wouldn't be recorded and wondered if the diners were okay with being filmed.

But it only took a few seconds for Spencer to realize that the cameraman appeared to be focused on Marc and Perry and not the ones receiving the food or anyone else for that matter. All the viewer would see was the back of people's heads.

After donning the mandatory pair of plastic gloves, Spencer took his post and started handing out two slices of bread per person. It didn't take long for him to understand why Dani had repeated her portion speech so many times. A lot of the folks requested extra pieces.

Service went quickly and they were nearly out of food when it became apparent that the last dozen or so folks in line would not get a plate. Spencer looked around and motioned to Dani who hurried toward him.

When she got close enough, he whispered, "We only have five portions left. What are we going to do when we run out?"

Dani kept her voice low. "Slow down handing out the food a bit. I'll go start making peanut-butter-and-jelly sandwiches for the rest of them."

Hoping there wasn't a riot, Spencer nodded and passed the word among the volunteers to stall while

Dani got together an alternative meal. Then he handed off his bread duties and went to the pantry to see what was available.

While Dani made a couple dozen PB&J sandwiches, Spencer found a basket of apples and several bags of potato chips. They were plating the substitute dinner when he heard a commotion out front.

"Stay here," Spencer ordered as he edged past Dani and peered out into the dining room, sure that the knife-wielding crazy was back.

He blew out a sigh of relief when he saw that the problem was a woman trying to duck in next to a man who was gesturing for her to join him.

Cutting in a line at the food pantry was akin to cheating on an exam at West Point. At the least, it could get you thrown out, and at the worst, you might find yourself on the wrong end of a fist.

Spencer exited the kitchen and stepped between the woman and the rest of the crowd. "Sorry, ma'am, please go to the back of the line."

"That's my wife." The man tugged the woman toward him. "I've been saving her place because she can't stand too long on account of her bad knees and hips."

Spencer examined the frail woman and wished he could make an exception for her. But because they were nearly out of the hot meals, he just couldn't do it. It wouldn't be fair to the person whose dinner she'd eat.

Striving for a fair alternative, Spencer looked at the husband and said, "You're welcome to give her your spot or go to the back with her, but the sign clearly states that there is no saving places or cutting."

"But…" the man started, then sighed deeply, considered his options, and said, "I'll go to the back and she can have my place."

Spencer patted the guy's shoulder. "Good man." The poor fellow was nearly as skinny as his wife and Spencer wished there was a way both of them could have the hot food.

Watching the man trudge to the back of the line, Spencer saw someone staring at him. The person quickly ducked out the exit, but not before Spencer recognized him.

Although Spencer had only gotten a glimpse and the man certainly didn't look anything like he had in Chicago a couple of years ago, Spencer was pretty darn sure the guy had been Brock Ortiz. What was his former best friend doing in a food pantry line in downstate Illinois?

Chapter 19

Dani was relieved to turn over kitchen cleanup to the group that had volunteered for that task. Her crew had continued to serve food until there wasn't anyone left in line, but the last twelve or so people had been handed a plate with a peanut-butter-and-jelly sandwich, an apple, a small bag of potato chips, and a packet of cookies, rather than the meal they had been anticipating for the past hour.

It was cruel to be surrounded by the garlicky tomato-scented air and be stuck eating a PB&J. To smell the roasting lemon chicken, then to have nothing more than a cold sandwich to fill your stomach was just plain wrong.

Those people's disappointed faces haunted Dani. And she vowed that next month there would be more than enough food for everyone to get a hot dinner, even it meant dipping into her own Chef-to-Go supplies.

She was glad that the television crew had left once they'd filmed the baseball players serving a few people. She'd hate to have the viewers see that the hot fare had ran out before everyone got a meal.

Sadness for those last few folks was lodged in Dani's throat as she turned to talk to her staff. "Thank you all for helping out. We'd love to have you come again in November and bring your friends. It will be our Thanksgiving meal and we expect at least fifty percent more diners so we'll need as many hands as we can get, and also any donation of food would be appreciated." She passed out a list of ingredients. "These can be dropped off here between now and then."

Watching the expression of the volunteers as she spoke, Dani saw that most were nodding that they'd be back and comparing notes as to what they could contribute. Only Marc Chandler and Perry O'Toole exchanged glances and smirked at her requests.

Dani rolled her eyes. She was pretty darn sure she'd seen the last of those guys.

Her crew, including Marc and Perry, left as soon as she finished her speech. After they had cleared out, Dani went to the restroom and changed from her chef's jacket into her sweater, freshened her makeup, and combed out her hair. Exiting from the bathroom, she looked around for Spencer.

She was texting him to find out his location, when she heard, "I'll be here next month."

Dani hadn't noticed Udell Williams walking up

behind her and she jumped, then turned and said, "Great." She patted the big man's arm. "Maybe next time you can help out in the kitchen instead of having to work security, but we sure appreciated you helping to keep everyone safe tonight."

"Wherever you need me is fine." Udell ducked his head, then gave her a sweet smile. "I came with Perry and Marc because my Moms had to use the food pantry in our town a few times to keep my sisters and me fed. I send her what I can from my check, but the Middle American League doesn't pay much." He chuckled. "Heck. If I didn't get free lodging and food, I'd be screwed. I make more off-season working as a custodian, but Moms wants me to live my dream."

"Of course she does." Dani nodded, then frowned. "But I thought professional athletes made a lot of money."

"The ones on TV do." Udell chuckled. "All of us playing for teams like the Korn Kings are there hoping that we'll get noticed or improve enough to eventually get in the bigs."

"Does that happen often?" Dani asked. "How many players get into the majors?"

"Enough that we'd all do just about anything to be the lucky ones picked." Udell shrugged. "Think about it. We go from barely scraping by financially to earning millions. From obscurity to stardom."

"I can see how that would be an incentive to do whatever it took," Spencer said, walking into the kitchen and voicing what Dani had been thinking.

"Yep." Udell shoved his hands in his pockets and headed toward the back exit. "Anyway. I'll see you next month, Miss Dani."

"Terrific!" Dani beamed. "I'll be rooting for you at the next game."

Spencer looked at Dani thoughtfully, then said, "Are you ready to go?"

"Yep." Dani put her tote bag on her shoulder. "I'm starved."

"Me too." Spencer cupped Dani's elbow and they strolled outside and into the small parking lot. "Do you want to ride with me? I can bring you back to pick up your vehicle afterward."

"Tempting. But it's probably easier for me just to follow you." Dani smiled as they headed toward her van. When they reached it, she leaned a hip against the door and warned, "Just don't lose me since I haven't been to your place before."

"No way will I lose you." Spencer bent down and brushed his lips against hers. "I've waited too long to find you to let you disappear."

Dani opened her mouth to respond, but she noticed someone peeking over the trunk of the car in the next parking spot. Before she could point out the Peeping Tom to Spencer, the person caught her eye, took a stumbling step back, and melted into the night.

At that moment her stomach growled and Dani giggled. "We better get going before I take a bite out of the seats. See you soon."

Dani got into the van and waited for Spencer to get to his truck. A few seconds later, she saw Spencer's pickup idling near the parking lot exit and she hurriedly put the van in reverse and pulled up behind him. Ten minutes later, Spencer turned into his driveway and Dani stopped the van next to him. She hopped out and took the hand he offered her.

Lacing his fingers with hers, he escorted her into his town house. As soon as she stepped over the threshold, she was struck by the sterility of his home.

She could take in nearly the entire interior from the doorway. The living room held a single recliner, an old couch, a coffee table, and a television, which hung on the wall. The dining room was totally empty. And in the kitchen, a single chair was pushed under a small table. She couldn't see the bedrooms, but she'd be surprised if they were any less utilitarian.

Hmm. Maybe this was why Spencer liked hanging out at the mansion. There might be more of a crowd, but it had a much homier feeling.

"What do you want on your pizza?" Spencer asked interrupting her musing. "I like just about anything but pineapple on mine."

Dani thought for a moment, then said, "Pepperoni, black olive, and mushroom."

"Sounds good to me." Spencer dug his phone from his pocket and dialed. As he waited for his call to be answered, he asked, "How about a salad?"

"That would be great. Any vinaigrette dressing

is fine with me," Dani answered. "Shall I get out the plates?"

"Sure. They're in there." Spencer pointed to the cabinet next to the sink.

Before he could speak, Dani heard a voice from his phone say, "May I help you?"

While Spencer was busy ordering, Dani opened up the cupboard he'd indicated and took out two of the four dishes and two of the four bowls inside. The silverware drawer was equally barren, and she was looking for napkins when Spencer finished his call and tapped her on the shoulder.

"I use paper towels." He gestured to the roll on the counter. "What would you like to drink? I have beer, water, and milk."

"Water's fine." Dani looked around. "Is there another chair or should we sit in the living room?"

Spencer's ears reddened. "The second chair broke and I haven't replaced it."

"Oh." Dani headed into the living room without commenting and sank into the sofa. Cooking and serving such a big crowd had sapped her energy, and she rested her head against the back cushions.

She was surprised when Spencer joined her on the couch, since the recliner was obviously where he usually sat. Straightening, she took the bottle of water from him, unscrewed the lid, and drank half the contents in one gulp.

"You must be exhausted." Spencer turned her

slightly and massaged her shoulders. "I don't think I saw you take a break the whole time."

"Tonight was more hectic than usual." Dani luxuriated in the feel of his fingers digging into her tired muscles. "Probably because we got a late start when we had to wrestle the poultry away from the crazy chicken lady before we could even begin the meal."

Spencer frowned. "Tell me about that. I never did get the entire story."

"There's not much to tell." Dani shrugged. "This woman found out there would be a television crew and wanted to get publicity for her cause."

"What about the knife?" Spencer stopped rubbing and stared at Dani. "You could have been hurt. You should have called the police."

"The baseball players handled it." Dani examined Spencer and decided he wasn't being a jerk. He was just concerned. "I was never in any danger."

"Maybe." Spencer continued his massage. "However, just because they're physically fit men doesn't mean they couldn't have gotten stabbed."

"You're right." Dani had thought the same thing when Marc had disarmed Rocky. "That's why I originally sent someone to get the food pantry security. But when he didn't arrive, the players stepped in before I could object."

"Where was the guard?" Spencer moved his hands from her shoulders and started kneading her lower back. "I didn't see him all night."

"He never showed up." Dani shook her head. "Rumor has it, he's not that reliable, but the food pantry can't afford anyone better."

They both sank into silence as Dani relaxed under Spencer's soothing ministrations. She couldn't stop yawning and Spencer seemed to have fallen into a Zen-like state as well. Both were worn-out. The events of the last few days had finally caught up to them.

When the doorbell rang, Dani jerked into a state of semi-alertness and Spencer groaned before he slowly rose from the couch and trudged to the door.

After paying the delivery guy, Spencer brought the pizza and salad bowl into the living room and placed it on the coffee table. The mouthwatering aroma of basil and oregano brought Dani fully awake, and as soon as he flipped open the carton, she eagerly reached for a slice.

The only sound for the next fifteen minutes was chewing and the occasional moan from Dani as she enjoyed her first meal since lunch. Finally, her stomach full, she settled back on the sofa and relaxed.

Spencer glanced at the last piece sitting forlornly in the box and asked, "Are you sure you don't want that?" When Dani shook her head no, he coaxed, "How about some ice cream? I have your favorite."

"You do not." Dani leaned forward, grabbed a paper towel from the roll, and wiped her mouth, then tossed it on her empty plate. "I bet you don't even know my favorite kind."

"Blue Bell Pecan Pralines 'n Cream." Spencer raised a brow. "Right?"

"Wow." Dani got to her feet and gathered the debris littering the coffee table. "I'm impressed. I don't remember ever telling you that."

"I have my sources." Spencer grinned and followed her into the kitchen.

"Ivy." Dani's heart skipped a beat. She was touched he had gone to so much trouble for her. "I should have guessed that right away."

"Got it in one." Spencer reached for the freezer handle. "So how about we have dessert and compare notes?" He paused. "Unless you're too tired. It's nothing urgent. We could wait until—"

"No way." Dani opened the cabinet and took out the remaining two bowls. "If I remember correctly, the next time our schedules mesh isn't until Thursday."

"Right." Spencer scooped ice cream while Dani found the spoons.

Once they were back on the couch enjoying their treat, Dani said, "Okay. I have a few things I wanted to talk to you about."

"Go for it." Spencer turned slightly and gave her his full attention.

"I had an appointment with Vicki Troemel, Yvette's wedding planner, today." Dani took a breath. "Mr. Whittaker sent her to ask me to use the food that hadn't been served at the engagement party, but was still good, to cater Yvette's memorial service which is on Sunday."

"Seems a little tacky, but I guess it's better than wasting it." Spencer's expression was nonplussed. "Will they have the body that soon?"

"Evidently, Mr. Whittaker's good friend the mayor has assured him they will." Dani shrugged. "You probably know better than I do, but I'm guessing that the county medical examiner didn't exactly have a backlog of bodies ahead of Yvette to autopsy and has had plenty of time for any follow-up requested by the police."

"True." Spencer pursed his lips. "But if I was the officer in charge, I'd want to keep the vic until I had the perp. In case there was a need to reexamine the evidence. Then again, maybe Christensen is ready to make an arrest. Have you talked to him today?"

"Nope." Dani ate a bite of ice cream. "Anyway, the reason I brought up my meeting with Vicki is that in talking to her, it was apparent that she was in love with Franklin Whittaker."

"Interesting." Spencer narrowed his eyes. "That would give her a motive to get rid of Yvette. And Vicki was under the collapsed tent."

"Exactly." Dani nodded. "Plus, considering how demanding Yvette was as a client, Vicki was probably never more than a few steps away from her the whole evening."

"That's a good point." Spencer tapped his chin. "You should probably share this information with Christensen as soon as possible."

"I plan to call him tomorrow morning once I finish with the lunch-to-go prep." Dani had considered informing Gray right away, but she wanted to go over it with Spencer before telling the detective.

Spencer nodded, then asked, "What other things did you want to talk about?"

"Well…" Dani bit her bottom lip. "I had a visitor before Vicki arrived."

"Oh?" Spencer leaned forward. "Someone I know?"

"Uh-huh." Dani made a face. "It was Frannie Ryan from the *Normalton News*."

"I should have guessed." Spencer's expression twisted in distaste.

"Frannie was out of town and another reporter got assigned the murder," Dani said slowly, then stalling before giving Spencer the bad news, added, "Frannie and Justin got engaged."

"Okay." Spencer clearly wondered why Dani mentioned that. "Anything else?"

"Frannie said that she wants to get back to Scumble River fairly soon because she thinks the mayor is up to no good and it has to do with your friend the police chief."

"Mmm." Spencer frowned. "Did Frannie give you any details?"

"Nope. She was afraid she'd lose her exclusive." Dani sighed. "But you might want to give Wally a call and let him know something's up, even if you don't know what it is exactly."

"I'll do that." Spencer tilted his head. "What else did Frannie say?"

"She was ticked at being scooped and persuaded her editor to let her do a human interest story on Yvette," Dani explained.

"Shit!" Spencer's eyes darkened with understanding. "She knows about me?"

"Yep." Dani reached over and squeezed Spencer's hand. "Frannie said that if you'll talk to her, she promises to only ask reasonable questions."

"Reasonable to her may not mean the same as it does to me," Spencer protested.

"I understand," Dani assured him. "But if others talk about your past relationship with Yvette and you don't, Frannie could end up with only one side of the story. The one that doesn't put you in a good light."

"There weren't that many people who knew us as a couple. We weren't married that long and I was undercover for a lot of that time."

"Sure." Dani tilted her head. "But someone is always willing to spill the beans. And if they don't know anything, they'll just make something up."

Spencer cursed, jumped to his feet, and paced the length of the living room.

"Maybe we should talk to Frannie together." Dani rose from the couch and followed him.

"Okay." Spencer nodded reluctantly, then sighed and caressed Dani's cheek with one finger. "You know, I really appreciate that you're taking this all so well. A lot of women would be upset with their boyfriend's ex-wife popping up like this."

Warmth spread through Dani's chest. She noticed the endearment he used back when he'd first arrived to help at the food pantry and wondered if it signaled a new phase of their relationship. Now Spencer calling himself her boyfriend made it seem even more likely.

Grinning, she joked, "Before I knew Yvette was your ex, she saw your picture on my phone and said how handsome you were. At the time I was a bit worried to let her meet you. So I guess the situation could be worse. She could have come to town to get you back."

Chapter 20

DANI DROVE HOME WITH SPENCER'S HEADLIGHTS shining in her rearview mirror. Knowing that she was almost too tired to see straight, he'd wanted her to leave the Chef-to-Go van at his place. When she'd insisted that she'd need it the next day, he suggested she could get one of the girls to bring her over to pick it up before they started the lunch-to-go prep.

Finally, when she'd pointed out that would mean setting her alarm earlier than her already crack of dawn wake-up call, Spencer had compromised. He'd follow her to the mansion to make sure she arrived safely.

Yawning, Dani turned into the driveway, parked, turned off the ignition, and bent to grab her tote bag from the floor. However, before she could grasp its strap, Spencer slid into the passenger seat.

He immediately said, "I wish we could carve out some time to be together before Thursday night. I'd love to come by after my pigsitting duty tomorrow, but the shift doesn't end until 3:00 a.m. and I know that's too late."

"Sadly, it really is." Dani blew out a frustrated breath. "I have to be up and cooking by six to get the lunch-to-go food ready in time. I try to have the bags packed by ten thirty for the students who pick them up on their way to their late morning classes."

"How about Wednesday?" Spencer asked, taking her hand and stroking her palm. "What time will you be done with your personal chef gig?"

"Unfortunately, it'll be later than usual." Dani reluctantly moved her hand away and unbuckled her seat belt. "It's a new client and they live in Morton. I'll be lucky to be home by midnight."

"We both work too hard." Spencer put his arm around Dani's waist and slid her across the bench seat toward him. "You need to hire some more help and I need to delegate more responsibility."

"Yep." Dani allowed herself to snuggle against his shoulder for a second. "But in the meantime, I really have to go inside and get some sleep."

They both glanced at the dashboard clock. It was well after midnight.

"Can you last a little longer?" Spencer asked. "I wanted to fill you in on what's been going on with me in regard to Yvette's murder."

"I'll try." Dani struggled to keep awake. "Start with how the meeting with Dr. Kayley went." She'd been concerned when he told her he would have to inform his boss about the situation.

"Surprisingly well." Spencer rubbed his jaw and Dani noticed the sexy stubble that had increased with every passing hour. "Dr. K was concerned, and while she was on board with me doing a little probing of my own, she did warn me to make sure the police want my help rather than view it as interference with their investigation."

"Good advice." Dani arched a brow. "Are you planning on following it?"

"Sure. Probably." Spencer grinned. "Okay, maybe. If I have to, I will."

"What do you mean by that?" Dani narrowed her eyes. "What did you do?"

"I asked my mentor to run a deep background check on Yvette," Spencer admitted. "Since our divorce, my only contact has been across a conference table at one of our attorneys' offices."

"Won't that sort of thing cause a flag to come up to the police?" Dani forced herself to straighten and put a little space between them.

"Nah." Spencer shook his head. "Hiram knows how to keep off their radar."

"Let's hope so." Dani bit her lip. "Do you think he'll find anything?"

"He's already discovered an interesting fact." Spencer's lips twisted. "It turns out that the guy Yvette was screwing behind my back, my then-friend Brock Ortiz, has gone off the grid."

"That is curious." Dani frowned. "I remember Yvette mentioning that she dumped him when he lost an arm while on duty. She had already met Whittaker at some fancy charity ball, and my impression was that although she said she didn't start seeing him until after Brock was injured, she actually hooked up with Mr. Billionaire right away." Dani tilted her head. "And a jilted lover treated that way is a great suspect."

"Yep." Spencer smiled wolfishly. "Even more so now that I caught him prowling around the very town where the murder took place."

"You've seen him in Normalton?" Dani squeaked. "Did you call Gray?"

"Not yet." Spencer scratched his chin. "I thought I spotted him just as we were finishing up the service at the food pantry tonight so I followed him outside. I couldn't get to him in time, but I did see him get into a beat-up black Dodge Charger and I got the plates."

"So why didn't you call Gray right then?" Dani had a bad feeling.

"I want to talk to Brock first." Spencer lifted a hand as if he knew very well that Dani would object. "Once I do, I'll turn him over to Christensen."

"It's not a good idea to wait," Dani cautioned. "What if he disappears before you find him? Couldn't keeping that info be considered obstruction?"

"Technically." Spencer seemed unconcerned with the thought of being arrested. "But if I can't locate him in the next two or three days, I'll go to the cops and report his presence. I just won't mention when I first saw him. No harm, no foul." Spencer squeezed Dani's hand. "For all we know, Christensen is already looking for him and that's why Brock was sneaking around."

Still concerned but knowing this wasn't an argument that she'd win, Dani took a second to consider what Spencer had told her, then said, "I wonder what your friend Brock was doing at the food pantry."

"Maybe he was here for the free hot meal." Spencer shrugged.

"But if he was hurt on the job, wouldn't he get disability?" Dani recalled her training in HR and added, "I think it's usually about seventy-five percent of his previous salary."

"But he's been off the grid," Spencer countered. "He probably hasn't been collecting it in order to stay invisible."

"That's possible," Dani conceded, then suggested, "But I think he might have been at the food pantry dinner because of you."

"What would make you believe that?" Spencer's tone was doubtful.

"First, describe Brock to me," Dani ordered. "Then I'll tell you."

"He's about my height. Short brown hair—at least that's how he used to wear it. Hazel eyes." Spencer paused. "And he was very muscular. He worked out a lot, but I don't know if that's still the case."

Dani nodded to herself as Spencer spoke, then said, "He must have come back to the food pantry after you chased him away."

"You saw him?" Spencer had been relaxed, but stiffened at her words. "Where?"

"When we were leaving to go to your place and you escorted me to my van," Dani explained. "I saw a guy watching us from behind a car."

"And the Peeping Tom looked like how I described Brock?" Spencer asked.

"Yes." Dani closed her eyes. "But his hair was to his shoulders."

"How about his arm?" Spencer asked quickly. "Was he an amputee?"

"He was wearing a canvas jacket, you know like the ones hunters wear, and besides, I couldn't see past below his shoulder."

"That's what Brock had on when I spotted him." Spencer grimaced. "But why would he be following me? What could he want?"

"Maybe he's gone crazy." Dani shuddered as a shiver ran down her spine. "If he killed Yvette, you could be his next target."

"Why in the heck would he want to get rid of me?" Spencer shook his head. "He's the one that nailed my wife, not vice versa."

"Unless Yvette claimed you were behind her dumping him. That you were the love of her life." Dani shrugged. "She didn't seem to care too much if she hurt someone. In fact, she sort of seemed to enjoy it." Dani glanced at Spencer to gauge his reaction.

Despite Spencer's obvious dislike of his ex-wife, Dani wondered if it hurt him to hear her described in such an unflattering light. How did he feel knowing that he'd married a woman like that? They probably should talk about what had made him fall in love with Yvette sometime, but she was too tired to go into it now.

Spencer seemed unfazed with Dani's less-than-flattering portrayal of Yvette. And after a moment he nodded his agreement with her assessment of his ex. Then he gazed out of the windshield and silently stared into the darkness.

Dani was just about to ask him what he was thinking about when he said, "Although in the scenario you suggested, since Yvi was marrying Franklin Whittaker, wouldn't he be the more obvious target for Brock?"

"I suppose, but I feel like there's something we're missing." Dani yawned. "And truthfully, my brain is too fried to function anymore."

"You're right and I'm sorry." Spencer took her in his arms. "You need to get some sleep and so do I. Call me when you take a break after the lunch-to-go sales. If I'm not tied up, maybe we can grab an hour together."

"That might work." Dani kissed his cheek. "Except for some ordering, planning, and recipe trials, I'm free all afternoon and evening."

Tuesday morning was a typical late October day in Illinois—dark, dank, and depressing. Instead of the glorious autumn full of colorful leaves that they'd all been hoping against hope for, they got the gray skies and drizzle common to the area. By this point, eighty percent of the population firmly believed that the state only had two seasons, summer and winter, and the other twenty percent were making plans to leave for Florida.

Dani wished she were one of the latter. She was already tired of not seeing the sun until nearly seven thirty in morning and having it disappear before six at night. Or maybe her bad mood was due to her lack of sleep and worry that Spencer was in danger from either Brock or the police. Or maybe both.

At 5:45 when she walked into her kitchen and flicked on the overhead lights, their glow out the windows was the only illumination around the gray-shrouded mansion. Rain beat at the glass, and when she gazed outside, she couldn't see any farther than the driveway through the fog.

While she waited for the coffee to brew, she switched on the radio, which was set to the university's student-run station. During the morning and early afternoon, it broadcast weather and news interspersed with selections of upbeat instrumental music. That changed to a hipper variety of tunes after classes were over for the day.

As Dani tuned in, the announcer was giving the hourly weather report. "High today in the lower sixties with wind out of the north, making it feel colder. Tonight will be in the forties with a chance of thunderstorms. No change is predicted for the rest of the week, so select your Halloween costume with that in mind."

Dani rubbed the goose bumps on her arms. She could put on a sweatshirt, but as soon as she started cooking, she'd be too hot and have to take it off.

Next up on the radio was the news, which mostly focused on activities around the campus. "In the early hours of Tuesday morning, three pledges from the Gamma Zeta Pi fraternity unleashed a flock of chickens in the Mu Nu Alpha sorority house. Campus security said the prank was in retaliation for MNA's pledges filling the GZP's game room with water balloons. No arrests have been made."

As Dani wondered which of Spencer's staff was forced to deal with that mess, the thud of footsteps on the stairs interrupted her thoughts. A second later, Starr and Tippi stumbled into the kitchen. Neither girl was a morning person, but they both had an eight o'clock class on Tuesdays and Thursdays, which meant Ivy was Dani's scheduled helper for the lunch prep.

"Good morning." Dani hurriedly dispensed her own cup of coffee. Her boarders often drained the pot with their huge to-go cups. The manufacturer claimed the machine brewed ten portions, but all the girls had massive travel mugs that emptied the carafe with a couple of pours. Once Dani had her precious caffeine, she asked, "How do ham-and-cheese quinoa cups sound?"

"Sure." Starr walked over and got out plates and silverware.

Tippi sat slumped on a counter stool and complained, "You promised waffles."

Dani barely stopped herself from snorting at Tippi's obvious lie. "Your other choice is bran cereal with bananas." There was no way she had said that she'd make them waffles. On weekdays, she tried to send them off with a healthy breakfast. "Or oatmeal."

"Fine." Tippi jutted out her bottom lip. "You made waffles for that detective. Clearly, you love him more than us."

How in the world did Tippi know that? Dani thought back. None of the girls were around Sunday morning and there hadn't been any leftovers. Then again, Tippi did have an extraordinary sense of smell. Dani was convinced the girl was part bloodhound. She'd probably gotten a whiff of the maple syrup in the air.

Ignoring Tippi's whining, Dani turned on the oven to preheat, then opened the fridge and grabbed the bowl of leftover quinoa from yesterday's lunch-to-go prep. While she was at it, she took out a carton of eggs, bag of shredded cheddar, and a block of parmesan cheese, as well as the shredded zucchini, green onions, and diced ham that she'd prepared before heading to the food pantry last night.

As Dani nudged the refrigerator door closed, Starr asked, "Have you ever wondered why the fridge merits a light, but the freezer is kept in darkness?"

Dani shrugged. It was too early to wax philosophical. Instead, she began to combine ingredients for her breakfast creation.

As she added some chopped parsley, salt, and pepper, she glanced up when Tippi muttered, "The refrigerator had a better agent."

Chuckling, Dani looked at Starr and asked, "Everything okay with you and Robert?"

"I think so." Starr poured herself a glass of orange juice and joined Tippi at the counter. "He's been awfully busy lately, but he says that pledging is over the day after Halloween and then he should be back to his normal work schedule."

"I'm glad things are going well between you two." Dani liberally coated muffin tins with nonstick spray and spooned the egg mixture to the top of each cup. "He seems like a nice guy."

Starr took a sip of her juice and beamed. "He invited me to his dad's birthday party next Saturday. Now I need to figure out a gift."

"Maybe Spencer would have an idea. You should ask him for a suggestion." Dani slid the muffin tin into the oven and looked at Tippi. "How's your plan to lure Caleb from the friend zone doing?"

"Good." Tippi smiled, then frowned. "Except he says he has to take that other girl to the dance because he already invited her."

"I warned you about that." Dani washed the mixing bowl and put it in the drainer.

"But he doesn't want me to go with another guy." Tippi pouted. "That's not fair."

"Caleb has a problem with you going with a guy, even if he's just a friend?" Dani asked, drying her hands.

Tippi made a face. "I don't really have any guy friends that won't want something more."

"Then I see Caleb's point." Dani glanced at the oven timer. There was another five minutes to go. "How are Ivy and Laz doing?"

"Don't ask." Starr shuddered.

"No. Maybe Dani should ask Ivy," Tippi said, thoughtfully. "I bet she could give Ivy some good advice."

"Definitely not." Dani shook her head. "If there's one thing I've learned, it's there are only two good reasons to give advice: if someone requests your input or if it's a life-threatening situation. Ivy hasn't asked me what I think, and although painful, you don't die from a broken heart."

Chapter 21

TIPPI AND STARR HAD ALREADY FINISHED BREAK-fast and gone upstairs to get ready for their classes when Ivy trudged into the kitchen and headed straight for the coffeepot. Dani hadn't seen her since Saturday night, and she was dismayed at the change in her young friend. The girl looked ten years older and a hundred times unhappier than her usual cheerful self.

Ivy's hair was unwashed and scraped into a ponytail, her eyes were dull, and she moved as if a boulder were strapped to her back. Sitting at the counter, she ignored the food Dani slid in front of her and wrapped her hands around her cup as if she were cold.

"I'm glad you're my helper today," Dani said with forced cheer. "It seems as if I haven't talked to you in ages. Sorry I wasn't around last night." She and Ivy usually binged on *Chopped* episodes on Monday nights. "Your uncle helped me at the food pantry dinner, then we went to his place and ordered a pizza. We were starved."

"That's okay." Ivy straightened, looking marginally perkier. "Did you have a nice time? Was the ice cream a surprise?"

"I did and it was." Dani beamed. "Thank you for being a part of it."

"You and Uncle Spence make a good couple." Ivy's smile slipped a little, but she took a breath and said, "That's something special and rare. I'm glad to be a part of making that happen anytime."

She and Ivy shared an understanding glance, then Dani said, "You better eat something because we need to start preparing the lunches."

Although it was barely 7:00 a.m., it would take them a couple of hours to get the food ready and another hour to get it packed. Dani consulted her list and began to gather ingredients and equipment.

Soon the scent of chocolate and caramel drifted through the air. Dani inhaled the tantalizing aroma as she prepared her delectable triple-layer shortbread bars for the Indulgent lunch bags.

Ivy was silent while she sliced the pastrami for the sandwiches that would also go into the Indulgent bag, but after she got through the ten pounds of brisket, she asked, "What does it mean when a guy tells you he'll be out of touch for a while and you can't contact him?" Without waiting for Dani to respond, Ivy continued in a shaky voice, "Is that him saying he's dropping you?"

Dani paused. Lying to Ivy and denying that possibility wouldn't make the situation any better.

"That is certainly one of the things it might mean." Dani finished mixing the shortbread crust, pressed it into the prepared sheet pan, and slid it into the preheated oven. "Did Laz tell you that?"

"Uh-huh." Ivy let out a long, sad sigh as she lined up a bowl of oil-and-vinegar coleslaw, a stack of Swiss cheese slices, and a squeeze bottle of Dani's homemade Thousand Island dressing. "He sent me a text Sunday morning while I was still asleep."

"I'm surprised he was up so early." While the shortbread baked, Dani turned her attention to the homemade barbecue potato chips that would accompany the pastrami sandwich. "Did you ask him why?"

Before she started to assemble the Rye Are You So Sad sandwiches, Ivy poured chocolate chips from the bin sitting on the counter into her hand, popped them in her mouth, and mumbled, "I couldn't. When I finally saw his message, it was already way past the time he said he was leaving."

Dani was thinly slicing potatoes on a mandolin, the scariest piece of equipment in her kitchen, and unwilling to risk her fingers, she paused before she asked, "Couldn't you send him a text?"

"His message said that he wouldn't have his phone with him."

Dani considered her response as she finished cutting the spuds and began to mix sugar, salt, onion powder, smoked paprika, chili powder, and garlic powder together in a large bowl. Should she say what she was thinking?

"It sort of sounds like Laz might be back in rehab," Dani finally admitted, glad Ivy couldn't see her concerned expression.

Ivy had finished assembling the Indulgent sandwiches and wrapping them, and when Dani spoke, she was on her way to store them in the commercial-sized cooler in the back of the kitchen. She stuttered to a stop, still holding the huge tray stacked with the Rye Are You So Sad entrée.

Ivy's voice cracked. "That can't be it. I have never seen him touch a drop of alcohol or smelled it on his breath."

The timer beeped and Dani fetched the short-bread crust from the oven, then put it on a rack to cool as she carefully chose her words. "From my experience in human resources, alcoholics can be sneaky."

Ivy didn't respond, but after she deposited the sandwiches in the cooler and pulled out the ingredients to make the Healthy side dish, pear and fennel salad, she said, "I have Mr. Hunter's phone number. Should I call him and ask? Would that be okay?"

"Let me think about that for a minute," Dani said, unwilling to give her young friend advice she hadn't completely thought through.

While she considered Ivy's question, she put the potatoes into a large bowl of cold water, separating the slices. Then she drained the water and repeated the process a couple of more times. Next, she spread out a layer of paper towels and put the potatoes on them to dry. Finally, she set her deep-fryer to 300 degrees.

Having come to a decision, Dani glanced in her friend's direction and watched Ivy toss the salad for a minute before she said, "It might not be wise to contact Mr. Hunter."

"Why not?" As Ivy spooned the pear and fennel into compostable plastic bowls and snapped on the lids, her brows met over her nose, a clear sign of her bewilderment. "Mr. Hunter told me to call him anytime."

"Rehab isn't something that every family is comfortable with discussing openly," Dani cautioned as she tested the shortbread crust, found it had cooled enough, and poured the caramel layer over it.

"But that's the thing." Ivy deposited the salads in the catering refrigerator, then came back and started slicing kale, avocado, and cucumber for the Healthy entrée. "His father is cool about it. We talked about Laz's addiction when I met him a few months ago. Laz's mom, not so much."

"I see." Dani nodded as she spread melted chocolate over the caramel and put the bars in the refrigerator to harden. She was impressed with Ivy's willingness to address a difficult issue. "In that case, maybe a phone call wouldn't be a bad idea."

"What should I say?" Ivy grabbed a bulk package

of whole grain tortillas from the pantry and dealt them out along the counter like playing cards.

"Good question." Dani put a quarter of the potato chips in the fryer.

"Maybe I could just tell him about the text and say I wanted to make sure Laz was okay." Ivy smeared a tortilla with hummus, then layered the veggies she'd cut on top. "Or would I just sound pathetic, like a girl who didn't know she'd been dumped?"

"Let me ask you a question." As each batch of chips came out of the fryer, Dani poured seasoning mix into a sieve and dusted it over them, gently tossing the slices so that they coated evenly. "You've always maintained that you and Laz are just friends. Is that true?"

"Not exactly." Ivy sprinkled raw sunflower seeds and then rolled the tortillas, packaging them in plastic wrap and depositing the Kale Blazers in the fridge next to the Indulgent sandwiches. "But it's only been a few months since his fiancée died, and we didn't want people to think he was that kind of guy."

"Right. Because most folks don't know that he and Regina weren't exactly a love match." Dani finished with the chips and since the first batch was already cool, she started portioning them into compostable cello bags. "Is Laz's father aware of your true relationship?"

"Yes, but his mom isn't." Ivy shrugged. "She was a huge fan of Regina and wouldn't take it well that he was already dating again."

"Why didn't you tell me and your BFFs the truth?" Dani was a little hurt that Ivy hadn't confided in her.

"Tippi and Starr might slip and say something to our mutual friends on campus." Ivy peeked at Dani from under her lashes, then said, "And you didn't seem to think Laz was boyfriend material for me, so I wasn't sure if you'd be disappointed in my choice."

"Then that's my fault for making you feel that way." Dani stopped what she was doing, stepped over to Ivy, and hugged her. "At first, I was just concerned that you and Laz didn't seem to have much in common. Once I got to know him better, I realized that you actually did mesh very well. And I really like him." With one last squeeze, Dani returned to her position behind the counter, then said, "Besides, it would take a lot more than disagreeing on who you choose to date for me to be disappointed in you. I think you're pretty darn terrific."

"Right back at you," Ivy said as she grabbed the red-and-white-striped sacks.

Dani stifled a yawn. "If Mr. Hunter knows you're Laz's girlfriend, I'd just call, tell him about the text, and ask what's up."

She checked the clock. Her early-bird customers would be there in half an hour and she still needed to get the Healthy dessert bars made. They were cutting it close.

Dani melted butter over low heat and stirred in sugar-free marshmallows. Once they softened, she removed the pan from the burner and stirred in mini twist pretzels, pumpkin seeds, dried apricots, and oats.

"Should I talk to Mr. Hunter in person?" Ivy gathered the entrées and side salads from the catering fridge and started filling the lunch bags.

"If you want to do that, you could invite him and Mrs. Hunter to dinner tonight," Dani offered. "I'm free and could whip up something."

She used a spatula coated with cooking spray to press the pretzel mixture into the prepared cookie sheet, drizzle it with sugar-free caramel topping, and sprinkle it with salt, then put the pan aside to set. Once that was done, she took the tray of Indulgent dessert bars and cut them into squares, slipping them into the same type of bags she'd used for the chips.

"That would be awesome." Ivy continued to assemble the sack lunches. "But it would only be Mr. Hunter. He and his wife are divorced."

"Okay." Dani smiled. Everything was done except for the Healthy dessert bars. While they cooled, she got out her cash box and set up her credit card reader. "Just let me know if he can make it."

"Six thirty for dinner sound right?" Ivy asked, and when Dani nodded, she wiggled her fingers in farewell and dashed out of the kitchen.

Shaking her head, Dani smiled. Having Ivy, Tippi, and Starr living with her had turned out be as much of a blessing as inheriting Mrs. Cook's property. They were good girls and their rent was a big help, as were the hours they worked for her as partial payment for their room and board.

Dani ran her hand fondly across the four-sided stainless-steel island that had two commercial stoves, a griddle, a broiler, a salamander, a sink, a pot-filler, and a built-in ice container integrated in the counter-top. She glanced at the restaurant-sized refrigerator against the back wall. It was amazing that the kitchen designed by Mrs. Cook was exactly what Dani needed for her company.

Simultaneously handling the trio of businesses was tough, but the mansion's setup made it a lot less stressful. The kitchen was spacious enough to prep all the food that she would need for her catering gigs, and with the installation of the pass-through window that she'd had put in near the back door, it made selling the lunch-to-go meals a snap.

Dani was the type of chef that cleaned up as she cooked, but there were always a few items that needed washing, and she was placing the last dirty bowl into the dishwasher when the service bell chimed. She dried her hands, straightened her apron, pasted on her professional smile, and went to greet her first customer of the day.

Sliding open the window, Dani recognized one of her regulars and said, "Good morning. Which lunch do you want today?"

"I want the Indulgent, but I'll take the Healthy. My track coach isn't happy with my weight." The boy tapped his credit card on the machine attached to the narrow shelf, then taking the red-and-white-striped paper sack Dani handed him, he waved and said, "See you tomorrow."

Dani wished she had half of the young man's willpower. Smiling, she watched the boy hop onto his bike and head toward the university.

It was a little after two by the time Dani sold the last lunch-to-go and finished cleaning up the kitchen. Grabbing her cell from her pocket, she noticed three missed messages. One was Ivy confirming that Mr. Hunter would be there for dinner. The other was from Spencer, telling her that their tentative plans for a late lunch were a no-go because he had a guard out sick, which meant he had to fill in for the man. And the third was from Vicki Troemel saying she had stopped by the mansion last night and dropped off the signed contract and check for the memorial meal. She wanted confirmation that Dani had received it from Starr.

Unlocking her phone, Dani texted Spencer that she understood his absence, informed Ivy that supper would be ready, and assured Vicki that she had indeed gotten the contract and check. Then, after grabbing a Diet Coke and the only leftover Kale Blazer wrap, she took a seat at the kitchen table and called Gray. The message from the wedding planner had reminded her that she wanted to contact him.

He picked up on the first ring and asked, "Everything okay?"

"As far as I know." Dani chuckled, thinking he sounded more and more like the big protective brother she never had and always wanted. "Have you found out anything new about Yvette's murder?"

"Nothing I can discuss." Gray's voice was guarded, which worried Dani.

"So you do have something?" Dani asked. "Like a likely suspect?"

"We're following some leads, but no one stands out from the pack."

"If you're interested, I have a few thoughts on that," Dani offered, then realizing she was starving, took a quick bite of the wrap.

"Sure. Let me grab the file." Gray rustled some paper. "Shoot."

"First, I need to paint the scene." Dani took a hasty sip of her soda and then gave him a summary of the wedding planner's visit.

Before she could go on, Gray said, "No one told me they were releasing the body to the family. Are you sure the service will be Sunday?"

"Vicki told me that the mayor personally spoke to Franklin Whittaker and guaranteed him that he'd be able to have the memorial for Yvette on that day." Dani took another bite of her lunch as she waited for Gray to stop swearing.

"It sure would have been nice if someone told me that." Gray cursed again. "But hey, I'm only the lead detective on the case."

"Sorry." Dani wasn't sure why she was apologizing. It wasn't her fault. Then again, she was the one bearing the bad news.

After a few seconds, Gray said, "So I'm guessing that wasn't the information you called about since you had no idea I didn't know."

"Right." Dani quickly swallowed the last of the wrap, then said, "I was wondering if you ever considered Vicki as a suspect?"

"Not really," Gray said slowly. "She had opportunity, but the only motive we could see was that Yvette wasn't exactly nice to her employees."

"Which would give me and everyone else that worked for her a motive." Dani's stomach roiled and she was suddenly sorry she'd wolfed down the Kale Blazer as it threatened to make a reappearance.

"Exactly," Gray agreed. "So why are you bringing up the wedding planner?"

"Bear with me." Dani wasn't sure if Gray would think she was being silly or not and she wanted him to listen before making up his mind.

"Okay." Gray's tone was a bit lighter. "I'm ready for your theory."

"When Vicki came here to finalize the details from the engagement party contract, she looked awful, almost as if she'd been ill." Dani frowned at the memory. "Plus, she was dressed like she'd just rolled out of bed."

"And that was unusual?"

"Definitely. Every other time I've seen her she radiated professionalism."

"Hmm."

"She told me that Franklin Whittaker was being attacked by his vendors and guests," Dani said, then crossed her fingers and added, "In my previous profession, one of my biggest talents was being able to read people. And Vicki's passionate defense of Mr. Whittaker was more than just that of a loyal employee. Her body language, and the way she said his name, made me think she was in love with the man."

"Which would give her a strong motive to get rid of Yvette before she married the man Vicki loved." Gray's tone was thoughtful.

"Exactly." Dani smiled in relief that Gray wasn't ridiculing her train of thought. "And the murder obviously wasn't planned. So Vicki just might have seen her chance and taken it."

Dani could hear some commotion in the background and Gray said hastily, "I'm being called to a meeting so I'll have to talk to you later."

"Okay."

"Thanks for the tip." Gray disconnected and Dani let out a sigh.

Mission accomplished.

Chapter 22

DANI DID A HASTY SEARCH THROUGH HER RECIPES and then inventoried her supplies. If she wanted to offer Laz's father any kind of sophisticated meal, she needed to run to the grocery store.

And considering both Mr. Hunter's social status and business contacts in Normalton, she definitely wanted to wow him with her cooking. The chicken noodle casserole she'd planned to serve the girls that night just wouldn't cut it.

Well aware that Laz's grandfather had provided the funds for NU's new library, Dani had a good idea of where the family was on the list of who's who. Near the tippy top. The Hunters were among the elite of the town's upper crust and she couldn't afford to make a bad impression.

When Dani had originally conceived her company, she'd known that most of her personal chef clients would have a decent amount of discretionary income. What she hadn't realized at the time was that in order for the catering arm of her business to be profitable, those were the types of people she would need to attract to that part of her enterprise as well.

The wealthier the individual, the more likely that they would throw huge, extravagant events. Sometimes several a year. They didn't care about the cost. Wanting the best of the best, whether it was for little Jerry's bar mitzvah or little Carmen's quinceañera or their annual holiday extravaganza, as long as their friends and acquaintances were awed, they'd happily pay Dani's invoice.

It had only taken one or two instances of supplying food for the parties thrown by the well-to-do for Dani to realize that there was good money in cultivating their patronage. And those people, the one percenters, chose their vendors almost entirely via word of mouth, which meant Dani needed to produce a stellar meal for Mr. Hunter.

Sprinting upstairs to take a quick shower, Dani's mind raced with the future booking possibilities if she dazzled Laz's father with her food. As soon as she was clean and dry, she hastily pulled on a pair of jeans and a sweater. Then, grabbing her handbag, she jumped into the van and headed for her favorite grocery store.

While she loved farmers markets and boutique food shops and utilized them whenever her client's budget allowed, since she was footing the bill for tonight's dinner, she drove to a larger supermarket where the prices were more in her budget and the variety couldn't be beat.

The rain had stopped an hour ago, but just as she pulled into the lot, the sky opened up again and she was drenched by the time the store's first set of automatic doors swished shut behind her. She used an entire packet of tissues to dry off her face and arms, but the rest of her was still wet as she pushed her cart inside the local Meijer. She shivered and rubbed the goose bumps on her arms as the overcooled air surrounded her.

Ignoring the mouthwatering aroma of barbecue ribs wafting from the nearby deli, Dani headed into the produce section. She retrieved the list from her purse and quickly skimmed it, then picked up cucumbers, cherry tomatoes, baby arugula, and alfalfa sprouts for the arugula salad.

Next, she selected a small pumpkin and a bunch of parsley for the risotto. And finally she nabbed the last bag of Meyer lemons for the tart.

As she moved to the next aisle, she remembered that she hadn't called Frannie Ryan to set up the interview with Spencer. He had agreed to give Frannie half an hour Thursday night before his date with Dani, and she had said that she would make the arrangements.

Stopping in front of shelves containing every imaginable kind of rice, Dani's gaze skimmed the array for arborio as she fished through her purse for her cell. Locating the sneaky device hiding under her makeup case, she sent a quick text to Frannie:

Are you available Thursday at five thirty to talk to Spencer?

Frannie instantly answered: Yes.

After spotting the rice she wanted and putting it in her cart, Dani typed: Meet us at the mansion. You have thirty minutes and only reasonable questions will be answered.

A short pause and Frannie responded: Okay.

Dani wasn't sure what to make of the emoji rolling its eyes that Frannie included, but it was probably a reaction to the word "reasonable."

Shaking her head, Dani made her way to the meat aisle where she checked the price of beef fillet. The whole tenderloin was twelve dollars a pound and she'd need five steaks. She dug through the refrigerated case until she found a small package. It was a little less than five pounds and she only needed three for tonight's dinner, but she had a private chef gig Wednesday evening and the remaining two pounds would serve her clients and their two guests perfectly.

After gathering a few more items, Dani got into the checkout lane. Over a hundred bucks later, Dani placed the bags in the van's built-in chiller, then climbed behind the wheel.

Exiting the grocery store's parking lot, she was glad the rain had stopped again. Although she had never fully dried off, at least she didn't have to battle traffic in a downpour. Driving in a college town was crazy enough without adding bad weather to the mix.

As she steered the van toward home, Dani considered what she needed to do first. With Mr. Hunter arriving for dinner at six thirty, Dani had less than three hours to cook and change into something that made her appear to be a cool, competent professional.

She'd tackle her wardrobe selection later; her immediate objective was to get the food for the night's menu started. And the lemon tart was number one on her to-do list.

Once Dani was home she put away her purchases, then while she put on her yoga pants and T-shirt, she checked her business voicemail. After she was re-dressed, she returned a couple of calls from prospective clients and sent Spencer a text confirming his interview with Frannie.

Finally, she was free to cook and as she bustled around preparing the food, Dani had a sudden feeling of déjà vu. Several months ago, she'd had Ivy invite Laz to a fancy dinner in order to pump him for data about the death of his fiancée. Now his father was her guest so that Ivy could ask him about his son's whereabouts. She hoped this meal would turn out as well as the previous one, both in deliciousness and information.

As it always did when Dani was in the kitchen, time flew by and she ended up with less than fifteen minutes to shower and put on a pair of nice black slacks and an emerald-green silk blouse. The doorbell rang while she was slipping her silver hoop earrings on and she finished adjusting them on her way down the stairs.

When she opened the door, an older version of Laz smiled at her and held out his hand. "You must be Ms. Sloan. My son has spoken of you often. Especially your wonderful skills as a chef."

"That's so sweet of him." Dani shook his hand and said, "Please call me Dani."

"And I'm Henry." He wore a navy suit with a pale-blue, striped dress shirt. His coordinating tie probably cost as much as Dani's whole outfit, including the shoes and jewelry.

Ushering Henry inside, Dani said, "It's nice to meet you. You look a lot like your son. Or I should say he looks a lot like you." She saw a flicker of sadness in his blue eyes, but he blinked and it was gone. Leading him into the kitchen, she continued, "I hope you don't mind eating in here. The formal dining room is just so…"

"Formal?" Henry suggested.

They were both chuckling when Ivy burst into the room, and as she hugged the older man, she said, "Mr. Hunter, it's wonderful to see you again."

"It's Henry, remember?" After giving Ivy's shoulder a squeeze with one hand, he turned to Dani and presented her with a bottle of wine. "I understand from my son that you have a no-alcohol policy in the mansion, but I hope you'll save this and enjoy it with someone special."

"Thank you." Dani accepted the gift and put it on the counter. In order to remove any temptation from the girls or their guests, she'd take the wine to her suite later. "I'm sure I will."

While Dani put the finishing touches on the meal, Ivy showed Henry to his place at the kitchen table and sat next to him. A few minutes later, Starr and Tippi came down for supper, and after introductions were made, they slid into their usual chairs.

Once everyone was seated, Dani served the first course. While they dug into their rocket salads, Henry charmed them with tales of his college days. He'd been quite a prankster and his fraternity was still trying to outdo some of his practical jokes.

The conversation stopped momentarily while Dani served the pumpkin risotto and fillets, but picked right back up as they sliced into their steaks. When the girls had first moved in with Dani, they would only eat well-done meat, but she had slowly trained them that expensive beef was best enjoyed at a perfect medium rare.

Now Dani glanced nervously at Henry, wondering if he would appreciate the correct temperature or if she should have asked his preference. She was relieved when he beamed at her as a he chewed a bite of the fillet.

"This is delicious," Henry commented after tasting the pumpkin risotto. "I can't quite put my finger on the spice you've used."

"Sage and garlic," Dani said. "I'm glad you like it. The trick to a good risotto is patience. You have to stir continuously until the rice fully absorbs the stock and is al dente."

"Laz was certainly right about your talents as a chef." Henry continued to eat, commenting between mouthfuls. "I was sorry we couldn't hire you for the library opening, but my dad wanted to use the vendor he has always used. I am so sick of the same menu for every single event."

"I understand his wanting to stick to the tried-and-true," Dani said. "And it was your father's big day, so it's only right that he have who and what he wanted."

"As usual," Henry muttered, then returned his attention to the food.

When everyone was finished with the entrée, Ivy got up with Dani to help her serve the lemon tart. While Dani cut the pastry into six equal pieces, Ivy placed them on small plates, then adorned each slice with a dollop of homemade whip cream.

As they worked, Dani lowered her voice and asked, "When are you going to ask Henry about Laz? You know he might not stick around once we're through eating."

"I'll do it right after dessert. I asked Tippi and Starr to make an excuse and leave the kitchen as soon as they've finished, but I want you to stay," Ivy whispered and smiled when Dani nodded her agreement, then she raised her voice and said, "Would you like a cup of coffee or maybe some tea with your tart, Mr. Hunter?"

"Coffee, please. I take sugar and cream." Henry gave Ivy a fond look. "And I'd really like it if you called me Henry. Mr. Hunter makes me look around for my father, and believe me, he wouldn't be a welcome guest."

Once they'd all had their dessert and Ivy had handed Henry his cup of French roast, Dani waited for them to take a bite and then said, "I'm anxious to hear everyone's opinion of the crust. I used a new recipe from a magazine that substitutes oil and water for the usual butter."

Henry immediately said, "I think it's great. Really flaky and rich."

The others agreed, and as promised, the minute they were done, Tippi and Starr made their apologies and went back upstairs.

Dani started to clean up, figuring she'd be near enough to support Ivy, but far enough away so Henry wouldn't feel as if they were ganging up on him.

Ivy cleared her throat and said, "Mr. Hunter, I mean, Henry, I got a strange text from Laz on Sunday and I haven't heard from him after that message."

"Oh. He didn't tell you." Henry's shoulders slumped and he closed his eyes. "Although rehab really helped Laz, since entering law school, he's had a couple of slips in his recovery. He'd been doing so well. He's been clean and sober for over three years.

But the stress of maintaining his grades has just been too much."

Ivy murmured something Dani didn't catch, and Henry straightened his spine.

Taking a deep breath, Henry said, "After talking to his sponsor, Laz decided to attend a sort of refresher course at the rehab center. It's an intensive weeklong program, away from any contact with the outside world."

From her position behind the counter, Dani watched Ivy give Henry a hug and whisper something in his ear. He shot her a smile and nodded. Ivy and Henry chatted quietly for a while, then they got up from the table.

Henry looked at Dani, who was filling the sink with soapy water, and said, "Can I help you? I find it very soothing to wash dishes."

"I'll help too," Ivy offered. "Since Mr…I mean, Henry, is my guest."

"Nope. We've got this." Henry herded Ivy out of the kitchen.

Dani blinked, but didn't object. Clearly the man wanted to talk to her alone.

"I'm glad you were free to join us," Dani said as Henry started in on the stack of dirty pans and mixing bowls she'd piled near the sink. The plates, glasses, and flatware could go in the dishwasher, but not this stuff. "I know the invitation was short notice and you probably have a very full social calendar."

"Not really." Henry smiled shyly. "Except for

business events, I'm pretty much a homebody. I prefer sitting in front of my fire and reading."

"Really?" Dani picked up a sheet pan and a towel. As she wiped away the water droplets, she asked, "What genre is your favorite?"

"Mostly thrillers." Henry shook his head. "But after my experience Saturday night, I might have to read something milder for a while."

Dani set the pan aside and grabbed a bowl. "I had a pretty scary Saturday night myself. I was catering an event when the wind collapsed the tent."

"That was where I was too." Henry paused, one hand holding a scrub brush and the other the pan Dani had used to make the risotto. "I didn't realize you were the caterer for Franklin's party. By the way, the appetizers were amazing. I ate a ton of them."

"Thank you. I must not have noticed your name on the guest list." Dani smiled, then wrinkled her brow. "It's terrible what happened to Ms. Joubert. Did you know her very well?"

"Actually, I'd never met her before that night." Henry continued to wash the dishes. "Franklin and I have some mutual business investments, and I was only at the party because of that."

"So you're not friends with Mr. Whittaker?" Dani's mind raced. Maybe she could find out the inside scoop on the billionaire.

"No." Henry shook his head. "At most we're friendly acquaintances. Why?"

"Well…" Dani faltered. "You know Ms. Joubert's death wasn't an accident."

"I read in the paper that the police have deemed it a murder."

"I overheard someone say that Mr. Whittaker had paid her a million dollars just for accepting his ring and that after the formal announcement at the engagement party that amount doubled."

"And you're wondering if Franklin killed her to avoid paying up?" Henry chuckled. "You realize that he could have just called off the engagement."

"True," Dani conceded, then started putting away the dishes they'd washed and dried. While she considered what she knew, she continued to tidy up the kitchen so it would be ready for the next day's lunch-to-go preparations in the morning. Finally, she said, "But the whole cash for her hand in marriage seems odd."

"Franklin told me about that. Apparently, Yvette insisted he do that to prove he was serious about going through with the wedding because he'd been engaged a couple times before and never made it down the aisle." Henry finished the dishes and dried his hands on a paper towel. "However, Franklin wasn't a stupid man, so there was a catch."

"That makes sense." Dani had wondered about the weird arrangement, but written it off as an eccentricity of the very rich.

"Franklin had his attorneys put in a little gotcha

clause." Henry shook his head. "If it were me, I just would have found another woman."

"What was the catch?" Dani asked.

"If Yvette was caught cheating anytime after accepting Franklin's ring, she had to return the entire million." Henry smirked. "And if she had an affair after the engagement party, that million had to be returned. And if she was unfaithful after they were married, she got nothing when they divorced. No, wait." He frowned. "I remember that Franklin said the prenup gave her two dollars if she had sex with another man. You know, because of that saying."

"That saying?" Dani wrinkled her brow, then put her hand over her mouth to hide her grin. "Do you mean he was calling her a two-dollar wh—?"

"Exactly." Henry made a face. "So Yvette had more of a reason to kill Franklin than he had to murder her."

"Because of the insult?"

"No. Because a few seconds before the tent collapsed, I overheard the wedding planner tell Franklin that just before the party started, she'd caught Yvette with another man. Franklin was planning on calling off the engagement."

Chapter 23

SPENCER YAWNED AND LOOKED AT HIS CELL PHONE. It was almost 2:45. In a quarter hour, he could finally leave. It was mind-numbing to watch two pigs doing nothing but wallowing for so many hours. He'd played enough *Free Cell* and *Spider Solitaire* to qualify as expert on either game and had even browsed a few jewelry store websites looking for a Christmas gift for Dani.

Thank goodness his team only had to guard Hamlet and Oinkphelia for two more days, and those two shifts were assigned to Robert and Lavonia respectively. Sorority and fraternity pledging officially ended at midnight on Halloween, and the university administration had agreed that after the hell night ritual was over and the inductees became full-fledged members, the mascots would be safe enough with just the security cameras.

As Spencer watched the final minutes of his

torture tick down, he tried to think of another way to find Brock. His ex–best friend had proven better at disappearing than Spencer had expected.

There was no activity on either Brock's credit cards or bank accounts. He wasn't staying at any of the local shelters or at any of the low-cost motels in the area. And he wasn't in the homeless camp near the railroad tracks.

In the past six months, Brock hadn't been in touch with any friends or family. At least none that Hiram had been able to track down. And if he couldn't locate the disabled firefighter, Brock had to have truly crawled under a rock.

Spencer had arranged to take the day off from work tomorrow. After his pigsitting shift, he'd sack out until 6:00 a.m., then spend the day looking into every little hidey-hole that he might have missed on his first try.

When the alarm on Spencer's phone beeped indicating that at last he could call it a night, he jumped off his camp chair as if he'd been zapped with a stun gun and quickly gathered his equipment. While he made his final patrol of the barn, he ran through his mental list, checking to see if there was anything he needed his security team to do the next day while he wasn't on duty.

Nope. Nothing urgent.

The monkey business in Fox Hall seemed to have ended with the girl dressed as Pocahontas.

There hadn't been any other calls to Area 51 or any other students dressed as Native Americans pinned anywhere else.

Spencer could only pray that the stunt had run its course, and that the added security patrols had discouraged whoever was behind it. If he or she persisted in grabbing drunken students and staking them to the wall, at some point, one of the victims would end up hurt, if not dead. Odds were that someone would either fall down while they were unconscious or choke on their own vomit. Or any of a thousand possibilities that could result in a tragedy.

Spencer would like to know who was behind the prank, but he'd settle for that person, or group of people, just not doing it again. One thing he'd learned working at a university was to pick his battles.

Now as he jumped into his truck and drove back to his town house, Spencer thought of Dani. It was a shame that she'd been so tired last night. It was one of the few times that the girls weren't only one story away from them. He'd been hoping that since they finally had some privacy, they could share more than a couple of passionate kisses.

They both agreed that weren't ready to hop into bed together. However, there were other possibilities. Ones he'd been eager to explore.

But he understood Dani's dedication to the food pantry. After all, it was her compassion and giving nature that had first attracted him to her. The fact that she used what little free time she had to cook for the poor said a lot about her character and moral compass. She could have easily just written a check.

Spencer continued to daydream about Dani as he parked in his garage, went inside, and got ready for bed. Sliding under the covers, he imagined her beside him, nestled in his arms.

He fell asleep with a goofy grin on his face. And when his alarm woke him up, he realized that he hadn't had any of his usual nightmares.

While he was in the shower, Dani had texted a summary of her dinner with Henry Hunter, and Spencer quickly sent her a message advising her to update the police. He wasn't thrilled telling her to have even more contact with the detective, but he also didn't want Christensen thinking she was hiding anything. Bad enough that Spencer was holding off on informing him about Brock's appearance in town and that he had no idea how he would handle that little detail if he did find his ex-friend. Sadly, hearing from Dani was the last good thing that happened to Spencer that Wednesday. After stopping at every flea trap and dive within fifty miles of Normalton, he hadn't found a trace of Brock.

When Spencer finally got home around midnight, he sent Dani a text to say he was free, hoping that if she was finished with her personal chef job but still awake, she'd call him back. When there was no response, he fell into bed. Between the late night with the pigs on Tuesday and dragging his butt all over Central Illinois, he could barely keep his eyes open.

———

Thursday, while Spencer caught up on work at his office, he reached for the phone a dozen times to call Christensen and tell him about Brock being in Normalton. There was no use putting it off. He'd been everywhere he could think of and he wouldn't have any time to come up with a new search plan before meeting Dani and that pesky reporter at the mansion.

Despite his good intentions to the contrary, as Spencer pulled into Dani's driveway and walked up to the rear entrance, he still hadn't contacted the detective. Vowing that he'd do it as soon as he finished doing the stupid interview with Frannie Ryan, Spencer peered through the glass door to see if the coast was clear of irritating journalists and/or nosy nieces, then went inside the kitchen.

Dani greeted him with a soft kiss on the cheek. And while it warmed his heart, she moved out of reach before he could take her in his arms.

She gestured to the table and said, "Have a seat. Would you like something to drink? Or a snack to tide you over before dinner?"

"I'll take a water if you have it." Spencer selected the chair that kept his back to a wall and sat down, then added, "Something to eat would be great. I missed lunch."

Dani took a bottle of Dasani and a tray from the fridge. She placed them both in front of Spencer and his mouth watered at the sight of the slices of prosciutto, salami, turkey, various cheese, and gherkins on the platter. She returned with a little bowl of mustard and a basket of French bread rounds and crackers.

"Wow." Spencer shook his head and smiled at the sweet woman gazing at him. "I hope you didn't go to all this trouble just for me."

"Why wouldn't I?" Dani asked, wrinkling her forehead. "I figured you'd be hungry after work." She shook her finger at him. "And that was without knowing you hadn't eaten since breakfast. You need to stop skipping meals."

Spencer had to swallow a lump in his throat before he could answer. Even then, he wasn't sure what to say so he settled on an inadequate thank-you. No one had cared about his needs in so long, he was almost speechless.

As he was trying to come up with more eloquent words, the back door rattled and Frannie yelled through the glass. "I'm here!"

Dani ushered the reporter inside and told her to take a seat. Once Frannie was settled, Dani asked if she wanted something to drink.

"A Diet Coke would be awesome." Frannie took her tablet from its case.

Returning with the soda, Dani joined Frannie and Spencer at the table. Spencer noticed that she chose the chair between him and the reporter and cocked an eyebrow at her, but she just shrugged.

As soon as Dani was settled, Spencer speared Frannie with a hard look and said, "You have half an hour."

"Okay." Frannie pulled out her cell phone and said, "I'm recording this."

"Fine." Spencer wasn't worried about being on the record. He'd been in law enforcement long enough to be able to control what came out of his mouth.

"Then let's get started." Frannie reached into her tote bag and plopped a thick sheaf of papers on the table. "I've managed to dig up quite a bit on the late Yvette Joubert, but I need you to put a human face to my research. What attracted you to her?"

Shit! He should have realized how awkward this might be with Dani sitting right there. He glanced at her. She had an interested express in her pretty eyes and was leaning forward.

"Uh…" Spencer thoughts raced. "She was very attractive and when she turned her attention on you, it was sort of hypnotizing."

"Mmm." Frannie checked something off her list and shuffled through several pages before she asked, "You got married less than a month after meeting Yvette. Why the rush? Was she pregnant or pretending to be pregnant?"

"No!" Spencer stole another peek at Dani whose fingers were tightly entwined together. Her knuckles were white and he cursed himself for making her go through this. "I was going to have to leave for an extended period of time due to a job assignment and Yvi had been staying with a friend, but needed to find somewhere else because that friend's fiancé was coming back from his deployment. She told me that an ex-boyfriend was stalking her so she was afraid to live alone, and I suggested she move into my condo. She said she was uncomfortable living together unless we were married."

"Speaking of that." Frannie ticked off another item, then stared at him. "Exactly what law enforcement agency were you with back then?"

"That's irrelevant." Alarm bells went off in Spencer's head. All he needed was a reporter digging in to his undercover work. "I'm only willing to answer questions about myself as it is related to Yvi." Under his breath he muttered, "And damn few of those."

"Be that way." Frannie studied her notes, then asked, "What was Yvette's explanation for cheating on you with your best friend?"

As Spencer considered his answer, he heard a faint sound from near the sliding window and glanced over. Peering through the glass was Brock Ortiz. Or at least an appalling version of the Brock Ortiz that Spencer had known.

Leaping to his feet, Spencer raced out the door. Brock stood frozen, guilt and another uninterpretable emotion warred for prominence in his troubled hazel eyes. His shoulder-length hair blew around his gaunt face, and his once ramrod straight back was bent.

When his gaze locked on Spencer, he let out a whimper and slid to the ground. Concerned he was ill, Spencer rushed toward the man kneeling on the cement.

Rocking back and forth, Brock moaned, "I'm so sorry. So, so sorry."

Spencer squatted down beside his ex-friend and put an arm around him. Brock reeked as if he hadn't showered in weeks. The odor of cigarettes and alcohol surrounded him in a cloud of hopelessness.

How had this man, a man who had once been a decorated firefighter, come to this? Was it his career-ending injury? Or was it the coldblooded woman who walked away and didn't look back when she broke his heart?

Drawing Brock to his feet, Spencer guided him inside. After settling him in a chair at the table, Spencer looked at Dani and asked, "Could you get him some tea? He's shivering as if he's freezing. I think he might be going into shock."

Granted it was chilly outside, but Brock's coldness seemed to go beyond the actual temperature. He gave the impression that he was seconds away from hypothermia.

"Right away." Dani dashed toward the stove and turned the burner on under the kettle. "He smells as if he's been drinking heavily for a while, which means he probably has been skipping meals. There's a good chance that his blood sugar is low. See if you can get him to eat something."

Spencer nodded, but when he looked at his ex-friend's vacant countenance, he didn't think it was possible to make him accept food. He was clearly retreating further and further into himself.

"Brock, talk to me, dude," Spencer gently slapped his ex-friend's cheek, and although he turned his head to look at Spencer, he remained mute.

If something wasn't done soon, he'd become totally unresponsive.

Surprisingly, the annoying reporter had remained quiet and Spencer turned to her and snapped, "Shut off your phone's recording app."

"Sure thing." Frannie tapped the screen, then said, "You called him Brock. Is that Brock Ortiz?" Her eyes gleamed. "Your ex–best friend? The man Yvette cheated with while you two were married."

"It is." There was no use denying it. Spencer sighed. "I don't suppose you'll leave us alone and forget you ever saw him here?"

"No." Frannie scrunched her face. "Dani could order me out, but I'd just wait at her property line." The reporter gazed into space before adding, "And then my story would be based on speculation instead of fact."

Spencer felt helpless. Neither was the ideal option.

But because Dani seemed to trust the reporter, Spencer muttered, "Then we'll see how it goes."

A few minutes later, Dani placed a steaming cup of Earl Grey in front of Brock, took his hand, put it around the mug, and coaxed, "You'll feel better if you take a sip."

Brock looked up at Dani, nodded, and whispered, "It's nice and warm. I'm so cold."

"It will help take the chill away." Dani pulled the tray of food closer and gestured to it. "A bite to eat might be a good thing too."

Once again Spencer was struck by her kindness. Instead of being disgusted by the sad shadow of a man sitting at her table, she was trying to comfort him. She didn't seem repelled by his filthiness, just concerned that he wasn't feeling well and needed her assistance.

Brock slumped. "I'm sorry to be so much trouble. I remember when I used to be the one helping people, and now I'm just a pathetic loser."

"We all need support once in a while and that doesn't make us less of a person and definitely not a loser." Dani waited until he drank some of the tea and wolfed down a sandwich, then said, "You'll probably feel a lot better if you tell us why you're here and what happened."

Brock looked at Spencer who nodded and said, "Whatever you've done, I'm sure we can figure out the best course to take once we have the facts."

"I don't know where to start." Brock rubbed his eyes.

"How about the beginning?" Spencer suggested.

"But I probably shouldn't talk without a lawyer or something." Brock looked at all of three of them in turn. "Right?"

"You might need one eventually," Dani reassured him. "But right now, it's probably just better to tell us what happened so we know the best way to help you." She gestured across the table. "This is my friend Frannie. She's reporter and can make sure your side is heard. You know the court of public opinion is important."

"I'd be happy to share your story with my readers," Frannie said, a tad too eagerly for Spencer's liking. "Maybe start with why you cheated with your best friend's wife."

Both Dani and Spencer shot Frannie a dirty look, but Brock said, "Okay." He took a deep breath and turned to Spencer. "I'm really sorry I went behind your back with Yvette, but she was always calling me when you were away. She'd claim that she was scared of her ex or needed my help with stuff, and then she'd tell me how lonely she was with you gone all the time. When she asked me to hold her, and then we…you know, I couldn't say no to her. And after that one time, it felt like sort of a compulsion."

"I understand, bro. I fell for her damsel-in-distress act too. We both have that protect-and-serve gene and she used it against us." Spencer thumped Brock's shoulder, then jerked his chin at Dani. "And let's face it, I ended up with the better deal."

Dani raised her brows but let his statement pass without comment.

"So you had an affair with Yvette and she dumped Spencer for you." Frannie frantically typed into her tablet, then glanced up and said, "How long before it all went south?"

"Things were good, real good, for a while. At least until I was injured." Brock glanced at his empty sleeve. "At first, I thought she'd stick by me, but then I recognized that a woman like Yvette could never be with half a man like me, so when she broke things off, I was okay, but that was before…"

When Brock didn't continue, Spencer asked, "What happened?"

Brock thumped the table and snarled. "I found out that she'd been seeing Whittaker behind my back even before my accident. She'd been sneaking with him since she met him at some benefit dance we attended."

"Is that when you decided to kill her?" Spencer asked. "When you realized she'd been cheating on you while everything was still supposed to be good between you two?"

"Kill her…" Brock stuttered, a look of confusion on his face. "I didn't kill her."

"But you said you were so sorry." Spencer wondered if he'd misheard.

"Sorry that I betrayed you and our friendship." Brock shook his head. "Over someone like Yvette."

"She was a hard woman to say no to," Spencer

said, then glanced at Dani, who met his gaze with a tiny smile of agreement.

"All I wanted to do was make her feel as bad as me." Brock shook his head again. "To pay her back for what she did to both of us."

"So, you…" Spencer prodded.

"I figured once a cheat always a cheat." Pain etched the lines around Brock's mouth even deeper. "Something I should have realized a lot earlier."

"Yep." Spencer couldn't keep himself from agreeing.

"I started following Yvette." Brock shrugged. "I might have gotten a bit obsessive about it. I abandoned everything, even foregoing getting my prosthetic arm. I spent all my time watching her. I knew that I'd eventually catch her screwing around. Then I'd tell Whittaker and he'd dump her like she dumped me."

Frannie pounced. "And of course you did catch her. When did you find out?"

"I knew she'd been seeing someone, but I could never get a clear look at the guy or any kind of proof." Brock's nostrils flared. "She'd been really tricky until the night of her big engagement party. Then I saw her get into her car with this guy and I waited. She must've thought because the Mercedes windows were tinted no one would see her, but the front windshield wasn't as dark and I had the perfect view of her and lover boy getting it on.

"I took a video with my cell of them half-naked

and of the guy exiting the back seat of her car with her right behind him. They both were smoothing out their clothes and hair. I didn't get a good view of lover boy's face, but I figured Whittaker would probably still be able to recognize him since I heard Yvette say something to the guy that made me think he was on the Korn Kings team. And even if the video of him nailing her was too dim to make out much, their disheveled appearances made it obvious what they'd been doing."

"Did you show it to Whittaker?" Spencer asked.

If he believed Brock that he didn't kill Yvette, maybe the billionaire murdered her in a jealous rage. Spencer could certainly see that happening.

"I didn't get a chance." Brock's voice broke into Spencer's thoughts. "They were checking invitations at the entrance so it took me a while to slip into the tent."

"Then it collapsed before you had the chance, right?" Dani's tone was sympathetic.

"No, somebody beat me to the punch." Brock scrubbed his eyes with his fist. "When I finally got inside and found Whittaker, this broad had him cornered and was telling him all about it."

Dani leaned over to Spencer and whispered in his ear, "That had to be the conversation that Henry Hunter overheard between Whittaker and the wedding planner."

Spencer nodded, then looked at Brock and asked, "What was Whittaker's reaction?"

"He laughed." Brock wrinkled his brow. "I was kind of shocked about that. At least until—"

"That's all Whittaker did?" Frannie jumped back into the conversation.

"No." Brock lifted his chin. "He said that no one got away with making a fool of him and he'd make sure they regretted it."

"Both of them?" Frannie murmured licking her lips. "The guy too?"

"Right." Brock paused in assembling another sandwich from the tray of meats and cheeses Dani kept edging closer to him. "Whittaker said that when he found out who Yvette had been banging, he'd ruin the man."

"Then he didn't know the guy's identity," Spencer muttered almost to himself.

"No. But he said he'd get it out of Yvette even if he had to pay for the information." Brock shrugged. "I was going to offer him the video that I took since if anyone deserved a payoff it was me, but Whittaker headed toward Yvette so fast that I was still trying to get through the crowd when the tent came down."

"So Yvette's lover had the best motivation to want her permanently silenced?" Dani mused twisting a piece of her hair as she thought. "And I bet that's who killed her."

"I agree." Spencer studied Dani's expression. It was clear that she was recalling bits and pieces and putting them together.

Finally she said, "I think I know who it might be. I just need to see Brock's video."

All eyes turned to Brock.

"Do you have your cell phone with you?" Frannie demanded breathlessly.

"Sure." Brock dug in his pocket, swiped, and tapped, then handed it to Dani. "Take a look."

Chapter 24

AN HOUR LATER, DANI OPENED THE MANSION'S front door to Gray. As soon as she had verified that the man in Brock's video was the same guy she'd suspected was the murderer, she'd contacted the detective.

Although they had different reasons, none of the three individuals around her kitchen table were happy with her decision. Because of the notoriously bad relationship between journalists and police, Frannie worried that Gray would kick her out and she'd lose the story of the year. Brock was afraid Gray would arrest him for stalking Yvette and recording her without her permission. And Spencer's objection seemed more reflex than motivated by a good reason.

Dani had ignored the trio's protests, picked up the phone, and dialed. As a result of that call, Gray was now striding down the hallway ahead of Dani, throwing questions over his shoulder as he headed into the kitchen.

She wasn't sure how he knew that's where everyone was assembled. She hadn't told him where they were gathered. Maybe his previous visits had helped him recognize her habit. Either that or he could smell the food.

Walking through the doorway, Gray swept the room with a glance. Hurrying past him and heading toward the counter, Dani was just in time to see him narrow his eyes when he spotted Frannie.

Although Dani had mentioned that Spencer and Brock were with her, she hadn't said anything about the reporter's presence at the mansion. She told herself she hadn't included her name because Frannie's presence wasn't a key part of the story, but in truth it was probably because she didn't want to deal with his opposition over the phone.

However, there was no ducking the issue any longer. Not with Gray staring at Frannie as if she were a flesh-eating virus he'd found on his manhood.

Trying to mitigate the inevitable hostilities, Dani quickly said, "When Mr. Ortiz showed up, Frannie was already here interviewing Spencer about his previous relationship with Yvette. She has promised to keep everything since Brock's arrival off the record until you've made an arrest."

"Fine," Gray said through gritted teeth. "Speaking of that, would you care to enlighten me on why you think you know who I should be arresting?"

When Dani had phoned Gray, she had only told

him that she knew the murderer's identity and that Spencer's friend had video proof to support her allegation. She'd refused to name her suspect because she wanted to be face-to-face when she explained her reasoning.

Although the detective had pressed her for details, she'd maintained that it would be simpler to show him than try to describe the recording. With that, he'd finally given up, and agreed to drop what he was doing and drive to the mansion to meet with her.

"I think's it best if Spencer starts by introducing his friend who is the person who made the recording we're going to show you." Dani gestured to Brock, then waved Gray to the seat next to Frannie. Once he was settled, she asked, "Before I sit down, is anyone hungry or thirsty?"

"I'd love a cup of your French roast. The swill at the station gives me heartburn." Gray smiled at Dani for the first time since he'd arrived, and she felt the tension leave her shoulders.

Hoping that the detective was beginning to adjust to being summoned to the mansion without being given any details, Dani said, "Coming right up."

"And since I'm guessing none of us are getting any supper," Gray continued, "whatever you have to eat would probably be welcomed by us all."

Brock had polished off the charcuterie platter, so after handing Gray his coffee, Dani removed the tray and put it in the sink. Then she pulled out the leftover

Thursday lunch-to-go entrées and desserts. These were the sandwiches that had turned out less than perfect and desserts that hadn't been a uniform size once they were cut. Putting them on serving dishes, she placed the food on the table, then brought out plates, silverware, and napkins.

Once everyone had something to drink, Dani slid into the chair next to Spencer and concentrated on what he was telling Gray about Brock. While she'd been assembling their impromptu dinner, Spencer had explained who Brock was and how he'd ended up at Dani's house.

Now Gray looked at Brock and asked, "Why were you following Spencer?"

"I knew he'd been looking for me since he spotted me Monday at the food pantry." Brock rubbed his eyes. "When I saw him there, I wasn't sure how to approach him so I ran away and hid out with an old firefighter buddy. He'd left the CFD and took a job in the private sector down here, so I was pretty sure no one would associate me with him." Brock twitched his shoulders. "But while I've been laying low, I've been keeping an eye on Spencer. Finally, this afternoon, I got up my courage to face him."

"Why were you at the food pantry?" Gray asked as he loaded his plate from the trays in front of him.

"For the free hot dinner." Brock ducked his head, clearly embarrassed. "I sort of went crazy when Yvette left me. I dropped off the grid, so I haven't had access to my disability pay."

"Then how did you find Spencer tonight?" Gray's expression was skeptical and Dani could tell he was far from convinced that Brock hadn't killed Yvette.

"These past few days while I was watching him, I found out that he was the head of campus security, so I waited outside his office until he left," Brock explained. "I followed him here, and once I saw how happy he was with Dani, I figured he'd be willing to accept my apology for screwing Yvette when they were still married."

All eyes turned to Dani, and Spencer ran his finger down her burning cheek, then he picked up her hand, kissed her palm, and said, "You're exactly right, bro. Turns out you did me a solid when you opened up my eyes about Yvi. You showed she really wasn't worth my time and effort."

"Okay." Gray had taken out his memo pad out when he sat down and now he looked up from the notes he'd been making. "Let me see if I've got this straight. Mr. Ortiz was engaged to Yvette after Spencer started divorce proceedings, but before she ended up with Franklin Whittaker." When they all nodded, the detective continued, "Spencer spotted Mr. Ortiz on Monday and rather than report his presence in the area to me, decided to look for his ex-friend on his own."

Suddenly starving, Dani grabbed a curry powder, dried fruit, and slivered almond chicken salad sandwich, then before taking a bite commented, "I told him that was a bad idea."

Spencer rolled his eyes at her before he looked

at Gray and said, "Sorry. This whole thing with Yvi has gotten to me more than I realized, and I haven't been thinking straight. I just wanted a chance to talk to Brock before we involved the police."

"Mmm," Gray mumbled through a mouthful of cognac-marinated beef tenderloin sub. After he swallowed, he said, "Don't let it happen again. Fellow law enforcement or not, friend or not, there's only so much slack I can cut you."

"I understand and it won't happen again." Spencer gave a firm nod, then said, "Anyway, once Brock showed up here and we got through the personal stuff, he told us he'd been following Yvi."

"Did you see who killed her?" Gray asked, quickly swallowing the sip of coffee he'd just taken. "Is that the video?"

"Sadly, no." Dani shook her head. "He recorded Yvette hooking up with a guy just before her engagement party. And it wasn't her fiancé. Remember I called and told you that Mr. Hunter said Yvette had been caught cheating and the woman who caught them told Whittaker?"

"So you think Franklin Whittaker killed her?" Gray guessed, his shoulder slumping. "We've cleared him. There are two witnesses that confirm that he was pinned under a table with them. They were with him the entire time until they were freed by a first responder and then they accompanied him when he looked for Yvette and consequently found her body."

"Whittaker isn't our suspect." Frannie finished her smoked salmon roll-up, licked the cream cheese from her fingers, and smirked. "Try again, Detective."

Gray shot the reporter a cold glare and retorted, "I'm not the one who claims to know the murderer's identity." He looked at Dani. "That would be you."

"Right." Dani tapped her chin. "Where was I? Ah, yes. Brock explained that his intent in following Yvette was to catch her cheating on Mr. Whittaker, tell him, and ruin her chance to marry the billionaire."

"I knew she was cheating for a while, but I could never get a look at the guy's face or get any kind of proof." Brock confirmed what Dani had said, then added, "That is, until Saturday night. I recorded her screwing lover boy and then the both of them getting out of the car."

"Again." Gray was clearly getting frustrated. "Whittaker didn't do it."

"I promise you he isn't my suspect." Dani reached across the table and patted the detective's hand, earning a glare from Spencer.

"Okay." Gray polished off his sandwich and took a deep breath. "Go ahead."

While Brock explained his delay in getting into the tent and then the conversation he overheard between the wedding planner and Whittaker, Gray took notes and ate cornflake-chocolate-chip-marshmallow cookies.

Finally, he interrupted Brock and asked, "You're sure the wedding planner doesn't know lover boy's name?"

"I am." Brock crossed his arms.

Spencer snatched the last red velvet brownie just before Frannie nabbed it, then said, "However, Brock did hear Whittaker vow to find out who he was and ruin the guy, even if he had to pay Yvi to reveal the man's identity."

"Whittaker was on his way to confront Yvette when the tent collapsed, but he never got a chance to get the information from her," Frannie said, triumphantly snatching the remaining cornflake-chocolate-chip-marshmallow cookie out from under Gray's questing fingertips.

"Which is why I'm ninety-nine percent positive Yvette's lover killed her." Dani grinned. "He was the only one who had something major to lose if Yvette was alive and able to talk to Mr. Whittaker. And by major, I mean getting a spot in the major leagues. Not only does Mr. Whittaker control his career in the Korn Kings, Vicki told me that Mr. Whittaker has recently invested in the majors as well."

"So you were able to identify him on Mr. Ortiz's recording?" Gray asked, then scanned the table obviously looking for the cell phone in question.

Brock slid the device over to the detective and said, "It's set to go. Just hit play."

While Gray watched the video, Dani said, "Because I already had a good idea of who it was, I can tell who it is, but I doubt it would hold up in court."

Gray narrowed his eyes. "Maybe our techs can clean up the footage and we can get a better view, but right now no one could make out who's on the recording without prior knowledge of the man's identity." Focusing on Dani, Gray said, "I give up. Who is the guy?"

"Marc Chandler." Dani smiled. "After hearing everything Brock had to say, I remembered a few things that I've learned, observed, or overheard the past few weeks and put two and two together."

Dani held up her index finger. "First, I recalled that Tippi told me that if Marc played as well in the upcoming final postseason games as he had during the rest of the season, he was a shoo-in to be called up to the major leagues. That means he has a lot at stake, and being kicked off the Korn Kings team would ruin him. Especially if Whittaker put the word out that Marc was let go because he was playing poorly or was injured."

"Whittaker has the power to ruin any number of people," Gray objected.

Ignoring the interruption, Dani added another finger to the one she already had up and said, "Second, I heard Perry O'Toole, one of Marc's teammates, teasing him at the food pantry about a woman he'd been seeing. One that he was keeping a big, dark secret. And during that same conversation, Perry said that Marc's hookup hadn't been around the past few days, which corresponded with the time period since Yvette's death."

"That's not exactly conclusive evidence," Gray murmured, but he sounded less skeptical this time.

"Third, Perry also mentioned that Marc is some

kind of survivalist who knows all kinds of takedowns and holds." Dani tilted her head. "My understanding is that an individual like that would likely know that a pen through the eye socket was a viable weapon that would kill someone."

"Good point," Gray conceded. "Anything else?"

"Besides that Marc looks like the guy in the video?" Dani asked. "Not really. But you said you had a print on the ink cartridge. Can't you match it to him?"

"Maybe." Gray pursed his lips. "However, I'm not sure what we have is enough to compel him to allow us to fingerprint him."

"Couldn't you connect him to the pen?" Dani asked. She was frustrated that evidently knowing who killed Yvette and having enough proof for the police to act on it were two separate things. "You said that it was a unique design and very expensive."

Frannie perked up. "Was it a green-and-gold Mont d'Eau fountain pen?"

"We haven't released the description to the public." Gray's brows rose in alarm. "How do you know that? Did Dani tell you? Is there a leak in my department?"

"Nope." Frannie beamed. "But last spring, I did a piece on the Korn Kings. Franklin Whittaker likes to motivate his players, and one way he does it is special gifts. He awards a custom-designed green-and-gold, which are the team colors, Mont d'Eau fountain pen to any player that makes a grand slam or pitches a no-hitter."

"So, if everyone Whittaker has given a pen can produce it and Marc can't…" Dani trailed off.

"We might have enough to compel his fingerprints." Gray nodded, then sighed. "However even if we get his prints and they match, he can claim he lost the pen. And the video is too dim to use as proof."

"But you can check around to see if you can find any corroboration that Marc was having an affair with Yvette," Dani suggested.

"Or." Frannie rubbed her hands together. "You can ask Franklin Whittaker to help you get a confession."

Chapter 25

ONCE FRANNIE HAD PERSUADED GRAY THAT Whittaker was his best chance of getting Marc Chandler to admit he was the killer, the detective had left the mansion with a promise to let them know if the billionaire agreed. But so far, Gray was maintaining radio silence.

Nearly two full days had passed and Dani was growing more restless with each passing minute. Although Gray had assured her that Marc would have round-the-clock surveillance until the police were ready to arrest him, she was afraid the baseball player would disappear if he got wind that he was the prime suspect in Yvette's murder.

Meanwhile, in between catering a community Halloween party Friday evening and working a personal chef gig on Saturday afternoon, Dani had tried to distract herself by prepping for the luncheon following Yvette's memorial service on Sunday.

Dani didn't even have Spencer to take her mind off the murder. He'd warned her that he'd be swamped with the campus Halloween activities, as well as their aftermath the next day, and that he probably wouldn't be able to contact her before he picked her up on Saturday.

And it was after that date that Gray finally called. Dani and Spencer had returned from dinner and were relaxing in the mansion's family room, watching a movie with the girls, when Dani's phone played the *Dragnet* theme song. She snatched it from the coffee table and walked into the hallway with Spencer following her.

"Did Whittaker agree?" she demanded, way too impatient to bother with the usual hello, how-are-you pleasantries.

"He did." Gray's voice was amused. "Mr. Whittaker was actually thrilled at the chance to be a part of bringing Chandler down."

"To get justice for Yvette?" Dani suggested.

"Nope." Gray chuckled. "To get revenge on the guy who had made a fool of him by having an affair with his fiancée."

Dani glanced at Spencer and said, "Evidently, Whittaker isn't as forgiving as you are."

"I didn't forgive Brock until I met you." Spencer kissed her on the nose.

With warmth flooding her chest, Dani turned her attention back to the phone and asked, "How's the whole thing going to go down?"

"Whittaker suggested that we do it tomorrow between the memorial service and the lunch," Gray answered. "He's made it clear to his players that they are all expected to show up, so Chandler will already be at the country club. Whittaker will call him onto the veranda for a private chat in the gazebo. We'll have several officers stashed within listening distance."

"Well, I hope I get to see you all make the arrest," Dani said.

"Sorry, that can't happen." Gray's tone was sharp.

"Actually it might." Dani smiled at outmaneuvering the detective. "I'm catering the luncheon."

After emitting a string of curses worthy of a Navy SEAL, Gray cautioned Dani to steer clear of the action and hung up. When Spencer kissed her good night, he reinforced the detective's warning to stay well away from the police sting.

Once Spencer left, Dani headed to bed. She wanted to be well rested for the next day. Although she fully intended to remain tucked safely in the country club kitchen, she would definitely be keeping an eye on the operation. While being held hostage by one murderer was enough of that type of excitement to last her a lifetime, watching a murderer being apprehended wasn't something she was willing to miss. Especially since she was the one who had figured out his identity.

Sunday dawned bright and clear. It had warmed up to the high seventies and everyone at Mass was acting as if summer had returned. Women had gone back to their lightweight skirts and blouses, while men wore khakis and short sleeves. However, knowing this was but a brief respite, Dani wasn't about to unpack the seasonal clothes she'd just put away and settled for dress slacks and a silk tunic.

After Dani got back to the mansion, she beelined to her suite and took off her church outfit. Out of respect for the occasion, she chose a black chef's jacket instead of her usual red, then pulled on the matching pants and her comfy nonslip Dansk clogs.

Once she returned downstairs, Dani loaded the van and headed to the luncheon venue. Ivy, Tippi, and Starr, along with two additional servers, were scheduled to arrive at the site half an hour before the meal to serve the entrées and desserts.

Country club personnel were taking care of the table setups and manning the two bars. They would also be responsible for the cleanup.

Vicki Troemel met Dani at the rear entrance of the imposing clubhouse. While the front was in a Mediterranean style, in back an expansive veranda overlooking trees and a tennis court ran the length of the building. From what Dani had been told, the lower level held activity and exercise rooms, while the restaurant, banquet hall, and kitchens occupied the main floor.

As Vicki helped Dani unload the van and take everything inside, she explained, "The memorial observance is being conducted at noon by Serenity Lake. We should be back here about fifteen minutes after that. Please plan on serving the meal at one."

"No problem," Dani assured her.

She'd decided to offer the guests a choice of lamb, red wine, and rosemary potpies or a Veracruz-style red snapper. Because there was no RSVP, she just had to hope that close to an equal amount of diners would select each option. She had a dozen extra of both, but if all the diners decided they preferred one dish to the other, there would be a problem.

Dani's mind flew to the arrangements. The potpies were ready to go and would be put in the oven half an hour before they were scheduled to be served, but she planned to prepare the fish entrée in the clubhouse kitchen. All she had to do was sauté the already chopped onions and garlic, then add capers and caper juice, diced tomatoes, olives, and jalapeño peppers.

At that point, she'd add the oregano, spoon half the mixture into the casserole dish, place the fish filet on top of the veggies, season them with salt, black pepper, and cayenne pepper, then pour on another layer of tomato mixture. After that, she'd squeeze lime juice over it all.

The recipe only took fifteen minutes to bake, so the snapper would be the last thing in the oven.

Meanwhile, she'd prepare rice for the fish and sour cream smashed potatoes for the potpies.

Vicki touched Dani's shoulder, bringing her out of her thoughts. "Did you get my message about providing some light appetizer trays?"

"Yes. But since you didn't give much warning, I had to go with what I could source quickly and had time to prepare," Dani answered as she began to unload the carts and organize the kitchen. "I sent the additional invoice to your email and will expect a check tomorrow morning at the latest."

"That will be fine." Vicki wrinkled her brow. "Mr. Whittaker just didn't want people drinking on an empty stomach. What do you have?"

"I've got lemon-flavored sun-dried tomato hummus, goat-cheese-and-pesto bites, turmeric curry deviled eggs, and antipasto skewers."

"Wow!" Vicki beamed. "Mr. Whittaker will be impressed that you could come up something that great at the last minute." She glanced at her watch. "Okay. I have to go change into my dress and pick up Yvette's ashes from the crematorium. I'll see you back here at twelve fifteen. Please have the appetizer trays waiting for us when we return."

When Vicki left, Dani began preparing the ingredients for the fish recipe. While they were sautéing, she arranged the assembly line for the dessert. Thankfully, the cake and hand pies were done and all she'd have to do was plate them and add a scoop of ice cream on the side when the diners were ready for their sweet course.

As she worked, Dani glanced around the kitchen and saw there was a glass door that opened onto the country club's veranda. Evidently, it was there to provide food service to those seated at the tables on the patio.

A few minutes later, she spotted Gray as he led several men onto the veranda. They all had earpieces wired into radios clipped to their shoulders. She watched him direct his troops to concealed spots scattered around the gazebo.

Turning away from the door, Dani wondered exactly how the police would obtain usable proof that Marc Chandler murdered Yvette. Illinois was one of the few states that allowed recorded evidence only if both parties gave consent, but maybe if the officers could hear what he said to Whittaker, they could testify.

Dani was fixing the rice and smashed potatoes when Ivy, Tippi, and Starr arrived along with the other two girls who had been hired to serve at the event. She immediately put them to work assembling the appetizer platters.

Dani and the girls were just taking the trays into the cocktail space when Mr. Whittaker stepped into the room. A distinguished-looking man in his fifties, he was tall and lean, with attractively styled silver hair. Wearing an expertly tailored dark suit with a crisp white shirt and a silk necktie, he was exactly how Dani had pictured him.

He walked over to Dani, introduced himself, and asked her to call him Franklin, then said, "I had intended to meet with you after the engagement party. I wanted to thank you for all your hard work on that event." He sighed. "Sadly, we never got to that part of the evening."

"I'm so sorry about how that night turned out." Dani shook the hand he offered her. Considering everything she knew, she didn't think it was wise to offer him her sympathy for the loss of his fiancée, so after a brief moment of silence, she asked, "Is there anything I can do for you right now?"

"Nothing, thanks." Franklin smiled. "Detective Christensen informs me that you are the one who figured out who murdered Yvette."

"I am." Dani was surprised Gray had told Franklin about her, but then again, since they were asking for his cooperation, if the billionaire demanded to know, the police were hardly in a position to deny him the information.

"In that case, I think it's only fair that you get to hear Chandler's confession." Franklin lifted his chin. "However, just be warned that there is a slim possibility that you might be called on to testify." He paused, then shook his head. "But he'll probably take a deal."

Dani considered the offer. Neither Spencer nor Gray would be happy if she accepted. However, after her experience with her ex-boyfriend, she'd vowed that she'd never allow herself to be controlled by another man's wishes again, so she was going to do what she wanted.

Beaming at Whittaker, Dani said, "I would love that. How will it work?"

"Detective Christensen has agreed to have you with him in the prime listening spot next to the gazebo." Franklin glanced at his heavy gold watch. "You should probably get out there pretty soon. Chandler is due in fifteen minutes."

"Absolutely." Dani nodded enthusiastically. "I'll get the entrées in the oven right now and alert one of my employees to take them out when the timer goes off." She hesitated. "Thank you for thinking of me. It's really very sweet of you."

The tips of Whittaker's ears reddened and he squeezed her shoulders. "From everything I've heard about you, you're a very special woman."

With that, he left and Dani stood for a moment wondering exactly who had been telling him about her and what they'd been saying.

Blinking, she shook her head. That wasn't important right now. What was crucial was getting the food in the oven and herself outside and hidden before Chandler arrived.

Ten minutes later, she and Gray were squatting among the bushes along the side of the gazebo. Three foot-long redwood slats formed the bottom of the octagonal structure and ended in a railing. The rest of the building was open, except for the columns supporting the roof.

As she'd predicted, Gray hadn't been happy to see her. He grumbled as he fitted her with a Kevlar vest and had given her strict instructions about her expected behavior. Mostly, she was to be quiet, stay still, and shelter in place if anything went wrong.

Franklin was already seated at a table that had been pushed against the back wall. Dani could just make him out through a space between the wooden slats. He seemed as cool and calm as if he were in his office about to have a routine meeting with any one of his thousands of employees.

Dani's knees were already aching when Marc Chandler arrived a few minutes later. She really needed to get back to doing yoga.

Marc strolled into the gazebo with a smirk on his handsome face. He wore a suit, but his shirt was unbuttoned at the throat and his tie was stuffed into the breast pocket of his jacket.

Without an invitation, he took the seat opposite his boss and drawled, "You wanted to see me?"

Franklin retrieved his cell phone from the inside pocket of his suit jacket, put it on the table, and tapped the screen.

Marc cocky grin faded. "What're you doing?"

"As you know, I record all meetings with my employees."

"Oh." Marc's forehead creased. "Should I have my agent here?"

"You can, but I doubt you want anyone else to hear this conversation." Franklin took out a leather notepad and flipped it open. "I had an interesting discussion with Detective Christensen about my fiancée's death."

"What's that got to do with me?" Marc's tone didn't convey the slightest interest.

"He had a video recording of you exiting Yvette's Mercedes just before the engagement party."

"I...I..." Marc stuttered, then seemed to pull himself together and said, "Yvette asked me to help her find a gift for you. I was showing her suggestions on my phone and she felt faint, so we sat down in her car for a bit."

"There's also video that was shot through the windshield of the Mercedes showing your bare ass pumping like you were drilling for oil." Franklin crossed his arms. "Any other lies you want to try?"

"It... I... The thing is..." Marc's gaze bounced around the gazebo like a ball on a roulette wheel, and for a second Dani was afraid he'd spotted her, but then he took a deep breath and said, "I'm sorry, man. The first time I slept with her, I had no idea that she was your fiancée."

"And all the times after that?" Franklin's voice had icicles hanging off of it.

"Then she threatened to tell you I raped her unless I continued with the relationship."

Dani wasn't sure she believed Marc, but on the other hand, from what she knew about Yvette, Dani wasn't completely able to rule out that the woman had been coercing him.

"And you couldn't have Yvette accuse you of that, could you?" Franklin's chuckle was anything but amused. "Because you knew, if I believed her, I would have ended your career."

"Exactly." Marc nodded like a bobblehead doll. "She had me by the short hairs."

As if tired of the current subject, Franklin abruptly demanded, "Let me see your team pen."

"Why?" Marc stiffened, then quickly said, "I mean I lost it. I was devastated and I've been looking everywhere for it."

"Well, it's your lucky day." Whittaker's smile reminded Dani of Scar's in the *Lion King* movie. "The police found it. Of course, I doubt they'll return it to you even after your trial."

"The police!" Marc's voice cracked. "What do you mean? Where did they find it?"

"Just where you left it in Yvette's ocular cavity." Whittaker shrugged. "They have your prints on it. You might as well confess."

"That's not possible," Marc protested, then seemed to realize what he'd said and hurriedly added, "I mean it wasn't me. Someone must have picked it up from the floor during the chaos when the tent collapsed."

"Let's not play games. You may have wiped your

prints off the outside of the pen, but you forgot to wipe them off the ink cartridge."

"That doesn't prove anything." Marc swallowed audibly. "Someone still could have found it and used it as the weapon."

Franklin ignored Marc's protest and leaned forward. "You obviously overheard Vicki telling me she had caught Yvette cheating. Then heard me saying that if necessary, I'd pay my dear fiancée for the name of her lover. And you knew Yvette would expose you if it meant getting her greedy hands on more of my money."

"No. No. No." Marc's head swung back and forth in denial. He was clearly starting to lose it.

"Here's the thing." Franklin's voice softened. "I know how manipulative Yvette could be, and I understand how none of this was your fault."

"That's right." Marc nodded.

Dani looked at Gray, who rolled his eyes. Neither of them believed the billionaire was that empathetic, but they hoped that the perp was more trusting.

"So, just to satisfy my own curiosity, tell me the truth." Franklin cajoled.

"Why would I do that?" Marc wrinkled his brow. "That would be admitting to murder."

"Do you remember how, after you had your little breakdown," Franklin asked, patting the younger man's hand, "I kept you on the team and made sure no one knew why you took several years off from playing?"

Marc nodded. "That was really terrific of you. I would have never been able to come back from that if you hadn't helped me. Coaches would have been afraid that I wouldn't be able to take the stress of the game."

"Well, now I need your help." Franklin's voice broke, but Dani was pretty darn sure he was acting. "In order for me to get any kind of closure about Yvette's death, I need to know the truth."

"I know I owe you and I want to help you." Marc was silent for several seconds, then seemed to make a decision and asked, "If I tell you, will you keep me on the team and not sabotage my chances for the majors?"

Dani glanced at Franklin's cell phone and saw that the wily billionaire had casually laid his notepad on top of it. She wondered if Marc had forgotten he was being recorded.

"Of course," Franklin assured him. "Someone with your talent needs to play for the Cardinals."

Marc frowned. "I thought you were a Cubs fan."

"Right," Whittaker agreed, then hastily added, "but Normalton roots for the Cards."

Marc shrugged. "I don't care who I play for as long as it's the bigs."

"So tell me the truth," Franklin encouraged.

"I didn't want to kill her," Marc started slowly. "But you're right, I did overhear your conversation with that wedding planner and I panicked."

"Understandable. Yvette was about to ruin your

life." Franklin patted the younger man's hand again, then prodded, "Tell me what happened after that."

"I hurried over to Yvette and offered her a percentage of my major league salary in exchange for her not to tell you I was her lover." Marc's lips curled. "But while she was bargaining for a bigger cut and demanding the agreement in writing, the tent collapsed and a pole knocked her out."

"And you…" Franklin urged.

"And I decided that she was a leech and didn't deserve a penny of my hard-earned money." Marc's mouth tightened. "I knew from my survivalist training that sticking something into a person's eye socket would kill them, so I grabbed my pen and shoved it in. Then I pulled it out, wiped off my prints, and shoved it back again."

"You killed her to save yourself some cash!" Whittaker pounded the table.

Marc jumped, then muttered, "I saved you money too."

"I don't give a rat's ass about the money!" Franklin thundered. "What I care about is the fact you betrayed me. After I did everything to help you in your career, you screwed my bride-to-be."

"I told you she didn't give me a choice," Marc whined.

"No one betrays Franklin Whittaker." The billionaire's complexion was so red Dani feared that he was about to have a stroke. "And I'm going to make sure that you serve every minute of your sentence. I'll attend all your parole hearings and play the distraught fiancée card."

"What?" Marc's face was purple. "You promised that if I told the truth, that would be it."

"Just like you and Yvette"—Franklin gripped the table's edge, perhaps to stop himself from taking a punch at the man—"I lied."

"Yvette deserved to die!" Marc screamed. "And you know it."

Dani watched as every cell in the billionaire's body went rigid, then he relaxed and smiled.

"Perhaps." Franklin replaced his notebook in his pocket, picked up his cell phone, and rose from his chair. "But I'm still turning this over to the police."

"Can't you give me a break?" Marc appeared suddenly to come out of a daze. "Kick me off the team, but let me slide on the murder?" He grabbed the billionaire's arm. "Please!"

"No." Franklin shook Marc off, then raised his voice. "Detective Christensen, he's all yours."

Epilogue

W OW!" FRANNIE RYAN RUSHED UP TO DANI AS they all gathered on the dock waiting to board Franklin's yacht. The fifty-two-footer was easily the largest boat in the marina. "This was so generous of Mr. Whittaker. Imagine arranging for us all to take an evening cruise on the Illinois River and sending his own personal chef along to make us dinner."

"He said between our experiences with the tent collapsing at the engagement party and helping find Yvette's killer we'd all earned it." Dani gestured to Frannie's fiancé, Justin, who was busy taking pictures. "He included our significant others to make sure we really enjoyed ourselves."

The billionaire had been extremely grateful to have the matter of his fiancée's murder settled. There would be no trial. Marc had agreed to plead guilty to second-degree murder and Franklin credited Dani and her friends with the quick resolution that had saved him from a great deal of public embarrassment.

A mischievous expression danced across Frannie's face and she said, "It's a shame that Detective Christensen couldn't be here."

"Police officers can't accept gifts," Spencer explained as he joined the two women. He slipped his arm around Dani's waist and added, "At least he's getting a letter of commendation. Whittaker is sending copies to the police commissioner and the mayor."

"What a cool guy." Ivy played with the tie of her black-and-white polka-dot jumpsuit.

She stood holding hands with Laz, who had returned from his mini-rehab seeming much less stressed. One of his takeaways from that week had been a resolution to acknowledge that he and Ivy were dating. Mrs. Hunter had grudgingly accepted his announcement, but Dani was glad that Laz spent more time with his father than with his mom.

As Starr hugged Robert's arm, she said to him, "I'm just glad you were able to get the night off." She shot Spencer an impish grin. "Thank goodness the campus Halloween madness is over and you're finally back to your normal shifts."

Spencer raised an eyebrow. "Has Robert complained that he's being overworked?"

"Not at all, boss," the young security officer protested and whispered something in his girlfriend's ear that made her shrug.

Tippi sauntered up to the group with Caleb holding her elbow to steady her as she picked her way across the wooden dock in stiletto heels. Once the Halloween dance was over and the gallant Texan's obligation to the girl he'd previously invited was honorably discharged, he and Tippi had been inseparable.

Looking around, Tippi asked, "Are we the last ones to arrive?"

Dani shook her head. "We're expecting one more."

"I told you Brock declined, right?" Spencer asked. "He wanted to return to the city and start putting his life back together as soon as possible."

"It's not Brock." Dani bit her lip. "It's my father." She checked her watch and shrugged. "But maybe he won't show up."

"After you helped get his company's foot in the door with Whittaker, he'd better keep his word to you," Spencer growled.

Ivy quickly stepped in and changed the subject, "So, Unc, whatever happened with the mysterious happenings at Fox Hall?"

"Those two incidents were it." Spencer shoved his hands in the pockets of his black dress slacks. "We've put in new locks and installed a lot more cameras, so I hope that discourages whoever was behind the tomfoolery."

Dani poked Spencer. "My money is still on a ghost from the Native American burial site." She snickered. "Deadbolts and cameras won't stop a spirit."

"At least Oinkphelia and Hamlet are safe." Robert chuckled. "Did you all see the video of the pledges dressed up as hogs at the Hell Night Luau? That was their punishment for failing to snatch the college mascots."

Spencer made a face. "All that fuss about those animals for nothing." He sighed and shook his head. "But I guess the whole point of most of what campus security does is to prevent problems from occurring and we definitely stopped the Greeks from pignapping the swine."

Before anyone could comment, Jonas Sloan arrived. He hurried toward the group, stopped in front of his daughter, and awkwardly gave her a hug.

Spencer held out his hand and said, "You must be Dani's father. I'm her boyfriend, Spencer Drake."

"Boyfriend?" Jonas glanced at Dani. "I didn't realize you were dating someone."

"We're fairly new." Dani glanced between the two men, hoping there wouldn't be any tension. "And you and I haven't had that much contact since I broke up with Kipp."

"I'm sorry about that." Jonas looked down. "I really thought he was the one for you. I was afraid you were throwing away your chance at happiness."

"I know. I should have been more honest with you about Kipp." Dani inhaled. "He never treated me very well, but you liked him so much I didn't want to disappoint you."

"I...I need to stop making you afraid of that," Jonas admitted. "I plan to try."

Dani was silent for a moment. She had her doubts, but she'd give her father a chance.

She took his hand and led him a short distance from the group where they could have a little privacy, then she pointed up at the sky. "I like to think that those aren't stars. That they're actually windows to heaven. And that their light is Mom showering us with her love and letting us know that she's fine until we join her."

Jonas enveloped Dani in what felt like the first real hug he'd given her in years. They stood silently for a long moment, then broke apart and returned to the others.

Smiling, Dani said, "We should all get on board. Appetizers are at six and I know how annoying it is for a chef when a client is late."

~

"What did you think of the cruise?" Spencer asked from where he was sprawled on the yacht's sofa.

"It was terrific. The couples all appeared to have fun." Dani leaned forward from her corner of the couch and selected a tiny red velvet cupcake from the tray of desserts sitting on the table in front of them. "I was a little worried that my dad would feel like a fifth wheel, but he and Justin seemed to really hit it off."

"They did. I overheard their conversation about technology and manufacturing. If journalism doesn't pan out for him, I think Justin has a future in industry. Did you know he was a double major at U of I and got a BS in computer engineering?"

"I did not." Dani licked the icing from the cupcake. "But I'm not surprised. Just from talking to him, I suspect that his IQ is in the genius range."

Spencer patted the cushion next to him, silently inviting Dani to scoot over. "I'm curious as to why you didn't tell the others that Whittaker offered you the yacht for an overnight stay."

"Well…" Dani remained leaning against the couch's armrest, ignoring Spencer's silent invitation to move closer. Tonight, she wouldn't let him distract her with his kisses. "I was happy to share my reward with everyone, but I also wanted a little time without some crisis popping up."

"Like Ivy, Starr, or Tippi having a fight with their boyfriends?" Spencer's wry grin made Dani giggle.

"That or another ghost attack at Fox Hall." Dani popped a mini-black-bottom-brandy bite into her mouth, reminding herself to ask Franklin's chef for the recipe. "The hull of this boat is pretty effective at blocking cell phone signals so unless we're on deck, no one can reach us."

"Ah, so I was included in your alone time." Spencer teased, "I thought maybe you just let me stay because I drove us here."

"You found me out." Dani snapped her fingers. "I only kept you around so I'd have a ride home tomorrow. It's too expensive to get an Uber from Peoria to Normalton."

"I knew it." Spencer chuckled, then said, "You never did tell me how you ended up witnessing Chandler's confession."

She knew neither he nor Gray were happy about her actions. But if she and Spencer were to be together, he had to be able to accept her decisions.

"Franklin arranged it with the police because he thought that since I had figured out the murderer's identity, I deserved to be there." Dani bit her lip. "And I decided to take him up on his offer because I needed to make sure that I hadn't jumped to some conclusion and implicated an innocent man."

Spencer nodded slowly, then reached down and nabbed the last bite-size frozen key lime tart. "I can appreciate that."

When he didn't comment further, Dani breathed a sigh of relief and broached another touchy topic. They might as well get it all out in the open right now while they had the time and the privacy. "What did you think of my father?"

"I still don't understand why you helped him get a foot in the door with Whittaker."

Dani wasn't sure why she did it herself, but she tried to explain. "He's not a bad man. He didn't abuse me and I never went without anything."

"Neglect is a form of abuse."

"I wasn't neglected," Dani protested. "He just

didn't have a lot of himself left to give to me. My mom took that part of him with her when she died."

"He was a parent." Spencer scowled. "He owed it to you to make more of an effort."

"He did, when I was younger, but I think once I moved out, it was almost as if he'd been abandoned again." Dani's voice thickened. "He'd never been warm and fuzzy, but that was when he really grew distant."

"Humph." Spencer snorted his opinion.

"Anyway…" Dani knew she wouldn't change Spencer's mind and was touched that he cared that much about her to be angry about her father's behavior toward her. "Dad seems to be trying now and I'm going to give him a chance."

"Of course you are." Spencer's voice was affectionate. "That's just who you are."

"I sure hope so." Dani brushed a tear away, then leaned over and poked Spencer's arm. "And don't pretend you're so hard-nosed. You're giving Brock a second chance. I heard you tell him you'd make a couple of calls and see if you could find him some security work once he had his prosthesis."

"That's nothing." Spencer took a sip of brandy before he said, "Besides, Brock did me a favor. He got me out of a loveless marriage that would have just become worse as time went by. Taking that into consideration, he was the reason that I was free when I met you."

Dani's heart turned to mush. Spencer was so

sweet. He'd been making his feelings about her clearer and clearer, even though she hadn't reciprocated.

"Aw, what a nice thing to say." Dani leaned toward him and cupped his cheek. She looked into his beautiful dark-blue eyes and risked exposing her inner self to him. "But the truth is, I think being with you and having the girls in my life has made me a better person. I was actually a lot like my dad before. I tended to keep to myself, I had very few friends, and I guarded against any feelings that might expose me to being hurt."

Spencer kissed her gently on the lips. "Me too."

"So maybe it's the combination of us together that makes things click."

Spencer tried to take her in his arms, but Dani scooted back against the sofa arm. "Hey, I have a question for you. Will you ever be able to tell me about your previous work?"

"It's probably better if I don't." Spencer stood up, took Dani's hands in his, and raised her up beside him.

"But that's not fair. You know all about my past." Dani took a step away from him. "If you're still not ready to trust me with all of yours, we need to take it slow until you do."

"It's not that I don't trust you. I just think you're safer without that knowledge." Spencer moved behind her, rubbing her shoulders. "And it's getting harder to ignore the physical attraction between us, isn't it?"

"Uh…" Dani gulped, then said in a breathy voice,

"But passion fades and I want to make sure we have more than that before we take the next step."

"Okay." Spencer kissed her neck.

Dani felt herself melting, but tried again to put the brakes on. "You understand. I don't want to be hurt again."

"Neither do I." Spencer turned her around and leaned his forehead against hers. "We can take it as slow as you want as long as we're always moving forward."

Dani looked past him out the yacht's floor-to-ceiling windows. The moonlit water was mesmerizing and made her realize just how happy Spencer made her.

Listening to her heart, she pressed her lips to his and murmured, "That's a promise I can keep."

Acknowledgments

Thanks to Rebecca Aygarn Talkie for the great Ouija board line.

About the Author

© David Stybr

Denise Swanson is the *New York Times* bestselling author of the Scumble River mysteries, the Deveraux's Dime Stores mysteries, and the Chef-to-Go mysteries, as well as the Change of Heart and Delicious Love contemporary romances. She has been nominated for *RT Magazine*'s Career Achievement Award, the Agatha Award, and the Mary Higgins Clark Award.

TART OF DARKNESS

Chef-to-Go Mysteries

New York Times bestselling author Denise Swanson serves up a delightful cast of small-town characters and a deliciously mysterious murder!

Right when Dani thinks she's hit a dead-end in her career, she unexpectedly inherits an enormous old house in a quaint college town. This gives her the perfect opportunity to pursue her true passion—cooking! So Dani opens Chef-to-Go, preparing delicious, ready-made meals for hungry students attending the nearby university, as well as providing personal chef services and catering events for the local community.

But just as Dani is relishing her sweet new life, a student is murdered and Dani becomes one of the primary suspects! She'll have to scramble to clear her name and save her business before the killer reappears—perhaps to silence the new chef forever.

"Fast-paced and fun—as is Swanson's style—
***Tart of Darkness* is utterly unputdownable."**
—Julie Hyzy, *New York Times* bestselling author

For more Denise Swanson, visit:
sourcebooks.com

LEAVE NO SCONE UNTURNED

Chef-to-Go Mysteries

New York Times bestseller Denise Swanson serves up another delicious cozy mystery!

It's the beginning of the university's fall semester, and Dani can't wait for the college students to return to Normalton, Illinois—after all, without them, there is no one to support her Chef-to-Go business. But Normalton University's orientation week is marred by murder, along with a series of car-jackings and sightings of a mysterious creature in a pond on campus. And with the whole town feeling unsettled, Dani finds herself dealing once again with the infuriatingly handsome Spencer Drake, the head of security at the university.

But as the trouble in Normalton draws worryingly close to home, Dani realizes that if the killer isn't caught soon, she may be the next one who is found scone cold dead.

"Fans of Joanne Fluke and Diane Mott Davidson will enjoy the cooking frame, the sympathetic characters, and the small-town setting."
—*Booklist*

For more Denise Swanson, visit:
sourcebooks.com